THE
TOWN
THAT
TIME
FORGOT

ELIZABETH
DONLEY-LEER

THE
TOWN
THAT
TIME
FORGOT

ELIZABETH
DONLEY-LEER

woodhall press

Woodhall Press | Norwalk, CT

Woodhall Press, 81 Old Saugatuck Road, Norwalk, CT 06855
WoodhallPress.com

Cover design: Asha Hossain
Layout artist: L.J. Mucci

Library of Congress Cataloging-in-Publication Data available

ISBN 978-1-954907-88-1   (paper: alk paper)
ISBN 978-1-954907-89-8   (electronic)

First Edition
Distributed by Independent Publishers Group
(800) 888-4741

Printed in the United States of America

This book is dedicated to the most driven, caring, loving, dedicated, critical, enduring, opinionated, and difficult to love woman I have ever known. You pressed me everyday of my life to reach for my dreams and goals even when I was not sure what those dreams were. You are my hero and always will be. To my mother Betty Ann Winkley Donley Schulman Bradley Bobosik. You are ever with me and although this life accomplishment has happened a couple of years too late for you to see firsthand, I know you are looking over my shoulder with great pride and encouragement to proceed. Your unbelievable life story, adventures, and brave endurance have been the ultimate story telling inspiration and source of writing material that any writer could ever hope for. Without them and without you I would not be the woman I am today. My only regret is that you are not here to see this accomplishment in person.

Preface

Although I understand different regions of the world experience things differently within the same era, the people and settings in this book are representative of the way things were when I spent my teen years growing up in southern California in the 1980s. As such, the characters have been developed using my firsthand experience of living in the era in California as a teen/twenty-something. My experiences on the east coast of the United States happened much later in life, so the basic setting and character development in this book is a compilation of my life's experiences and may not be exactly the way you remember people and places in the 1980s. I hope you enjoy this fictional story inspired by many of my life's real-world events.

1

The Making of Mr. Blanchard

As he sat in the back of the church being shunned by his supposed Christian peers, listening to the minister pontificate his own beliefs as law, Blake remembered his own childhood growing up as an orphan within these very walls. He remembered the way some of these very parishioners would tease and bully him because of his unusual appearance. As if it were his fault, he had gray hair by the time he was fifteen, or that he could eat whatever he wanted and remain rail thin. They would taunt him about the paleness of his skin, until he could take it no longer and would become violent in the name of self-preservation. And then, somehow the adults would make him out to be the bad guy. He did not remember his parents or how he had come to live in this place almost two decades ago. The only memories he had were of the horrible childhood he had here, and being force-fed the Christian philosophy the hypocrites bullying him wanted him to live by.

But today would be different. Today he turned 18 or at least that is what he was being told. He would finally become free of this place, whether by choice or by force according to orphanage guidelines. This place he had thought of as home from before he could speak would no longer have a hold over him. As miserable as his time spent at this religious institute of compassion and charitable giving was, his life could have been much worse. He could have ended up in one of the many workhouses or forced apprenticeships by the time he was five or six like many of the other residents were made to do.

It was only by happenstance that the same odd and off-putting appearance that made him the laughingstock of bullies, also kept him from being sent to any of the work institutions where most institutionalized children ended up. Those in charge of running these workplaces would take one look at him, thinking he was sickly or would cause havoc within their work environment, and reject him. This did not mean he didn't have to work for his keep, though. His caretakers saw to that. They made him work even harder, doing chores that were normally performed by adults at the orphanage grounds to make up for his inability to earn wages for the institution.

He didn't remember his arrival at this place of torment, but he had been told he was abandoned on their front doorstep wrapped only in a shroud of black fabric inside a wooden crate. A label in a foreign language with a name burned into the outside of the crate were the only indications of where he had come from. Those who found him decided to call him what they thought was written on the side of the crate and that's how he became Blake Blanchard.

Beyond that, he knew nothing about who he was, except who he had been forcibly taught to be by his keepers. As of today, he would be released to the outside world to fend for himself and learn the ways of those men who lived beyond the confined protection of the orphanage grounds.

Now that he was forever free of this place which he had dreamt of leaving for so long, Blake wasn't sure where he would go. All he knew was that he wanted to be as far as humanly possible from the place and the horrible people who ran the facility and dwelled within its walls.

With his few meager possessions flung over his shoulder, Blake never looked back as he walked down the only road that led into the town that had taught him all he ever knew. The people who had bullied and taunted him relentlessly, implanting a feeling of worthlessness into his self-perception, would no longer reign over his existence. It was his turn to decide who he was and would be. His only focus going forward would be on the future and finding a place where he belonged.

Little did he know he would soon come to a crossroad that would forever change his life and the way he perceived himself and those around him.

#

Blake wandered from town to town looking for work and a place to call home. But every town was the same; ridicule, doors slamming in his face, and people wanting nothing to do with the odd-looking stranger who dared to approach them. It was as if he had never left the orphanage at all or the tiny town that encompassed it.

He tried to convince himself that the poverty and oppression of the time made people more fearful and skeptical than they would normally be. However, the more times he experienced the same reactions, the more he began to believe his fellow man was the problem and not the many wars, empirical rule, blight, and famine that spread throughout Europe during the 19th century. Afterall, wasn't it mankind who was the cause of all the prevalent issues facing humanity in the first place?

It had been six months of wandering since Blake left the orphanage. As thin as he was before, his bones now protruded, giving him the appearance of a walking skeleton. Meals were few and far between; typically consisting of what limited items he could either steal from those who curtly sent him on his way, or that he was able to catch in the wild using his minimal hunting and foraging skills. He now found himself cold, hungry, and lost sitting at the water's edge near a rarely used foot bridge wondering if life was worth the struggle.

He stared at his reflection in the nearly frozen water, saying to himself how easy it would be to end his misery by simply slipping into the cold water that slowly flowed in front of him. The chill of the water would only hurt for a moment and then all the pain and discomfort that he dealt with on a daily basis would be gone. The urge became stronger as he felt his body slowly slipping down the embankment and the water permeating his shoes, soaking his already frozen toes.

The water gradually rose up his legs, sending a temporary burning sensation throughout his limbs as his torso fell into the shallow water. By the time his head sank into the water, there was no feeling left within his frail body. He lay there with his eyes closed, wondering when consciousness would cease when suddenly he heard a voice beckoning to him.

"Blake! What are you doing?" The voice bellowed.

Unconsciously, Blake heard himself responding to the disembodied voice while he waited for darkness to take him. "I am ending my suffering."

"But, why would you want to do such a thing, when you have such a glorious future ahead of you?"

The voice's response caught Blake off guard. He had only known loss, misery, and hatred. How could his future be expected to be glorious, he thought to himself. "You must be thinking of someone else," He replied to the voice.

"No, my son. It is you I am thinking of."

"Your son? I have no father. Nor do I have a mother. I have no one on this earth to call family."

"True. Your mother died in childbirth, unable to bear the gift I had given her. So, no you do not have anyone on that place you call earth to call family. But you still have family. You are my son. You are the glorious gift of my unholy union with your mother."

Blake's mind swirled with confusion, thinking to himself, 'there's no one here. These must just be my last coherent thoughts as life leaves my body.'

As if he could read Blake's mind the voice replied, "No, Blake I am real. You may not be able to see me now, but I am as real as anything you have ever known."

His thoughts spiraled out of control at that last response. 'How can that be? Can it be that the god who my caretakers had so viciously beat into me is real? Could it be that I am his chosen one?'

"Hahaha...Well...you are the chosen one. But I think you have the wrong father in mind." An ominous voice continued to laugh at the thought of Blake being a son of God, as it ridiculed his thoughts.

Blake's mind went blank at that response, and he lay there both frozen in body and in thought.

"Yes son, you are the creation of the supernatural. But of the fallen, not of the risen."

At that moment, Blake felt a mixture of emotions. He was scared at the concept of being the son of Satan and thrilled at the idea on not being part of the human race, with all its hypocrisy and pious beliefs. He wasn't sure what to do with this newfound knowledge.

Sensing his confusion, the voice encouraged him to accept his existence for what it was and fulfill his destiny. "Your difficult life has not been by coincidence, my son. I placed you with those who would teach you the true nature of man so that when you were old enough to join me, you would be able to fulfill your mission with confidence and without compassion for those who have tormented you. You shall be my right hand among the humans who dwell upon that plane of existence."

"Why can't I come live at your side, father? Why must I live in this place that hates me so?" Blake didn't understand why anyone would want their offspring to live in such conditions.

"Sadly, my son, you are half mortal. To live at my side as such, you would have to forsake all that is glorious about you as my spawn. However, should you choose to reside among the mortals and devote yourself to fulfilling my will, your pain and suffering will be rewarded. All that is needed is for you to take my hand and feel the eternal warmth of my power."

A hazy being crept into Blake's conscious mind. His hand was outstretched beckoning Blake to join him. Without thought with his eyes still shut, Blake could feel his hand rise out of the water reaching for the being which reached out to him from within his mind. When their hands touched, Blake could feel a warm sensation begin to work its way up his fingertips, along his outstretched arm, and migrate throughout his body.

"There you have it my son...my gift to you...my gift of warmth and eternal grace within my realm. No more shall you be cold, or suffer from human conditions such as hunger, poverty, and want. All I ask for in return, is your unconditional loyalty to act as my agent among the human-world."

The feeling of warmth brought new hope to Blake and a renewed sense of worth to his being, and he replied, "Yes, father. I am your loyal agent and will serve you amongst the human-world."

"You have made a fine decision, my son. From this point forward you will refer to me as Master and have the full protection of me and my army. Great things lie ahead for you within my ranks."

With his body now feeling warm, and toasty Blake opened his eyes to find his body still submerged in the frigid stream. A smile stretched across his face as he sat up, realizing he would no longer be cold no matter his environment and he pulled himself from the water.

Blake noticed his reflection in the water had changed substantially. No longer did he look eighteen. Now, his skin looked withered and aged. His pale color had turned to look more like ash than flesh, and his eyes were a dull grey that matched his prematurely grey hair. At first, he was startled by his new appearance. Then, as he began to realize that his hunger pangs and deep aches in his bones from being cold had vanished, a sense of contentment took over. An unfamiliar sense of confidence took the place of his self-loathing as he crossed the bridge to embark on his new life with a new purpose and mentor to protect him.

###

The years progressed quite normally for most, but for Blake, time seemed to stand still. From the moment when he made his vow to his father, his appearance changed little. He had seen humanity at its worst and its best during his travels. Blake was loyal to his master throughout the decades of training; following his orders and fulfilling his role in helping bring about the master's plan for the fall of humanity. He stirred the pot of hatred and greed wherever he had the chance, traveling throughout Europe, Asia, and eventually landing in the U.S.

Following the first world war, the U.S. was a breeding ground for greed as the industrial revolution began, hatred toward thousands of unwanted immigrants flooding into its ports, and suffrage for those demanding equality in a time of rampant inequality. This made it the perfect place for Blake to establish roots and feed into the environment that his master worked hard to promote.

He took up residence in a manner house just outside the city limits of the small farm town of Oakwood, establishing his dark presence. Locals found his presence unnerving to their normally peaceful and cohesive way of life. Life may not have been easy in this rural town, but the people were a community and worked hard to help one another, which made it a good place to live and raise children. Blake's presence undermined the fabric of the town, and its citizens continually shunned him, trying to make him leave. This only encouraged Blake to stay and continue his master's unsettling work for dominance.

Blake did everything he could to corrupt the citizens of Oakwood and proudly flaunted his anti-Christian beliefs in this predominantly Baptist town, intentionally making townspeople fearful of him. He wanted them to talk about him and let their imaginations run rampant with what went on in his home behind closed doors; because the human imagination was much more creative and evil than he or his master could ever invent.

It was all part of his master's plan to transform this small community from a God-fearing place to a corrupt, selfish atmosphere. Instilling doubt in the power of God with a strong supernatural being living nearby provided the perfect opportunity for good people to reach out for a reliable, albeit darker, solution in desperation when times were bad, and they wanted immediate results.

Oakwood was but one such small community that Blake's master strove to take ownership of. He had many such agents established in small communities around the globe, taking over more and more of the human race's spiritual futures. Having a foothold in these smaller God-fearing areas provided him with a greater gain when he implemented his larger-scale mayhem, making it harder for good to endure.

Oakwood was a strong community with lots of family ties, which made it difficult for Blake to have influence over, until 1940 when Joe Wilson accepted Blake's offer to help him win the Mayoral election. Joe was desperate to win, having been on the town council for several years and wanting to move up the political ladder. His numbers were waning, though as he was running against the incumbent who was quite popular, even though he had accomplished little for the community during his time in office.

The circumstances made it the ideal time for Blake to approach Joe with his offer to help him win, in exchange for Joe having Blake's home incorporated into city limits. Blake knew that being part of the city limits would afford him more opportunities to stir things up because he would then have voting rights. Plus, the idea of him being within city limits would anger the residents of Oakwood, making it a double win for Blake and his master.

Joe knew he could help his community grow and flourish if only he were elected, but his reach was small when it came to voters. That made him vulnerable to Blake's influence and proposal, of which Blake took full advantage. Joe knew there might be a little backlash about incorporating Blake Blanchard's property into the town, but it wasn't anything he couldn't deal with. And besides, the good he could do for the town greatly outweighed the small uproar that would ensue over such a minor map change. So, Joe accepted Blake's offer, wishing not to know any of the details as to how Blake Blanchard would fulfill his end of the arrangement. Plausible deniability, he thought. Seeming as though Blake could read his mind, he looked at Joe before walking away and said, "Now you're thinking like a real politician." Joe stood there stunned wondering if he had made the right decision.

Joe's numbers began to improve little by little, but not enough for Joe to win. His anxiety rose wondering if Blake could really do what he said he could. He decided to call Blake and discuss the current situation. The phone rang only once before a deep voice answered, "Hello Joe."

"How did you know it was me?"

"Who else would it be this close to the election?" Blake loved to taunt those humans who dared to deal with him. "What can I do for you?"

"I'm concerned with the poll numbers. I'm still behind and the election is in two days. I thought we had a deal."

"We do have a deal. The deal was that you would win and then my property would be incorporated into the city limits. What would it look like if I simply changed the polls overnight? Someone might get suspicious, don't you think?"

"I guess so. But this is cutting things too close for comfort."

"Don't worry, Joe. Everything is well in hand. Go work on your acceptance speech and continue your campaigning as normal. Let me worry about the rest."

Joe hung up the phone even more uneasy than before their conversation, after hearing the dial tone return. He decided there wasn't much else he could do, other than campaign and hope for the best and returned to his campaign office to continue the fight.

With one day until the election, Joe was down in the polls by twenty points and he was sure there was no way he could win. He spent the day shaking hands, introducing himself to people, and doing the typical end-of-the-election campaigning hoping for a last-minute upset.

Then, at 5:30 that evening, the call came in from campaign head-quarters; Fred Davis, the incumbent, had died of a massive heart attack. With only Joe Wilson and Fred Davis on the Ballot, Joe would become Mayor by default. It wasn't exactly how Joe wanted to win the election, making his win bittersweet.

The phone rang again as Joe sat silently digesting the situation. This time it was Blake Blanchard. "Hello Joe. Did you hear the good news? Your adversary is dead. You won."

"I wouldn't call Fred Davis dying good news." Joe was disgusted at the way Blake was gloating over the win and loss of a man's life.

"Well, you have won. My end of the deal is complete. Now don't forget to fulfill your end." The phone disconnected and Joe stood there for a long time contemplating what he had done. Did Blake somehow have a role in Bill's heart attack? Was his death on Joe's hands? Shaking his head, he realized there was nothing he could do about it now and after all, he never asked for anyone to die. He chose to believe it was all a coincidence, but just in case Blake did have something to do with it, he had better fulfill his part of the deal.

2

The Letters

It had been a typical morning for the Wilson family, breakfast together as a family minus one very important member, minor chitchat about what the day had in store, and a few pleasantries regarding how everyone slept. This was followed by hurried departures as Joe left for city hall, Eddie went off to do whatever he did throughout the day, and Hillary cleaned up the kitchen before running her daily errands, leaving Amy on her own for a while.

Amy sat in the rocking chair on the front porch just like she did every day at this time. A soft breeze blew a strand of her long brown hair across her face and tickled her nose, making her sneeze. Her oldest brother, Greg, always teased her about how softly she sneezed and would let out a playful laugh. Remembering this, made her wish the postman would hurry up and arrive, hopefully bringing a letter or two from Greg.

She knew the mailman's schedule by heart by now. She wanted to be the first to read all her brother's letters and waited patiently for the mail to arrive each day so as not to miss one. It had been weeks since they had received a letter from Greg, which was normal. There would be long stretches of time with nothing and then a bunch of letters would arrive all at once adorned with foreign post-marks. He tried to write as frequently as he could, however, being in the middle of a war zone made it difficult to do.

So far, his military travels had taken him through North Africa, to Ireland and Scotland, and last they heard he was in Britain getting ready to be deployed to Italy. If it weren't for the war, these letters of his travels would have seemed spectacular.

Her brother was a wonderful writer, and his letters captured the imagination with their vivid details and colorful descriptions. He tried to keep them positive so as not to worry his family, while also keeping them informed on what was happening abroad. This was not an easy task with the violence and destruction that usually surrounded him, and each letter became darker in tone, which worried Amy.

Her brother had always been kind and gentle. That's why it surprised her when he was one of the first to enlist once the U.S. entered the allied forces. He had told her that he hated the idea of killing someone, but he hated the idea of genocide more. And that if he was living a life of freedom, it was his responsibility to help those who could not help themselves. Greg saw what was happening in the German concentration camps as just that, a group of people unable to defend themselves and in need of assistance.

He was only a baby when his father shipped out towards the end of World War I. But he had grown up listening to his father speak of the horrible things that happened and watched his father's face carry worry reading the papers seeing it all happening again. This time the evil at the gate was Hitler. And his hatred of Jews, or anyone who he did not see as part of the "perfect race," or "Aryan Nation" had spread through Europe like wildfire. It was far worse than anything Amy's father's generation or the generation before had ever seen. That's why her brother chose to put his life at risk for people he had never met, and his family understood even if the idea of him being on the battle lines terrified them.

Amy's thoughts were interrupted when she heard Lewis, the mailman approaching the Wilson family mailbox. "Hi Amy. You're looking nice today."

"Thank you, Lewis. Anything from Greg today?" Amy was almost halfway down the driveway before she spoke.

Lewis shuffled through the envelopes in his hand before stopping at a stack of letters rubber banded together. "Looks like you hit the jack pot today, little lady."

Amy grabbed the letters out of Lewis' hand, turned and ran back up the driveway as she yelled, "Thank you, Lewis. See you tomorrow."

Lewis smiled placing the rest of the Wilson's mail in the box, and waved good-bye, "See you tomorrow. Happy reading."

The rubber band had already been removed and Amy was sorting through the stack of letters by the time she reached the front porch. Her hands trembled with excitement as she looked at the postmarks and put them in order of date, with the oldest one on top. Three letters in all.

Her mother was at the grocery store and her father was busy working at city hall, making this the perfect time to sit down and read them without interruption. So, she climbed back onto her perch in the rocking chair and opened the first letter, careful not to tear the postmark. Her mom and middle brother liked to save them in a book as a gift for Greg when he got home to remind him of all the wonderful places he had seen. It was their way of ignoring the fact that he was fighting in a war, not on vacation.

May 10, 1943
Dear Family,

I hope my letter finds everyone safe and well. Thank you for the care package that you sent. I received it last week when our mail finally caught up with us. Keep sending the cookies, jerky, and chocolates. The guys in my unit all must have one of your snickerdoodles every time they arrive, so I guess your cookies are world-famous now, Ma.

Other than missing the springtime weather and all of you in Oakwood, I am good, so don't worry about me. The weather here is cold and wet. I never thought about it being winter on this side of the world when it is summer on our side of the world. Thankfully, the army supplied us with quality boots and rain gear so we're able to stay as dry as possible while we hike from one location to another or hunker down in a muddy foxhole someplace waiting for the fight to come to us.

Our deployment to Italy was changed at the last minute and we were sent to France instead to help prepare for allied troops coming from Italy. Not sure what the plan for that is, I'm too far down on the totem pole to be given those details. And if I were, I probably wouldn't be allowed to talk about it anyway, but whatever it is, sounds big. Half the guys I know had their orders changed at the last minute to clear a path for troops.

The other half have been sent to try and liberate prisoners from different concentration camps. What this guy Hitler and his Nazi army are doing over here is beyond evil. Only the devil himself could gas hundreds of people at a time like they were cockroaches and bury them in one mass grave site.

Getting from one place to another over here is a real mess. Hitler's armies have taken over the train stations so that they can monitor who is going where and capture any Jews who might be trying to escape to Switzerland.

The architecture here is beautiful, what hasn't been bombed to hell, that is. The French people have been very friendly to us. They love the allied troops, and the French resistance is everywhere helping to keep us safe and battle this evil son of a bitch. Some of the people I have met have lived in their homes for three generations, and now their homes are nothing but rubble and they have only what they can scavenge or have on their backs. The children love when U.S. troops come through, since most of us have chocolate as part of our rations. Chocolate has become a form of currency over here with more value than cash.

I met a little girl last week who reminded me of you, Amy. I gave her some chocolate and she gave me some of her mom's homemade bread. Then we sat and talked for a bit as best we could with the language barrier. You would be surprised at how much English they speak and understand here in France. They hate when Americans try and speak French though, because they say we butcher it. I guess that makes Americans good at butchering two languages, French and English. Haahaa…I'm sure glad you made me take my English studies seriously in school, Mom. Some of these guys sound like they've never been to school a day in their lives, and they don't look a day over fifteen.

Well, give Dad a big hug for me, and say hello to Lewis. I better get some rest while I can. We're supposed to be moving out again shortly. I'll write when I can.

Love Always,
Greg

Amy wiped a tear from her eye as she finished reading the first letter, missing her brother even more than before. The image of her big brother sitting hunkered down in a muddy hole, waiting for men with guns to come was simply too much for her to bear. She took a minute or two to compose herself before opening the next letter, still being careful not to tear the postmark.

17

May 16, 1943
Dear Family,

I know it has only been six days since I wrote you last, but it feels like a lifetime. Before we were able to pull out, an air raid struck, bombing the little town we were in. I'm alright, so don't worry. But the little girl I was telling you about was killed along with her mother when the building they were staying in collapsed from a bomb blast. My heart sank as I pulled her from the rubble and held her in my arms. This kind of thing happens so frequently over here that it is making it harder and harder to care about anyone. We barely had time to bury them before we were forced to evacuate and head to our next location. They say it's darkest before the dawn, well it is turning black over here. The light better appear soon, because we're tired of this crap.

I'm sorry to start my letter with so much doom and gloom. It has just been a tough week. My feet have blisters from all the walking and trudging through rocky fields and embankments, trying to work our way around enemy troops. I guess if the sun were out, this would be some beautiful countryside though. We have traversed so much territory in the past week zigzagging from one country to another, I'm not even sure where we are anymore. It's weird how close these small countries are. It's like being able to drive through the New England states in a day or two because of how clustered they are.

I miss your cooking, Ma. Every time I must eat one of these K-rations, I cringe and then close my eyes and make myself try and believe it is your pot roast. My imagination is not that good though, so I choke it down and pray we get to go home soon.

Well, I just got word to get packed up, because we are moving out again. So, I am going to have to keep this letter short.

Give my love to everyone,
Greg

Amy burst into tears as she folded the second letter and returned it to its envelope. Her brother sounded miserable and worse than she had ever known him to be. After a few minutes of sobbing, she pulled herself together, and opened the next letter hoping for better news.

July 8, 1943
Dear Family,

I don't know how long it has been since I wrote last. I just know that it has been a while. We've been all over France, then trekked through Italy and are now on a boat heading to the island of Sicily. Thankfully the weather here is much warmer, even if I still haven't seen the sun, and the water is like a picture out of a postcard, crystal blue depths with green shorelines. I'm told this is the best time of year to be on the water here since it's calm, which makes it easier to cross to Sicily. It's funny that to get dry, I had to be on a boat in the Mediterranean. Although, with the amount of cloud cover there is today, I may not get to stay dry for long.

It's hard to make friends over here. But I did get close to one fella from North Carolina over the past few weeks. He was new to our regiment, and we were able to connect about home life, even though he wasn't from our neck of the woods. I would have loved for you to have met him, Mom, when we got home. Unfortunately, he ended up going home before me, in a pine box, during our first battle as we entered Italy. Forward troops had supposedly cleared the area, but we were ambushed as soon as we entered town. We took cover in an old bombed-out building. But before we knew what hit us, we were surrounded and taking heavy fire. We lost a lot of good men that day. It made me sick to watch my brethren being killed right in front of me, their blood splattered on my face and flowing through the street like a small stream.

I'm still having a hard time understanding why I am still alive, and they are not.

None of what is going on over here makes any sense. Women and children being torn from their homes, beaten, some even raped and killed all because they are different than us. Entire families being slaughtered like animals, while their possessions are stolen and shipped back to Hitler's private hoard. Churches are not even safe from theft, destruction, and murder. The amount of hate that fuels the Nazi armies is beyond comprehensible. And, if Hitler had his way, he would be all the way to the U.S. spreading his hate by now. He's like an evil virus that spreads and contaminates everything within its path if not treated early.

The war seems to be ramping up for something big to happen over here. There's never a quiet moment now that we're traveling through Italy. The allied troops have been encountering more and more resistance and hand-to-hand combat than we've had until this point. Our superiors are telling us to prepare for even more resistance when we land in Sicily. We're expecting to have to fight Italian troops as well as Germans. The allies are fighting both Fascists and Nazis since they have partnered up against the allies. There's supposed to be air support, but if the weather holds, we may be on our own. Either way, I'm ready to shoot me some Fascist and Nazi sons of bitches. It's time for some major payback for my buddies who paid the ultimate price to these assholes. Knowing I took out as many of them as they did our regiment's boys will help give me some peace of mind. At least that's what I keep telling myself as I prepare for battle once more.

I'm just ready for all this needless violence and destruction to be over so I can come home.

My love to all,
Greg

Amy's mom walked up just as she was putting the letter back into its envelope. She could see tears streaming down Amy's face and became alarmed. "What is it, Amy? Is it Greg? Is he alright?"

Amy nodded to both of her mother's questions as she tried to regain her voice and composure. "Yes, Mom. It's these letters from Greg. I've never heard him sound so miserable and angry."

This made her mother set down the bags she was carrying and sit beside Amy, taking the letters from her hand. "Let me see those." The letters were still in date order like Amy had sorted them when Hillary glanced through them. "Maybe from now on you should wait to read your brother's letters with the rest of the family. They are obviously too much for you to handle."

The thought of Amy not being able to handle what was in Greg's letters ran a chill up Hillary's spine. Amy was a strong tomboy of a girl. Growing up with two very active older brothers had made her that way. With that thought, she decided to wait until Joe got home to read the letters. "Come on. Help me put these groceries away and start dinner. It'll take your mind off things."

Amy nodded in agreement to help ease her mother's concerns and felt better when she saw the worry lines fade from her mother's face, but she knew nothing would stop her from thinking about what her brother was going through.

Dinner was ready when Joe got home from the office as usual. He greeted Hillary with a gentle peck on the cheek as he entered the kitchen. Even though she smiled back at him, Joe could see that something was bothering her, "What is it?"

"I'm worried about Amy. We received some letters from Greg. She read them before I got home from the grocery store, and now she's just not acting herself."

Did you read them?"

"No, I wanted to wait until you got home to read them. But Amy says Greg is not himself in the letters and she's really worried about him. Will you talk to her?"

Joe nodded at Hillary and went to find Amy. He found her sitting on the old swing in the back yard deep in thought. "Hey there, June Bug."

Amy loved her father's pet name for her and looked up with a smile upon hearing the words. "Hi, Dad. What's up?"

"That's funny I was about to ask you the same thing. Your mother is worried about you."

"I'm fine. I just had a weak moment or two." Amy felt like she had to be strong for her parents and Greg.

"Talk to me June Bug. What's going on in that little head of yours?"

After a minute of looking at her father as if nothing was wrong, Amy finally decided to tell him what was bothering her. "It's the tone of Greg's letters. They are so dark and angry. I have never heard him like this."

Joe's face drew serious hearing Amy's words. He knew all too well how war can change a person after having been in the last world war when he was about the same age as Greg. It took him a long time to overcome what he had seen, and he still had the occasional nightmare, especially now that his eldest was overseas fighting a relentless enemy. "Fighting in a war has that effect on people. It's good that he is writing about it, getting those dark feelings out into the open. It's better than him bottling them up like I did. It'll help him return to the Greg we know and love when he comes home."

"Have you read the letters?"

"Not yet. I will read them later with your mother and Eddie after he gets home from work."

"I would think twice before showing them to Eddie, Dad."

Joe looked at Amy with a bewildered look. "Why? We've always let him read Greg's Letters."

"I know, but you know how Eddie always wants to follow in Greg's footsteps and already has a few impulse control issues, especially when it comes to this war. I'm afraid he might do something rash after he reads how angry Greg is in his letters."

Amy's words triggered her father's worry lines and the two sat silently side-by-side on the swing set, lost in their own thoughts for a long while before Joe felt ready to reply, "Okay, June Bug. I will take your advice and read the letters with your mother alone first, and we can decide if it is a good thing for Eddie to read them or not together. Does that sound good to you?"

"Yes. Thanks for the talk, Dad."

"Any time, June Bug. Anytime."

That night Joe and Hillary sat down and read the letters together. They now better understood their daughter's reaction to the letters and decided it would be best not to show the last two letters to Eddie in hopes of avoiding any impetuous acts. Their hearts sank at the thought of their eldest son being in harm's way and at the ripple effect that it was having on their entire family.

"Did you see the paper today? There are another fifteen boys from our small community on the obituary page and thirteen on the wounded in action list." Joe's voice was filled with anger. "This war is decimating our community."

"Yes. I saw the paper this morning. They were talking about it at the grocery store. I recognized one of the names on the Missing in Action list as being a boy from Greg's graduating class. They were on the basketball team together."

This was a little too close to home for Joe and he reached over and gave Hillary a hug. Greg enlisted shortly after graduation along with half of his graduating class. "As tough as it would be to hear your son has died, I can't imagine what it would be like sitting and waiting, not knowing if they are dead or alive being tortured somewhere." Joe's comment made Hillary cling to her husband that much tighter.

###

A knock at the door sent Amy and Eddie running to see who it was. They both reached the front door at the same time and froze in place as they looked through the screen door at the man in the Western Union uniform. It used to be exciting to receive a telegram, now it was a paralyzing experience. The man at the door looked back at them without expression, knowing what they were thinking and said, "I have a telegram for Mr. and Mrs. Joe Wilson." Working for Western Union had become one of the grimmest jobs in town, because they were the individuals who had to deliver the worst news possible about a families' loved ones abroad.

###

"This is the house. I'll take it." Amy opened the door and reached out for the envelope.

"I need you to sign here, Miss."

After signing for the telegram, Amy, with her brother shortly behind her, took it to the kitchen where her mother was doing dishes. "Mom...It's for you and Dad."

Hillary looked over at her daughter to see what she had, and her knees buckled, dropping the dish she had been drying as she recognized the all too familiar envelope in Amy's hand. It made a huge crash shattering into a million pieces on the floor in unison to the way her heart now felt. Her voice caught in her throat as she yelled, "Joe!"

Eddie and Amy both reached out and caught her, then helped her to one of the kitchen chairs, lying the envelope on the table. The three just stared at it afraid to read what it had to say.

Since it was Saturday, Joe was home from work. He hurried into the kitchen reacting to the shrill panicked voice of his wife to see his family staring at something on the table. He opened the telegram and read it first to himself, and then aloud for the others. Tears flooded his eyes making it difficult for him to see what he was reading, causing him to stutter.

August 1, 1943
Mr. and Mrs. Joe Wilson
    The Army deeply regrets to inform you that your son Gregory Joseph Wilson Private First Class was killed in action in the performance of his duty and in the service of his country. The department extends to you its sincerest sympathy for your great loss.

The message was short and to the point, bringing the remaining three Wilsons to tears of anguish. Amy ran to the swing in the back yard as her father tried to console her mother and Eddie ran out the front door letting it slam behind him. They all needed some time alone to process the horrific information they had just received.

Amy's mind raced with thoughts, 'It can't be true.' 'He just wrote to us last month.' 'There must be some kind of mistake.' But in her heart, she knew her brother was dead. The brother who had taught her how to ride her bike and stopped Peter Armstrong from picking on her in the second grade. The brother who had always protected her and had a positive word to cheer her up when she was sad, was gone. Who would cheer her up now? These thoughts only made the tears flow faster and harder as she sat there watching the sun go down unable to move, remembering what a great big brother he had been.

Eddie awoke early the next morning wanting to be out of the house before the rest of the family got up. He couldn't face them after the news they had received the day before. Anger raged through him, overpowering the sadness that he felt over the loss of his brother. All he wanted to do now was kill as many Nazis as possible. This was what permeated his existence when he entered the Army recruiter's office.

He remembered all the times growing up with his big brother, how Greg had taught him to throw a spiral football pass, teaching him how to talk to girls, and the many backyard campouts they had together, while he signed the recruitment papers. These memories only solidified his decision to enlist and avenge his beloved brother's death.

His family would not be happy about his decision. But it didn't matter now. He was nineteen and in charge of his own life. If he wanted to avenge his brother's death while protecting his country from the evil that threatened it, he could, and would.

3

The Master Plan

"Hello, Master. How are you today?" A dark skeleton-like figure stood in front of a silhouette of a man-like creature whose outline resembled that of a gargoyle more than a human. Its eyes blazed red creating the only light in the room. The creature sat silently upon his throne strumming his fingers impatiently, as the shadowy figure in front of him sank to his knees in reverence.

"How do you think I am?" The creature responded with disdain, as though he had been unintentionally insulted. "Enough of the pleasantries. Let's get on with your progress report. I have other disciples to meet with today in addition to you. How is the ownership of Oakwood going?"

"Yes, your unholiness. The people of Oakwood are becoming completely distraught over the number of recruits being taken from their small community and sent to the front lines. Your plan is working thus far, My Under Lord." The stick figure of a man reported. "The number of souls coming home in caskets is increasing with every deployment as we had hoped, and families are becoming desperate to protect their remaining children from such events."

"Good. All those years of plotting and manipulating to bring this town to its knees, and to have your dwelling included in the town's city limits have finally come to fruition. I think it is time for you to approach them with my offer. An offer that they shall not soon forget one way or another." The sinister figure growled in delight.

"Your wish is my command, sire. I shall contact Mayor Wilson today with your generous offer."

"The sooner the better. He must convince the counsel to sign before he hears of his second son's unfortunate situation, or our leverage will be gone."

"Understood. The town council meeting is tomorrow morning, so I shall make sure he understands that it is important that this opportunity not pass by," the kneeling servant replied.

"See that you do! Now, be gone with you," the silhouette ordered, waving his hand, sending ash and embers flying across the room. With that, the man before him rose to his feet, bowed his head one more time and retreated from the cavernous room.

The rising sun made the slender man flinch upon leaving the chamber as it met his eyes. He had forgotten to draw his blinds before passing through the sacred temple's doorway to meet the unholy entity to which he was loyal. He preferred the dark and only came out in the daytime to tend to business that could not be handled after the sun went down. Some in Oakwood said it was because his skin was so fair that the sun scorched his flesh when it was exposed to the rays of the sun. Others said that his skin was so fair because he avoided the daylight, and that his flesh scorched from his dealings with the devil. No one knew for sure, but everyone was sure that he was in league with the underworld in some manner. They even went as far as to say his name Mr. Blanchard was given to him by the devil as a joke about his paper white skin.

Remembering the things his fellow townspeople said about him made him think 'if those who gossiped about him only knew what the much younger version of himself looked like, they would be left speechless.' He remembered how dark his hair and tanned skin had once been when he was a small child before hitting puberty when his appearance changed. It seemed like just yesterday, when it had been more than a hundred years since he had been offered immortality and signed his soul and allegiance over to his master. Master had succeeded in making the idea of eternal life and immeasurable power seem impossible to resist. What he didn't realize was that to have this power and immortality meant living in the dark and foregoing the long days of basking in the sun, fishing, boating, watching sunrises and sunsets; all things that he had once loved as a small child when life was good, even in the orphanage.

After his eyes reacclimated to the light in the room, Mr. Blanchard picked up the phone and called Mayor Wilson at his office. "Good afternoon. Mayor Wilson's office. How may I help you?" a soft professional female voice answered the phone.

"I'd like to speak to Mayor Wilson. This matter is of great urgency." The voice on the other end of the phone was commanding and absent of emotion, in contrast to his statement of urgency.

"I'll have to check if he's available. Whom may I say is calling please?"

"Tell him it is someone who has a solution to Oakwood's frontline issues." The voice said.

"Yes, Sir, but may I have a name?"

"Tell him what I said. He'll want to take my call," Mr. Blanchard insisted.

Frustrated, the young secretary placed him on hold and dialed Mayor Wilson on the intercom. "Sir, you have a gentleman on line one who says he has a solution to Oakwood's frontline issues. He won't provide his name and insists that you take his call. What would you like me to tell him?"

Mayor Wilson was intrigued, but took a moment to think about it. What could this man be referring to? The only frontline issues that he could think of right now, were the many young men from their small community being killed in the vicious war over seas. But how could this person have a solution for that? The curiosity got to him. "Go ahead and put it through, Miss Barkdale."

"Mayor Wilson speaking."

"Hello Joe," a cocky voice from the other end of the phone responded. "Long time, no speak."

"Who is this? How do you know my name?"

"You mean to tell me you don't recognize my voice after all this time?" The voice chided.

"Am I supposed to know you?"

"It's me, Mr. Blanchard."

Joe turned pale when he heard the name of the person on the other end of the phone. "Why are you calling me? I have no business with you."

"You mean no **more** business with me, don't you, Joe?"

Joe's mind reached back to a few years prior when he was running for Mayor and was behind in the poles. Mr. Blanchard had been living on the outskirts of town for years at that time, wanting to live within town limits. He approached Joe with a plan to get him elected in exchange for Joe having the city limits expanded to incorporate Mr. Blanchard's property. Joe had no idea why he wanted to be incorporated into the town or what Mr. Blanchard had in mind to get him elected, but he agreed. "You said that business was complete, and we were square. You did whatever you did. And I fulfilled my end by having the town limits expanded. What do you want with me now?" Joe never wanted to know if Mr. Blanchard had a hand in his opponent's heart attack just before the election, making Joe the Mayor by default. And he didn't want to know now. What he did know is he didn't want to be indebted to this sinister individual.

"It's not what you can do for me, Joe. It's what I can do for you," Mr. Blanchard answered. "I know the numbers of fallen young men from our small community are increasing exponentially, including your eldest son." He paused to savor the sadness he could feel coming through the line. "I'd hate to see you lose the last of your name lineage to the madness happening so far from home." Hearing Joe's breath stagger, he paused again to enjoy the pain he was inflicting through his words.

"What do you think you can do to stop the madness and protect our town and my son?" Joe's voice was mixed with anger and sadness at the same time.

"It's not what I can do, but what he whom I serve can do. I am only the messenger. And you must understand before I tell you, that this offer is a one-time opportunity, and you'll only have 48 hours to either accept or reject it. If you reject this offer, your son and the rest of the town's young men are in the hands of the fates, which is not looking good for you or the town at the moment. Do you understand?" Mr. Blanchard continued to tickle Joe's insatiable curiosity with his words.

Even though Joe knew he should not listen to this man's offer, his curiosity and desperation got the best of him. "Yes, I understand. What's your offer?"

"Good. My employer has connections in high political positions who can make sure that the men from Oakwood are no longer shipped to the frontlines, but instead are sent to areas of service out of the reach of danger. He is willing to do so and place this lovely town of Oakwood under his protection, for a small price." Mr. Blanchard stated.

31

"I see. And what would this miracle cost the town of Oakwood?" Joe answered with skepticism.

"Only the town council would be responsible for the cost, and their successors, of course. That's not so bad, is it?"

"Let me know the rest of the fee before I answer that."

Mr. Blanchard sneered, "an annual human sacrifice to be completed on the day of the signing of the contract. Each of the council members must sign the contract in order to make it valid, and the council members shall be the only individuals to know of this arrangement. As long as the annual fee is paid, the town and its citizens shall remain safe and continue with their peaceful pre-war lifestyle."

Joe couldn't believe what he was hearing. "You want us to commit murder? Why would we possibly consider such a thing?"

"I can think of a few reasons. To save your last remaining son for instance...Or for the greater good even. After all, one life per year could save the town many more in return." In contrast to the subject being discussed, Mr. Blanchard seemed to be taking great pleasure taunting Joe.

This jolted Joe back to the reality of his dead son and the life-threatening situation that his youngest son was now in. "And if the council fails to pay this fee in any future year, what happens?" Joe couldn't believe he was seriously considering this, but if it could save his son and the sons of so many others, Mr. Blanchard could be right, forsaking one for the greater good of many had to be a virtuous action. Didn't it?

"In that case, the town shall be in breach of contract and as such, the town's protection will be terminated and the council members, and all of their surviving heirs will be cursed until the last one is dead." Mr. Blanchard's tone turned very serious. "I see," was all Joe could muster in response. They both sat silent for what seemed like an eternity before Mr. Blanchard closed the conversation.

"I know the weekly council meeting is tomorrow morning. I suggest you discuss this with your fellow council men and get back to me. Your deadline for acceptance and your first payment is midnight tomorrow."

Joe responded, "It might be a good idea if you were to explain the details of the contract to the council before I discuss it with them. Come to the meeting and I will turn the floor over to you to present your offer. Then the council will discuss this and take a vote."

"I'll be there promptly at 11:15. Enjoy your day," Mr. Blanchard said with an evil laugh of contempt, knowing Mayor Wilson would think of nothing else and be in constant internal turmoil until the matter was concluded.

4

The Contract

One by one the town council members gradually filtered into the small conference room located next to the Town Hall. This is where council members had been having weekly meetings to discuss town business since the town was established in 1894. It was pretty much the same room in 1944 as it was when it was built fifty years prior, a professional, yet intimate setting with oak wood paneled walls matching that of the Court House. In the center, was a round oak table that seated twelve. The town founders wanted these buildings to reflect the dignity that they hoped would carry forward as the town grew. The council preferred to hold their meetings here because it encompassed a sense of collaboration rather than the stark formality of the Town Hall meeting room. This week's meeting, however, may have been better suited for the Town Hall.

"Hey, Bill, how are things at the mill these days?" Lou, a short balding man who ran the local grocery store, asked his fellow councilman as he entered the room.

"So, so...This war has us working double shifts to provide for the military's needs, but we are shorthanded when it comes to workers due to so many of our men and boys being shipped overseas. So, it's a balancing act these days. Have you heard from Tom?" the tall redheaded man replied. Their conversation was cut short before Lou could respond by Mayor Wilson entering the room.

"Hello, Mayor Wilson, any good news for us today?" Lou greeted him with a smile.

The mayor's face remained seriously grim. "I'm afraid not today," he replied. "We've had three more young men killed from our small community this week: the Harvey twins, and Mrs. Bristol's boy." This news attracted the attention of everyone in the room, bringing with it an overpowering sense of sadness. The men continued their commiserative talk and took their seats as the last of the councilmen arrived.

"So, what's on the agenda today, Joe?" Lou asked as the mayor shuffled through a pile of papers on the table in front of him.

"Well, we have ten more of our boys and men being shipped out today, so we need to make sure to get those families added to our community support list," the mayor responded, getting straight to work. Joe was normally a much more social man, but today's business demanded he remain serious.

"I can follow up on that," a younger blonde man chimed in.

"Thanks, Chris. That is much appreciated." Due to a childhood eye injury, Chris had been declared 4F and unable to fight with the other young men whose lives were being placed on the line every day. But he definitely made up for it in all that he did on the home front.

"That leads into our next piece of business today." Joe added with a pause, "The safety of our community and community members." As he spoke, a lanky man dressed from head to toe in black with a fire-red bow tie entered the small conference room. All eyes fell upon him, and whispers began to fill the room. "What is he doing here?" "This is a private meeting." "Who invited him?"

Joe, at 52-years old, knew only too well what a toll this world war and the previous one had taken on their town, having lost his eldest son the year before. His wife and daughter had never quite recovered from the loss and were heartbroken when his youngest son decided to enlist to fight the enemy who had killed the brother he idolized as a young boy. The day his youngest son enlisted was the day Joe decided he had to do whatever was in his power to make sure that history would not repeat itself in his family.

Noticing the men's whispers, Joe turned to face the grim figure that had the room abuzz, "Thank you for joining us today, Mr. Blanchard."

The whispers became questions as the council members openly voiced their disdain over this individual being present at their meeting.

"Mr. Blanchard is here at my request," the mayor explained. "He has recently approached me with a proposition that could keep our community members safe from this devastating World War that continues to take so many of our young citizens." Although everyone else in the room addressed each other by their first names, no one even knew if Mr. Blanchard had a first name, as no one wanted to be on a first-name basis with this man of the black arts.

"What could he possibly do to keep our boys from being sent to fight?" responded a resentful voice from the other side of the table. Chuck, a middle-aged man slightly past his prime, was not one to hold his feelings in when it came to Mr. Blanchard. "We have no desire to make any arrangements with a man of his character."

"All members of this community are welcome to speak to this council," said the mayor. "Please hear him out, as he does live within the town limits."

"Not because he is welcome here, but because he refuses to leave the town limits," Chuck responded.

Lou, being the first to help those in need, and the last to leave his store at night felt it was his responsibility to look out for those less fortunate than himself and was well-liked by the entire community. As such, he spoke in an effort to calm the temperament of the room, "Be that as it may, he is still a resident of the town and does as such have rights. Let's hear what he has to say."

Mr. Blanchard nodded to Lou and the mayor as if to thank them for their support, making the two men feel slightly uneasy, before beginning to speak. "Gentlemen, I have graced your presence today with an offer on behalf of my employer." Sarcastic mumbles at the employer reference could be heard around the table. Everyone knew that he really meant his devotion to what everyone else called the devil. Mr. Blanchard returned to speaking as though he did not hear the comments. "Through our business practices, my employer and I have built quite a collection of contacts, who with a little influence from my employer, would be willing to manipulate the system preventing your community members from being sent overseas."

"And how exactly would this be possible?" Chuck again spoke out.

"You see, my employer's many business contacts are very high-ranking individuals within the government and military, providing them with the ability to strategically place individuals in safe or stateside deployment details."

Chuck asked, "And why would your so-called employer want to help us? What's in it for him?"

"It has not skipped his attention that the number of Blue Star Flags has increased exponentially, blanketing our small community in recent months. And now it seems the gold stars are appearing in equal numbers. No community should endure such sadness on such a massive scale. It is for this reason that my employer is offering his assistance in keeping your children and community members safe." Mr. Blanchard paused as the room sat silently reflecting on all the deaths over the past few months due to the war; remembering how worry set in with each blue star that represented a young man being sent to war popped up in a neighbor's window. And the sadness that flooded the community every time a gold star flag took its place, meaning that this unfortunate family would be receiving their loved one home in a box.

"As to the price, it is but a small sacrifice," he concluded with a devious grin, then turned and headed for the door simply saying, "Your mayor can fill you in on the more tedious details as we have already discussed them. I will leave you gentlemen to your discussion. Please get back to me by the end of business today with your answer."

The men all instantly looked at the mayor and demanded to know what Mr. Blanchard meant by "small sacrifice."

Joe took a deep breath and with a heavy heart began to explain the fine print of the contract set before them. "We are being asked to..." pausing as if he might not be able to finish his sentence, "The conditions of the contract state that the town and its citizens, as well as their descendants, will remain safe, prosperous, and continue to live their peaceful lifestyle as long as they remain in the town and perform an annual human sacrifice on the date of the contract signing by the stroke of midnight." Gasps of shock and horror interrupted Mayor Wilson, but he continued anyway. "If the town breaks the agreement, the town and its citizens will suffer complete devastation. This includes any descendants of the original town people and those who have moved away. On a side note, I think it would be best if only the town elders and their collective of members entrusted with the responsibility of keeping the contract shall know of the contract or its details."

"Hold up a second." A timid man in his late forties spoke up with a horrified and bewildered look on his face. Jack was the newest member of the council and rarely spoke in meetings. "What exactly are you asking us to agree on when you say *human sacrifice*?" Even saying these words out loud sounded like speaking a foreign language to him. The rest of the men looked at him and then back at Joe, hoping that they too had misunderstood what had just been put before them to vote on.

Joe reluctantly defined what was meant as a human sacrifice, "On this date before midnight every year going forward, we shall take someone's life for the sake of our town and it's inhabitants' way of life."

An ominous chill spread through the room as these men attempted to absorb what had just been said. Chris was barely into his twenties and found it difficult to believe that these men who he thought so highly of for most of his life were considering taking one of their town's citizen's lives each year, "How would you decide who you would kill? Pulling a name out of a hat? Some unlucky soul who had made one of us angry the day of voting? Randomly walking out into the town and killing someone? I think this must be better defined." He felt as though he might be walking a fine line asking these questions and was trying diligently to sound like a team player even though he was still in shock that they were having this discussion.

Steve added, "And who would be responsible for carrying out this deed? Would it be a group activity? Would we do it by lottery? How could we force someone to do something that was so much against their nature?" Steve was about the same age as Jack and had never heard of such an insane proposition being brought before the council in the entire eight years that he had served as councilman.

Joe elaborated more on what he saw the process being, "I understand your concerns, gentlemen. It is unconceivable to think that we would kill one of our friends and neighbors for any reason, or that we would force one of our fellow councilmembers to do something that they did not believe in."

Bill finally spoke up, "Then what?"

"I have thought about this in great detail ever since Mr. Blanchard presented this proposal to me yesterday. As such, I have come up with the following contingency for the sacrifice stipulation of the contract, if you gentlemen would agree. With having regular tourism streaming through our town, it would not be difficult to choose an out-of-town visitor as the sacrificial lamb, shall we say, and create an accidental death situation for them to fulfill our contract." This clarification seemed to address the main concern that was being brought up and changed the tone of the conversation that continued.

Chuck couldn't believe what he was hearing. "You are seriously sitting here debating on performing annual human sacrifices? I can't believe this. This is not the same as when we agreed to fast-track Bill's proposal to clear cut the north edge of old Oak Wood Forest public lands without a community hearing just so we could all make a fast buck. This is murder."

Chuck's point did nothing to keep them from debating for hours on whether Mr. Blanchard and his employer could be trusted, how his employer could actually fulfill his end of the bargain, and if they could live with themselves knowing that they could have done something to keep their children and community members safe and did nothing.

Chuck made it clear he would not be part of such an evil plan and said, "You're worried about being able to live with yourselves by doing nothing when what you should be asking yourselves is will you be able to live with yourselves knowing that you were the direct cause of someone's death?"

In the end, all but one of these honorable councilmen who either had a loved one fighting overseas or had lost a loved one to the war voted to approve the contract.

Chuck, the one councilman who refused to let Mr. Blanchard corrupt the town he had been born and raised in, angrily left the meeting upon hearing the outcome of the vote.

The remaining five councilmen and the mayor stayed to discuss the terms of the agreement. It was decided that only the acting members of the council would ever know of the contract or its contents. Additionally, the position of town councilman would from this point forward become a lifetime position. This was an easy change to make since the position was not filled by community vote, but by councilmember recommendation and mayoral hiring. The unanimous thought on these decisions was that the fewer people who knew the better.

"Now that we have clarified these details, how do we change Chuck's mind or at least keep him from saying something?" Lou asked.

After a few minutes of silence, the men realized that neither of these two options would be possible. They knew that Chuck was an honorable man who would not have his mind changed or be kept silent if he felt strongly about something. Then they agreed that if a human sacrifice was needed to complete the implementation of the contract and ensure Mr. Blanchard's employer would help keep their loved ones safe, then Chuck would have to be the first. They could not risk Chuck's outspoken manner exposing their secret deal with the devil's agent to keep their community safe. These reputable men could not bring themselves to say that they were entering into a contract with the devil or agreeing to perform annual human sacrifices, so they simply used the less evil-sounding terms "agent of the devil" and "sacrificial lamb," even though they all knew what these terms really meant.

The mayor pulled a contract from beneath his pile of papers and each of the men signed it, all the while telling themselves that it was for the greater good of the community. All that was left was to decide who would fulfill the inaugural sacrifice and how they would choose

Chuck's successor. Joe felt as though he had put these men through too much already and said, "As I am the one who has instigated this arrangement, I will be the chosen agent to complete the contract terms this year. We can discuss his replacement at our next meeting." This seemed to place the other men's minds at ease for the time being.

When the last man had signed and left the room, Mayor Wilson called Mr. Blanchard to inform him that the deal had been made and the signed contract would be delivered by close of business. "All but one of the council members have signed, and the last holdout shall be signing in his blood since he will be the first sacrificial lamb. Will this be sufficient?"

Mr. Blanchard eagerly said, "Wonderful. Yes. That should suffice if it is done by midnight tonight. I will inform my employer that the deal has been made. He will expect your first annual sacrifice to be made by midnight tonight and then he will set in motion the required steps towards keeping your town's people safe and secure."

Before hanging up the phone the mayor solemnly replied, "It will be done."

5

Closing the Deal

Mayor Wilson sat in deep contemplation staring at the clock after hanging up the phone. He thought to himself, 'three o'clock, only nine hours to meet the deadline...but how would he fulfill this terrible sacrifice?' The longer he sat there watching the minute hand tick away, the more he realized it was only right that he would be the one to complete the task. How could he ask someone like Bill or Lou, who were already going through so much, to complete such an unforgivable deed? Chris was far too young and innocent; Steve, the council secretary, and Jack the newest member of the town council, who rarely spoke in town council meetings, were definitely too mild-mannered to be asked to complete the required atrocity. And it was doubtful that Chuck would choose to kill himself to help the cause, especially since he was against the agreement in the first place. This assignment was far too important to be left to chance. No, it was his idea to enter into this sad agreement in order to save their young men and their town; and he could not ask someone else to do something that he was not prepared to do himself.

Once the decision was now cemented into his mind that he would kill the first sacrifice himself, he began organizing a plan of action. The best way to accomplish such a thing without causing suspicion or an investigation within the community would be to make it look like an accident. Chuck had a standing in the community as a hardworking, honest citizen and anything less than an accident or natural causes would cause the community to demand an investigation. This would also go along with the criteria agreed to for future sacrifices. But first, Joe needed to know what Chuck was up to and where he could find him; so, he called both Chuck's office and his home, unable to locate him. Frustrated, he decided to take a walk around the town square to clear his head.

He had only been walking a few minutes when he came across Lou, who was sweeping the sidewalk in front of his small local grocery store. "How are you holding up, Lou? I'm sorry I didn't get to talk to you about what has been happening within your family. Things just seemed to get a bit overheated at the meeting. How's Mary? Have you heard from Tom?"

Lou looked up with a gentle, tired smile. "I'm hanging in there. I'm more worried about my wife these days. Although I must confess, today's events have made me a bit worse for wear. No word yet. Last we heard he was headed to Antwerp. That was a few weeks ago. Mary checks the mailbox two or three times a day looking for his letters, but I remind her that it isn't like he can just walk to the corner mailbox and send her a letter." Lou and Mary had been married for three years before being blessed with their son, Tom. They had been told that they would never be able to have children, so when he was born, he became the center of their world. This made it even harder on them when he enlisted at 18 and was immediately shipped overseas to the front lines.

This brought Mayor Wilson back to his original thoughts as he responded, "I'm sorry to hear things are affecting Mary so. I'll try and stop by and see her soon. Now, though, I think I need to find Chuck and speak with him and try and calm him down if I can." Joe didn't want to bring Lou's mind back to the real reason Joe was looking for Chuck.

Lou nodded as he agreed with Joe, "He did seem pretty angry when he left. We can't have him telling anyone what we've done, so that might be a good idea. I just saw him headed out of town with his rod and reel about fifteen minutes ago, so my guess is you'll find him over by the bridge crossing. He has a special fishing spot near the fallen oak tree. I'd try there first."

Joe smiled, "Thanks, Lou. I'll do that." Then the two men nodded and went their separate ways, Lou returning to his quiet, meditative sweeping, and Joe heading towards his car.

#

Chuck was still fuming over what went on at the town council, so he decided to close his accounting office early, grab his rod and tackle box and go cool down at his favorite fishing spot near the dam. He was sure the rest of the council would come to their senses once they had time to think things over, but he needed to decide what his next move would be if they did not. Chuck was content with knowing that there was nothing that the council could do to move forward as long as he refused to sign the contract since per the town guidelines, all council members were required to sign any contracts, agreements, or legislation for it to be considered official.

As Chuck approached the bridge crossing that sat just south of the power plant's dam, he could see that his usual spot was a bit wetter than normal and figured it had probably gotten a little shower earlier in the day, but it would still be a good place to set up for some fishing. He parked his truck where he normally did and worked his way down the embankment, careful not to slide off into the deep water. Chuck had never been a very good swimmer so the idea of falling in was one of his biggest fears.

When he reached his favorite spot, he set down his tackle box and leaned his poles up against the fallen oak. He set up his collapsible stool and stuck a couple of reel holders into the ground. Chuck had a multi-reel license that allowed him to fish with more than one pole, so he usually liked to set up two or three to increase his odds. He liked to do catch and release, but when the fishing was really good or a fish died, he would either have a fish dinner at his home for friends and neighbors or donate them to the local nursing home for the elderly and disabled fishermen who lived there and could not fish anymore due to their health.

The town's small size made the nursing home a one-stop shop for individuals who could no longer take care of themselves or live on their own, no matter how old they were. Although it may not have been the most conventional method of managing a community's needy, it turned out to be a much healthier arrangement than the traditional institutionalized manner of dealing with those with special needs. The younger residents liked to listen to the older residents talk about their glory days, which in turn gave the older residents a sense of self-worth, enhancing the emotional environment and making it feel more like a community than an institution where people would typically go waiting to die.

This evening he figured he would do some good after such a despicable town council meeting and attempt to reaffirm his faith in mankind. Chuck knew that a lot of these men were permanently wounded veterans of the first world war, and it made him feel good inside to give something back to them for all that they had done for this country. When he had his rod stands secure, he sat down and began to bait his hooks; one with garlic cheese bait, another with salmon eggs, and the third with a lure and old-fashioned worm.

When Chuck had everything set just right, he cast and placed the first two poles so that the current wouldn't tangle them and then climbed up on the fallen oak tree to stand just at a secure edge of the water where he was sure he could get out if he fell. He was somewhat confident in his balance, and this was a big fallen tree with plenty of stability. This wasn't the first time that Chuck had stood in this spot; it felt like a worn pair of shoes to him, he had stood there so many countless times over the years. It was probably the one place near water that he did actually feel confident and was a great location for casting a bit further upstream and out of the heavy current.

When he had settled in, he felt himself begin to relax a bit and tried to figure out what to do about the town council's plan. He considered each councilman carefully as to whether they would be a good source to approach first. Chuck wanted to find the most trustworthy and reasonable man who would have some pull with the other council members. It wasn't going to be easy to change the mayor's mind. He was pretty set on this arrangement going through.

Chuck gently wiggled his line, trying to entice the fish as his attention drifted into his inner mind while he contemplated each man's characteristics and his knowledge of them. He was instinctually fishing as he meditated deeply.

He immediately eliminated Chris, knowing that even though the mayor liked Chris, and that he was a conscientious young man, he had also been dating the mayor's daughter for the past year. This would give him an unintentional allegiance to the mayor.

Next, he considered, Lou, Steve, and Jack. Chuck knew that Lou had more than any man should carry on his shoulders at the moment and couldn't bring himself to add more for him to bear. Steve and Jack were generally very grounded, and moral men who took their roles on the town council seriously. But, although they had spoken up at today's meeting, they were generally very soft-spoken men who might find it difficult to stand up against the mayor and convince other councilmembers to join them.

That left Bill. He was a sound businessman, and an ethical community member, who could see both sides of most topics. He knew how to stand his ground in any discussion or debate. However, Chuck knew that it was common knowledge that Bill's son, Nathan, had been convalescing in the Naval Hospital in Pearl Harbor for the past few months after being seriously injured in combat. This made Bill a wild card when it came to changing his mind about the devilish proposal. But he was still Chuck's best option, so he decided he would approach him to try to change his mind later that evening, hoping Bill had some time to fully understand what was being asked of them.

Joe was cautious not to draw anyone's attention as he drove out of town, but as soon as he was clear from view his foot became lead connected to the gas pedal. He thought to himself, 'Only fifteen minutes ahead, and it's a thirty-minute drive going the speed limit to get to the bridge, so I should be able to catch up fairly quickly.' He knew that Chuck would be fishing for a while, but his nerves were beginning to fray at the task at hand, and all he wanted to do was get it done and over with at this point, making time an ever-conscious presence in the forefront of his mind.

He had only been driving about fifteen to twenty minutes when he noticed Chuck's truck up ahead, pulled off by the side of the road on a dirt patch. This brought him out of his blind focus of trying to catch up with Chuck, making Joe look at the speedometer. He quickly took his foot off of the gas as he realized he had been driving 85 miles per hour in a 55-speed zone. The last thing he wanted to do at this time was to draw attention to himself. Joe slowed down and pulled over a few hundred feet behind where Chuck was parked in an area that provided a fair amount of cover.

Joe waited and watched for a few minutes after turning off the engine to see if he could see Chuck. There was no sign of him. Chuck must have already headed down towards his fishing spot, giving Joe the perfect opportunity to complete his task, forever preserving the town he loved. That is how he had to think about things if he was going to go through with the terrible deed that needed to be done. He had to view it as the only way to keep the people of his town safe for generations to come in this time of uncertainty, sadness, and turmoil; otherwise, he would not be able to live with himself knowing what he was about to do.

After it was clear that there was no one around, Joe climbed out of his car and began to work his way towards the river and Chuck's favorite fishing spot. He hadn't been hiking very long when he could hear Chuck's voice as he softly spoke to the fish, attempting to lure them in. Speaking to the fish was one of Chuck's tried-and-true techniques; at least that is what he told everyone when he would return with the best catch of the day.

Joe slowly moved in the direction of the voice. He hoped he would be able to see Chuck from an angle with sufficient cover not to be seen himself. This would provide him with the chance to evaluate the situation before making his move. As luck would have it, Chuck was standing exactly where Joe had hoped he would be, on his favorite perch at the water's edge on the fallen oak.

Joe watched Chuck for what seemed like an eternity as he mustered his courage and then finally stepped out of the underbrush that he was using as camouflage. He startled Chuck as he called out, "Chuck! I thought I'd find you here."

Chuck almost stumbled from his landing as he turned to see who was calling his name. "What are you doing here?"

"I came to see if we could talk this thing out and come to some kind of agreement," Joe responded with a friendly tone, all the while noticing how unsteady Chuck looked standing so near the water. Joe intentionally blocked his path so that Chuck was unable to return to solid ground. Chuck was an outdoorsman and in significantly better shape than the mayor, who spent all his time behind a desk or in meetings. Joe knew that if things became physical, he would need all the advantage he could get.

"What's there to talk about? I'm not signing any contract with that man, and definitely not under the terms mentioned. I can't believe that any of you would either. I've known most of you since grade school and always thought of you as upstanding, God-fearing men."

Joe looked at Chuck with determination and attempted to make him see their point of view, "We are good men Chuck, and I am sorry that you feel so disappointed in us. You must see it from our side, though. Look at how much pain and loss has happened to this community since this war began. Our young men are being shipped off every day only to return home in body bags. We must do something to help save our community and this is the only option available." His voice began to ooze with desperation as he finished his plea.

"No, Joe. This contract is not an option, and not the way to save our community."

Joe bowed his head, moving steadily closer to Chuck. "I'm sorry that you feel that way, Chuck. We have known each other a very long time and I never thought something like this would happen…"

Chuck looked at Joe with sudden fear. "What are you doing?"

Joe lunged hard at Chuck, knocking him off his perch into the deep water. Chuck gasped for air and struggled to stay afloat and make his way towards the riverbank. He could not fight the undercurrent that continually pulled him further and further down. Joe stood there, almost catatonic, as he watched his friend struggle, eventually sinking for the last time.

When it was clear that Chuck was dead, Joe began to survey the scene and decided that it would look more like an accident if he were to tangle one of the lines in a surrounding tree and throw the rod into the water making it look as though Chuck had fallen in trying to dislodge the entanglement.

After he was confident that the scene was set, Joe carefully worked his way back to his car and waited until he knew no one was around, before starting his engine and heading back to town. His mind was a fog of thoughts, images, and emotions that set his focus adrift. He felt his soul blackening as he internally reconciled what he had just done, causing him to harden a little. Joe knew that he would never be the same man that he had once been.

That evening Joe delivered the signed contract to Mr. Blanchard at his home, with the agreement that Chuck's replacement's signature would be accepted in absentia for this one instance only, since Chuck was no longer able to sign the contract even if he had wanted to. As he approached the 18th century Victorian mansion that sat on the outskirts of town, Joe realized that this home that housed such a dark-souled man was impeccably maintained. It wasn't at all what you would think a home of an agent of the devil would look like. He had never given it much thought or looked too closely at it before now. It made him wonder how someplace that housed such an evil man could be as inviting as this house was.

Joe's thoughts came to an abrupt stop as he was met at the front door by Mr. Blanchard, almost as if he was reading Joe's mind, "You like my home, Joe? It's one of the many perks associated with working for my employer. Come in."

"That's okay. I'll stay right here. I simply came to deliver the signed contract and inform you that payment has been made."

"If you wish. I would have thought that you wouldn't want to be seen doing business with me out here on the front porch, from our previous interactions."

Joe suddenly became acutely aware that he was standing on the front porch of a man no one in town would want to be seen discussing business with, "You're right. Maybe it is best that this business be concluded inside." He shuddered as a chill ran up his spine when he heard the door lock behind him as he stepped inside.

Bill decided to take a walk before going back to work at the mill to try to come to grips with what had just occurred at the council meeting. He had never seen things so tense or had such an unimaginable topic be brought forth for discussion, let alone to be voted on. Even though he had voted for the contract, he now felt the need to reconcile his decision with his innate core values. As he walked around the plaza, he saw Lou mindlessly sweeping and decided to go check in with him, since they hadn't been able to complete their conversation before the meeting began.

Lou was looking frailer than Bill had ever seen him when he looked up as Bill approached. "Hey, Buddy. You doin' okay?" Bill's thoughts transitioned from his own sense of guilt to concern for his friend.

"I'm not sure."

Bill placed his hand on Lou's shoulder and guided him to the hand-carved wooden bench that sat in front of the grocery store and helped him sit down. It was a spot where community members often sat on a cool evening or hot afternoon to socialize or catch up in passing. Right now, it seemed to be more of a lifeline for these two men who were desperately searching for a moment of normality. "How's Mary? Any word from Tom?"

Lou's expression said more than his words ever could, "Last word was he was being deployed to Antwerp a few weeks ago." The two men sat silent for a few minutes as they remembered that the news from that region over the past few weeks was some of the worst so far during this unholy war. "Mary's going out of her mind with worry. And I...don't know how to comfort her during this period of unbearable waiting."

Bill's head lowered, understanding how difficult the waiting was. He and Marge had been on pins and needles waiting for information about their son before receiving the scariest telegram of their life telling them that their son had been seriously injured and was being shipped to Pearl Harbor Naval Hospital for treatment.

Lou sensed Bill's empathy and asked, "How is Nathan doing?"

"Sorry to hear that. We'll keep him in our prayers as always. We got a letter last week from Nathan saying he should be home next month as soon as he is released from the hospital."

"Thank you. I'm glad to hear he'll be home soon. I bet Marge is all abuzz."

"She can't sit still." Bill chuckled. "If she's not cleaning his room, she's knitting him socks. It's like she was pregnant all over again." They both laughed.

Sensing a slightly lighter atmosphere, Bill said his good-byes and reminded his friend to call him if he needed anything. Lou returned the sentiments, and the two men went their separate ways.

###

It had only taken a day before Chuck's body had been found by hikers, washed ashore down river and the news spread throughout the town like wildfire. Joe was relieved when the final incident report was filed by the Sheriff's office of Chuck's death being declared an accident. The investigation was short and straightforward once the investigating officers located Chuck's truck and reviewed his fishing site, causing the mood of this week's council meeting to be substantially different from how most past meetings started. There was little chitchat, and when each councilmen entered, he barely made eye contact with the others in the room as he took his seat at the table and waited for the meeting to begin. Joe was the last to arrive and the empty seat where Chuck normally sat rang out like a church bell when Joe began the meeting by tapping the gavel and requesting that Steve read the minutes of the last meeting.

Once the minutes were read, Joe continued the meeting by asking for suggestions for filling the empty seat that had everyone's attention. "I won't make light of why there is an empty chair where one of our friends once sat. Nor will I ignore that we have an important and difficult decision to make when it comes to filling his position. But fill it we must. So, does anyone have a recommendation as to who we can ask to take Chuck's position? Remember, he will have to agree to those same vows of silence, and to spend his life fulfilling the contract that we have now entered into." The room remained quiet while each member pondered who they might recommend for this very important and unethical position that had been created under the pretense of serving the greater good. Each of these men had made this decision to take on the burden that this contract carried. But none were sure they were willing to thrust that burden onto someone else, especially someone they knew and trusted.

Surprisingly, it was Chris who had a recommendation, "I believe the person who fills the empty counsel seat should be someone who loves this town and understands all too well what is happening to those being sent overseas to fight." Chris paused for a response from the others sitting around him. The rest of the men in the room nodded. "As such, I think my oldest brother Charley would be best suited for this position."

Charley was well known amongst the council members. He had been one of the first to be shipped off to fight and had just returned a month ago after being injured for the third time and discharged. He would understand better than anyone how vital it was to protect their town's citizens from being sent to fight in this bitter war. Everyone agreed that this was a great choice.

"Thank you for your wonderful suggestion, Chris. Charley would be a perfect fit. Do you have a recommendation as to how to best approach him with our offer?" Mayor Wilson asked.

Bill spoke up before Chris could respond, "My boy Nathan and Charley were close friends before Charley deployed, and he spent a lot of time at our house. Maybe I could take him out for a beer tonight to catch up and thank him for his service. Then when the time is right, pitch our proposal to him."

"What do you think, Chris? Would Charley be more amicable having it come from Bill?"

"Yes, I think Bill's idea would be the best way to handle this situation. He has always respected you, Bill, and I think he will be able to commiserate with you about Nathan and feel a bond he might not feel with the rest of us."

It was decided. Bill would be the one to meet with Charley, make the pitch to him and convince him to sign the contract as the seventh member of the secret council. If he couldn't close this deal, no one would be able to and then they would have a whole other hornet's nest to deal with.

6

Audition Time

Jim didn't like school and didn't want to go to college after having spent four years trudging through high school. He remembered his many arguments with his mother over going to college, though. "Why do I need college? I hate school."

"Because it opens you up to more options in life."

"That's bogus and you know it. Why can't I get a real job and just work my way up like Dad did?"

"The world doesn't work that way now. Without a college education you may not even be able to get a job doing anything other than flipping burgers or cleaning toilets. Is that how you want to spend your life? As someone else's maid."

"You're exaggerating as usual, Mom. Dad, would tell me to do what I want."

"You have no clue what your dad would have said."

"Oh! And you do?"

"You're damn right I do! Your father and I had many conversations on the topic and started saving for this important milestone from the time you were born."

"Whatever!"

"Your father would be so disappointed in you right now."

With that, Jim simply rolled his eyes and walked away. But he couldn't stop thinking about what she said, and it was that last response that always hit home with Jim making him change his mind about going to college.

It seemed odd to him that so many eighteen-year-olds he graduated with knew what they wanted to do for the rest of their lives. He had no idea what he wanted to be when he grew up. When thinking about a major, he decided writing for the school paper had been one of his favorite activities for his time in what he called "the internment camp." So, he went with journalism.

One of the first things Jim did during his first few weeks of college was sign up to write for the campus newspaper. As a result, he was asked to write an in-depth local news article as an audition for the paper's writing staff. He had three weeks to complete it and the topic would be completely up to him. If he was accepted, it would help the editorial staff decide which section of the paper he would best fit.

Picking a topic had been particularly difficult for Jim. Sitting in the local diner pondering the many topics that he considered, he realized he wanted something closer to home that provided a unique perspective on life in the area. And to show how much progress had changed the landscape and culture of the region in comparison to other areas of the country, or maybe a broader comparison of the world.

While he pondered his thoughts on how to approach this idea, he overheard several of the other customers chatting with the waitress about a tiny town a few hours away that was the ideal tourist destination for those looking to step back in time to a simpler way of life. The waitress spoke of how it was a quaint, quiet, friendly, little town built in the late 1800s and was the perfect place to get away to for a few days. Jim thought that would be an interesting contrast point to use in his paper on how progress has affected small-town America, and how one town managed to maintain its small-town values.

When the waitress came to Jim's table, he couldn't resist probing her for more information on the town he overheard her chatting about. After all, being nosey is an important characteristic for a journalist to have. "Excuse my eavesdropping, but I couldn't help overhearing you talking to that couple about a little town not too far from here. Would you mind telling me more about it?"

The waitress happily proceeded to tell Jim about the small town. "It's called Oakwood. Not a very big town and off the beaten path, but well worth the visit. It's a couple of hours northeast of Highway 20." She paused for a second and then continued, "My grandparents grew up there and my parents would take me to visit them when I was a child during school breaks. It has always been one of my favorite places to visit, which is why I enjoy helping passing tourists discover the hidden gem. The people there are friendly, and life is still simple as it used to be in the past. It's almost like a living time-capsule of values and a lost way of life. That's what makes it the perfect place to escape to for a few days of relaxation."

This information stirred Jim's curiosity, and he decided to do a little more research on this "time-capsule" town and maybe take a road trip. At the very least, it would be a quiet place to write his article without distractions.

"Thank you for the information. I may just have to check it out sometime." Then Jim smiled at the waitress who was waiting with pen and pad in hand and said, "I'll have scrambled eggs, bacon, and hashbrowns, with a side of pancakes, please."

The waitress smiled back at Jim. "Scrambled eggs, one, two, or three?"

"Two please."

The waitress continued, "Bacon, hashbrowns, and a side of pancakes. Would you like anything to drink?"

Jim responded, "Coffee, and a small orange juice, please. Oh, and the hashbrowns extra crispy."

The waitress smiled and repeated, "Coffee, small orange juice, and hashbrowns extra crispy. You've got it," before she walked away and put his order in with the kitchen.

Jim sat taking notes on potential directions for his paper to go as well as drafting out a rough outline while he waited for his breakfast. When his food arrived, he caught himself shoveling it in as if he hadn't eaten in a month so that he could get to the campus library and begin his research. He was surprised at how excited he was to dive into the work now that he had a subject.

Finishing his last bite and chugging his coffee, Jim paid his bill and set off for the campus library. He wanted to get to the microfiche machines before there was a wait. With only two machines there could sometimes be a line that would keep you waiting all day. He wanted to scan the newspapers for as much information as he could find on Oakwood before going there to be certain that he had enough to work with.

Speeding through the city on his motorbike, Jim nearly hit a parked car's mirror when a driver started to exit their vehicle, snapping him out of his trance focusing on how to proceed with his paper. The near miss caused his adrenaline to surge and a cold chill to run down his spine, intensifying his focus on the road.

His father had been killed in a car accident when he was a young boy, making him know all too well how dangerous driving was, especially when distracted. His mother was very upset when she learned that Jim had bought a motorbike and made him promise to be vigilant when driving and always wear a helmet. Jim did the best he could to be a safe and responsible driver, usually wore his helmet, tried to stick to speed limits, never drove intoxicated, and watched for pedestrians and parked cars. The last thing he wanted was to cause his mother the same pain that he watched his mother traverse after his father was killed by that drunk driver.

However, he was just about to turn nineteen and a college student, so there were times when his mind wandered, making him less careful than he wished to be. He had wanted to take a couple of years off from school before starting college to save up more funds and figure out what he wanted to do with his life. But when he told his mother, she told him it was college, a full-time job, or a place of his own. Their many previous arguments helped him decide college was the best course of action in the short term; at least until he could find a full-time job doing something better than flipping burgers or cleaning up after others. His mother had always told him that this was her rule, he just never imagined that she would enforce it when the time came. Boy, was he wrong.

Jim arrived at the library parking lot, removed his helmet and ran his hand through his hair to fix any potential hat hair before climbing off the bike. He grabbed his satchel and trotted off to the reference section of the library with his helmet tucked neatly under his arm. The librarian's assistant at the counter was a young grad student named Sharon who recognized Jim immediately when he walked through the door. She had developed a secret crush on Jim over the past couple of weeks, watching him come in, and always flashed a bright smile his way when she saw him.

Jim was pleased to see he was the first one to sign in to use the microfiche machines and hurriedly scanned the Periodicals Contents Index for anything containing the word "Oakwood," then grabbed a selection of listed national and larger east coast newspaper films to scroll through before sitting down at the newest of the two machines. It was the prize that every student tried to get since the older machine tended to overheat, making it important to stop and give it a rest every twenty or thirty minutes. This was a problem if you had a lot of research to do because it could easily triple the amount of time you spent in the microfiche room.

He decided it would be easiest to start from current newspapers and work himself backward, so he picked up the film dated with the most recent month and started feeding it into the machine. The first pass was spent looking for any content that contained the word oakwood. Since the town was so small Jim didn't expect to find much.

Jim was surprised, not sure if he was more surprised at how up to date the library microfiche department was, or to almost immediately stumble upon a short article about the small farm community town of Oakwood celebrating its 90th anniversary the previous month in the July 1984 *Gazette*. The article went on to describe the town and its history...

Established in July of 1894 by William Oaks, the local mill owner. The town of Oakwood began as a small immigrant community. This quaint little town has somehow managed to retain its old-world charm and values, with one of the lowest crime rates in the country, higher than average employment rates, and some of the best graduation statistics in the educational system. The simple way of life in Oakwood could easily be compared to that of an Amish community if they didn't encourage science and technology studies. An average Friday or Saturday night in Oakwood is spent at the local movie theater, having dinner at one of the handful of community diners, or attending a school dance. Bingo at one of the abundant community churches is another favorite pastime, while high-school football is almost considered a religion.

Reading the blurb on the town gave Jim the feeling that he had just passed through a wormhole into a different place in time.

He found himself reading the newspaper article for a third time, wondering how a community could manage to remain so ideal without having the plight that often-affected small communities in this ever-growing technological age. He took a few notes for himself about the town and his thoughts of things he wanted to follow-up on.

Town established 1894

Founder William Oaks mill owner

Main residents hard-working immigrants

Continues to be a quiet farm community with low crime.

How have they managed to keep crime low?

What is the secret to their peaceful existence?

How has technology impacted the way of life there and what have they done to minimize its negative impact on the community?

A little further back on the same roll of film, he came across a large advertisement in the June 1984 issue of several papers, for a contest being hosted by the town tourism board. It was the 15th year of an annual contest for ten lucky winners and a guest to win a fully paid trip to spend August 11th thru 15th in the town for the Oakwood Summer Festival.

On the next roll of microfiche, there was only one mention of the town of Oakwood in addition to the contest entry advertisement. It was in the Obituaries regarding a Boston man, named Ben Jones, who had accidentally drowned while visiting the picturesque town of Oakwood. The article stated that he had slipped on a wet rock while enjoying the local scenery and knocked himself unconscious before falling into a nearby stream. The date of the article was August 1983.

As Jim continued through the microfiche he found a few gazette postings about town Christmas pageants, Fourth of July picnics, farmer's markets, community celebrations, and the contest entry advertisements going back to 1969 when it started. Beyond that, there was very little written in the larger newspapers about the peaceful town of Oakwood. That's when he realized that there was nothing before 1969 listed about the town in any of the microfiche. This seemed strange with the town being established in the 1800s.

It became apparent that he would need to make a trip to Oakwood to peruse the local newspapers, community library, and any historical documentation that he might be able to locate. This would be important information for the comparison of the town's past to its current way of life.

7

The Impromptu Meet Cute

Concluding that he had found all that there was to find from the documents on file at the campus library, Jim cleaned up his area before leaving, tossing the pages of torn-up notes in the waste bin that sat next to the entrance, packing his notebooks, print outs, and pens back into his satchel, and placing the microfiche in the return bin for the head librarian to refile. She was insistent on doing that herself since she hated when they were misplaced by others attempting to do her job.

The librarian was normally a very nice lady, but if you wanted to see her get riled up, just put a microfiche film in the wrong slot and sit back and watch the show as she turned red and mumbled under her breath, putting things back where they belonged; all the while putting on a tight, rigid smile for those around her. Jim had intentionally done this once or twice in the short time he had been attending the university, after a classmate told him about her reactions, just to see her reactions for himself. However, he was focused elsewhere today.

Jim was caught off guard to see it was already a quarter to four and he had spent the greater portion of the day sequestered in the compact microfiche room. The lack of windows made the room ideal for reading microfiche. There was no sun glare to reflect off the monitor screens. The desks were old folding tables, and microfiche films were neatly organized by category and date in a specially designed file cabinet hanging on one of the walls. The room was an old storeroom that had been converted into a wing of the reference department for the microfiche. It was easy to lose track of time here due to the lack of windows and the stark dove grey room having no clock.

It surprised him to see the cute blonde grad student at the front desk was still working when he passed on his way out. She usually only worked a few hours per shift so he would either see her when he was coming in or when he was leaving, but rarely both. He thought she had a beautiful smile and gorgeous blue eyes. It always made him blush, which he did not typically do, when she would catch him watching her flip her Farah Fawcett-style honey blonde hair out of her face so that she could see what she was doing. He knew her name was Sharon, by her name tag that she was required to wear. Beyond that, he knew very little about the beautiful young woman. She seemed to be shy and spoke very little. This didn't stop Jim from regularly enjoying the sparkling smile that she would shoot his way when she saw him.

Sharon looked up from what she was doing to see Jim looking at her as he passed by and decided to be brave and speak to him. "You're still here?" she asked in a nervous voice.

Jim liked that she noticed and decided to stop for a moment and respond. After all, it was the first time she had spoken to him, so it would be rude not to.

"Now isn't that funny? I was just going to ask you the same thing," he answered with a crooked smile. "Aren't you usually out of here by now?"

Sharon was shocked to hear he noticed when she was there and when she wasn't. "Yes, but we received a large shipment of donated books and I have the task of sorting them," she explained. Jim realized at that moment he hadn't eaten since breakfast, and he was ravenous hearing his stomach make a loud gurgling noise.

He blushed and played off the unanticipated bodily sound saying, "Hmmm...my stomach seems to think you should call it a day and join me for a sandwich at the student hall. I have to say I agree with him."

Smiling she explained, "I would love to, but unfortunately I have three more stacks of books that needed to be sorted before I can leave," then asked, "Would you be willing to give me a raincheck?"

"A raincheck it is. I just hope it rains soon." Then watched her blush before asking for her number. She grabbed a piece of scratch paper from the desk, quickly wrote her number on it, and quietly handed it to him. The two gave each other one last smile before Jim wished her goodnight, turned and walked away.

Even at 4:00 in the afternoon, the early-August air was filled with humidity when Jim stepped out of the library. It had been a particularly warm day and Jim was glad that he had spent the brunt of it inside an air-conditioned building. It was hot days like this when moisture permeated the air that made it difficult for Jim to keep his helmet promise to his mother.

Usually, whenever he was tempted to ride without it, he just remembered how crushed his mother had been when his father never made it home due to the irresponsible driving habits of another, and he put on his helmet without hesitation. This was not one of those situations. The humidity made the heat unbearable, making the thought of cooler air running through his hair as he sped down the road too tempting to ignore.

Jim sat straddling his motorbike after fastening his helmet to the back of his seat, before turning the ignition and revving the engine to give it a good idle. While he let his bike warm up, he sadly reminisced about the policemen at the door all those years ago, coming to tell his mother his father had been killed by a drunk driver in an early morning car accident. Jim was only five when it happened, so the words meant little to him. All he knew was that his father had left for work the day before as he always did, but instead of him coming home that night, it was two police officers telling him and his mother the next morning that his father would never be coming home again. Jim knew little when it came to details of the accident but had strong memories of that day.

These memories stirred both a sense of devotion to his mother for the loss that they both shared, and at times a feeling of resentment towards his mother and the universe. Resentment toward his mother for becoming so overprotective and toward the universe for taking away someone so precious, when it seemed while he was growing up that most of his fellow students still had their fathers at home; at least until high school when divorce became the word of the day.

Shaking off the terrible memory, he began to crave pastrami on rye with a side of potato salad. His stomach grumbled again in agreement, and Jim set off for the student hall to satisfy his craving.

The hall was buzzing with students arriving for their dinner after a long day of classes, but it was still not as busy as it would be in an hour or so. Jim decided it would be a good place to eat and review the notes he had taken.

He found a table tucked away in a semi-quiet corner and placed his satchel on top of it to reserve the table while he went and got his food. The student hall eatery was set up cafeteria-style for all the entrees and then with self-serve kiosks for other items. The food was decent, and the price was right for students who were pinching pennies and a long way from home.

The scent of lasagna and fried chicken permeated the kitchen area as Jim stepped forward to order his sandwich, looking up, when one of the cafeteria workers asked him, "What'll it be?" before she looked over and recognized him with a smile.

This had been Jim's regular place to eat since moving to Milledgeville. "Let me guess, pastrami on rye, with a side of..." she stopped and looked at him for a minute while Jim grinned and wondered if she would say fries or potato salad knowing that those were his two go-tos. "Fry...no, potato salad tonight."

Jim laughed and said, "Yep! You nailed it." He didn't know her name, but this was a fun little game she liked to play with the students who she recognized as regulars, and Jim tended to eat a lot of pastrami sandwiches here at the hall when he was studying. They were consistently tasty, and the price was right. "Oh! And can I have a pickle with that tonight?"

Still smiling she responded, "Mixing things up a little tonight, eh?" and the two laughed in unison before she turned away and returned with a tray that contained a plate with a steaming hot pastrami sandwich, a large mound of potato salad, and a kosher dill pickle spear, then saying in a hushed voice, "I gave you extra on the pastrami and potato salad tonight. You look like you're getting a bit thin." And she winked before moving on to the next student in line. Jim nodded, took his tray, grabbed a soda, and paid the cashier before returning to his table.

He dove into his meal as soon as he sat down taking a large bite out of the sandwich that was piled high with tender pastrami. He hadn't realized just how hungry he was until the food hit his mouth. He found himself wondering if the girl at the library liked pastrami, and why he hadn't stopped to talk to her before. She would be receiving a phone call from him soon to schedule their raincheck date.

In all the times he had walked past her, he had never noticed how blue her eyes were. They were like two blue marbles made to look even more vibrant by the hint of jade green that outlined the ocean of blue making up her corneas. Thinking about them made Jim glad that she had finally spoken to him. Then he returned to his sandwich before opening his satchel and removing a stack of notebooks.

8

Developing a Plan

Jim spread the notebooks across the table organizing them by what was in each. One contained his schedule and daily planners, another contained his class syllabi and notes, and the last was the notebook that contained his notes from the library. This notebook had pockets where he had slipped the printed copies of the articles to keep them for future review if needed. This would be more convenient than running to the microfiche room at the library every time he needed to remind himself of their content. Pulling out a pen and a couple of different colored highlighters, he set them on the table next to the neatly organized notebooks.

Taking a sip of his soda, he opened the red notebook that contained his notes from the library and scanned what he had written.

He thought to himself that there wasn't much there and that he would have to find a lot more information before he would have enough to write this article. This prompted him to make a list of information that he wanted to compile so that he could stay on track with his research.

What prompted the establishment of the contest in 1969? Where did the funds for the prizes come from?

Who did William Oaks sell his lumber to before the town of Oakwood was established?

Why was there nothing prior to 1969 in any of the larger newspapers?

Who were the other founding fathers of Oakwood?

What are the crime stats, educational stats, and employment stats like going back through the town's existence? Were they always this good? If not, what happened to improve them? How did they maintain these improvements?

Completing his list, he opened his planner and looked over his schedule for the next few weeks to verify the best time to make a trip to Oakwood to visit the town records and get more information on the history of the town and its beginning. He figured that would be a one-day trip for data collection.

Looking at his schedule reminded him that this was his weekend to drive home and spend some time with his mother. He and his mom had agreed when he went away to school that he would make the three-hour drive home once a month to see his mom and fill her in on how campus life was going. This would be his first trip home since moving. Although he valued his newfound independence, he liked knowing that it eased his mother's mind to see him, and it turned out to be a perfect time to do his laundry.

Realizing that it was already Thursday, he figured that he would call Sharon for their raincheck, before he left to go home for the weekend and wrote himself a note along with her number into his calendar.

According to his calendar, he had a teeth cleaning on Monday afternoon, so the following Wednesday was the best opportunity for the first visit to Oakwood. That way, he would have a couple of days to organize his notes and get in a date with Sharon before making the trip to Oakwood. This trip would have to be on a weekday so that the government offices would be open.

Having finished his dinner and sketched out a general plan of how to proceed, Jim headed home. He was looking forward to a relaxing night in front of the TV with a cold beer before taking a hot shower and hitting the sack. Jim had easily obtained a fake ID shortly after getting settled into his new apartment so that he could drink even though he was only nineteen. After all, he was in college, and wanted to have the full experience. His mother would not approve, but what she didn't know wouldn't hurt her.

9

Oakwood 1969: The Sacrificial Hiccup

For more than two decades the small town of Oakwood's secret committee who had been delegated the responsibility of performing the annual sacrifice and keeping the secret had fulfilled its obligation year after year without fail. There had been the occasional issue with lambs going astray putting minor crimps in the sacrificial plan, like the year the lamb was two hours late to the festival party and the committee had to improvise the sacrifice turning it into a slip in the hotel bathtub in order to make the deadline.

Or in 1966 when they were almost discovered by the life insurance investigator who came to investigate one of the sacrificial lamb's deaths. They lucked out when he arrived in town the day of the sacrifice and they were able to solve two problems at once by having him die in a car accident on his way out of town, incinerating his paperwork that could potentially stir up a more detailed investigation.

Then in the summer of 1968, the unforeseeable turned everything upside down. For the first time since the signing of the contract, there was not one tourist in town and the sacrifice date was upon them.

This left the committee in a conundrum: who of their own community would be this year's sacrifice? How does one choose one of their neighbors and friends to kill for the sake of the common good? And once the sacrifice was chosen, how would they avoid this from happening again? These were questions that hadn't come up since the very first sacrifice in 1944. The majority of the committee members were too new to know what it was like to sacrifice one of their own. Joe Wilson, the former Mayor of Oakwood, on the other hand remembered all too well what it felt like to take the life of a friend and neighbor.

Having been raised into the culture of the sacrifice by their forefathers to be a member of this committee and hold the responsibility sacred above all else, the concept of taking one stranger's life to protect so many other lives didn't seem to bother the newer committee members. But those same individuals were taken aback by the idea of killing someone they knew.

Joe sat at home in the dark thinking to himself, 'How can I pass on this burden to someone else? After all, I was the one who started all of this with bargaining with the devil's representative.' He decided that he alone would be the one to bear this burden.

Joe had not aged well. At age 76, he looked more like 90. The responsibility of living up to the contract for the past twenty-four years, along with the memory of what he had done to Chuck, had taken their toll on the once social and jovial man. He and Chris were all that remained from the original six who signed the pact, with the last of the others dying two years ago. Joe, Chris, and Charley who had taken Chuck's place on the council were all who were left of the original Secret Circle of Seven. They alone remembered how difficult a decision this contract had been to make. And only he knew what it had been like to take a friend's life. If it were the last thing he ever did, he would not pass this feeling on to anyone else to bear. That was it then. At tomorrow's committee meeting, he would tell the other six that he would take care of carrying out this year's commitment and the committee should focus on creating a solution to avoid having this ever happen again.

Having made up his mind, Joe placed the empty whiskey glass that he had been babysitting for the last hour on the side table and went to bed. Tonight, would not be a good night's rest with so many somber details on his mind, but sleep was needed nonetheless if he were going to have the strength to face the committee with his decision tomorrow. He changed into his pajamas in the dark and climbed into bed hoping that sleep would soon come.

###

After a long night of tossing and turning accompanied by a parade of nightmares, Joe awoke with the sunrise. He slowly slid his legs over the side of the bed and stumbled to the bathroom before heading downstairs to make some coffee. The smell of coffee brewing wafted through the room gradually bringing full consciousness to Joe's body and mind.

He picked out his best power suit and favorite tie before getting dressed to attend the weekly town council meeting, also known as the meeting of the Sacrificial Order. At this point, the name "town council" was pretty much a smokescreen for the secret society to meet, although they did tend to regular everyday town business. Joe carefully thought about how to present today's somber topic to the committee as he got dressed. With only three days before the annual sacrificial deadline, there was no time to waste.

Being the eldest and longest-standing member of the council of seven, Joe was well respected, and everyone, including the current mayor, made a point of greeting him accordingly as he entered the town hall. "Good morning, Sir, how are you feeling today?" chimed a chorus of voices.

Joe nodded back to each of them, saying, "Good morning. I'm well, and you?" He knew this would initiate a brief round of chitchat and thought it was the best way to put everyone into a cooperative mood before broaching such a difficult topic.

As Joe settled into his usual chair at the round table, the sound of a gavel tapping on solid oak brought the seven men to attention, causing them to take their seats and focus on the current mayor with the wooden mallet in his hand. The mayor, Tim Berkshire, was in his mid-thirties who had been brought up in the community to follow in his father's footsteps as a member of the sacred order. He took his positions as mayor and on the committee very seriously. This made him less social than most of the other mayors who held his position but he was a genuinely kind and sincere man. Joe understood the pressure and responsibility that went with the position Tim held and respected this about him.

Tim greeted the men around the table as he called the meeting to order, "Good morning, everyone. This morning's agenda is pretty straightforward when it comes to town business. A stop sign request, a new repair on the old town hall, and some budgeting issues. However, on the agenda for the sacred order, we have something a bit less appetizing. Choosing a sacrifice for this year's commitment. With no tourists in town and the date only three days away, we have some serious decision-making to do. So, I suggest we deal with this matter first."

The rest of the men around the table sat silently looking at their laps not wanting to be the first to respond. Joe took this opportunity to speak up and take responsibility. "I have put much thought and consideration into this very issue over the past few days, and I have decided that I would like to take this burden off my fellow council members' shoulders. I alone should be the one to carry out this dreadful deed, since I brought forth this collaboration with Mr. Blanchard so long ago." The rest of the council sat staring at Joe, not knowing how to respond.

Tim spoke up, "Joe, that is very noble of you, but we cannot ask this of you. It is all of our duty as the sacred seven to carry this burden as a unit so that no one member should have to suffer through it alone."

But, before Tim could say any more, Joe responded, "Yes, that is how it was meant to be. However, except for the first sacrifice, no sacrificial lamb has been from our community. I alone know how difficult it is to choose someone you know to sacrifice and then complete the act. This is too important an action to be left in uncertain hands. That is why I am saying I will take charge of this year's sacrifice."

Tim sat in awe of what Joe was saying. No one had remembered that first sacrifice since they were all children when it happened. Charley was not a child at that time, but he had not joined the order until after the first sacrifice, making Joe and Chris the only reigning committee members who would remember what the first sacrifice was like. It was only now that the six men sitting in the circle with Joe recognized the premature aging that carrying this burden had done to Joe, each wrinkle its own reminder of that terrible day.

Tim asked, "Are you sure about this, Joe?"

"Yes, surer than anything I have ever been sure about. This is my responsibility this year. The council should focus on a plan of action to avoid having this situation happen ever again." With that, the other men sitting at the large round table nodded their heads and decided that would be the most effective use of their time.

The meeting continued with the normal everyday town council business as if the previous conversation had never happened. Everyone was eager to put that nasty business out of their minds.

Before closing the meeting, Tim reminded the council members, "It is our responsibility to make sure this year's circumstances never happen again. With that said, I want everyone to be thinking up ways that we can ensure tourism at this very important time of year and present your ideas at next week's meeting."

After the meeting, Tim pulled Joe aside to talk to him. "Joe, what have you got in mind? How are you planning on choosing a sacrificial lamb?"

"Tim, you are better off not knowing. The more you know, the more of a burden you will carry."

"Joe, I will carry this with me for as long as I live whether you tell me or not. So, let's talk this out and figure out the most humane way of handling this together."

Tim was not going to let this go and Joe finally gave in. "My thoughts are to choose someone who is already dying and in pain. Take them out of their misery." Joe knew a lot about misery and pain. "I want it to look like natural causes and not just another tragic accident."

Tim agreed that this sounded like the best course of action. What he didn't know was that Joe's second option if this plan didn't work out was to sacrifice himself for the good of everyone. He was tired of living with the memories of what he had done and found himself thinking more and more about this being his number one option instead of his number two.

"Since I retired a few years ago, I have been volunteering over at the nursing home and become quite familiar with its staff and residence, which provides me with a source of potential candidates," Joe continued.

Tim took a moment to think it all through and finally responded, "It sounds as if you have given this a great deal of thought and I would agree that your plan sounds the most humane. If you have this under control, then I will go ahead and focus on working with the others to develop a plan of action to keep this situation from happening in the future."

Joe nodded. "I think that would be the best use of your time and skills. I can manage this on my own."

"Okay, just keep me in the loop so I know what's going on, please," Tim concluded before turning and walking away.

On his way home, Joe decided it would be a good idea to stop by the nursing home, say hello, and do a little research. Sacrifice day was only three days away and he still needed to choose his sacrificial lamb as well as the best method for carrying out the gruesome task.

###

When he entered the nursing home, Joe was greeted by smiling faces from both staff and patients. Everyone was always happy to see him because he made a point of giving his attention and assistance to all who wanted it. Few visitors came to see the residents, which made Joe even more popular. It made him feel useful and happy to be needed again. Retirement has a way of leaving someone feeling obsolete and forgotten, which Joe found ironic since most people worked their entire lives away just to retire and enjoy themselves.

Sitting in a large, soft-cushioned armchair gazing out the window across the room, Joe saw Betty looking more frail than usual and lost in her thoughts. Joe admired Betty. She was only six years his junior, but had accomplished so much in her life. She had outlived four husbands, raised two daughters, three of her five grandchildren, and nine of her eleven great-grandchildren all while working for the town building department. This was quite an accomplishment. Joe's only real claim to fame was the secret arrangement with Mr. Blanchard, and that had to be a secret.

"Hello, Betty," Joe said as he approached where she was sitting.

Betty slowly looked over at Joe and gave him a weak smile.

"How are you today?" Joe continued.

"I've been better. But I'm still kicking," Betty said in her usual sarcastic manner. She was hard as nails on the outside, yet tender and loving on the inside. Her twelve-year battle with breast cancer had taken all of the fight she had left in her, but hadn't taken her wit away.

"Was today a chemo day? You are looking a little less chipper than usual." Joe asked.

"Are you saying that I'm looking old? What a thing to say to a woman." Betty replied with a wink. "Yes, today was an especially difficult round of chemo, followed by a less than inspirational meeting with the oncologist. I wish they would just say I'm being used as their lab rat and get it over with."

Joe noted that Betty was in an even more cantankerous mood today than normal.

"I'm sorry to hear that. Bad news?" Joe probed.

"Same news, different words. Chemo isn't working, we need to try something else, blah blah blah," she answered with a snarl. "Twelve years of this is enough for anyone. But here I am, still fighting."

"Have you seen your family lately?" Joe asked.

"My eldest comes to see me once a week as if it were her duty, but she lives a long way from here so it's tough for her to get here more often than that. Her sister and her kids stopped coming a long time ago unless they need something. Even when they came to visit it was really only because they wanted something. My other grandkids make an effort, but are too far away to come see me more than once a year," Betty replied with a heavy sigh and sad expression. "They all have their own lives and things to do."

Joe's heart ached for her. She had given so much of herself to so many only to be stuck in this place to die forgotten and ignored. Attempting to brighten her spirits as much as his own he asked, "Feel up to a round of checkers? Or maybe Swap Out?"

"Oh! You feel like getting your butt kicked by an old broad today, do you?" she answered with a cheeky smile.

"Aren't you the confident one? You don't always win," he responded. He blushed a little as Betty gave him a look that said, "Oh really?" and he added, "Well, at least not at checkers." Betty was the queen of Swap Out. Joe had never heard of it until Betty taught it to him. Her father had taught it to her, and she was a champion at the game. It was exactly like checkers with one difference, instead of trying to capture all your opponent's pieces, you tried to force them to take all of yours. It was much harder than it sounded. Joe could see the color coming back into her cheeks as she smiled at him. This made him happy.

"Well, go grab the checkers set if you're that eager to get your butt whooped." She replied with an antagonistic smile.

Joe smiled and went towards the game closet where he ran into her attending nurse. He saw the nurse watching them and took this opportunity to ask her nurse about Betty's diagnosis and prognosis. "How is she really doing?"

The nurse looked at him with a somber expression, "We've done basically all we can for her. Now it's about keeping the pain manageable and attempting to stop the cancer from growing into her vital organs."

Joe bowed his head and asked, "Is she in a lot of pain?"

The nurse nodded, saying, "Unfortunately, yes. We have her on a brand-new pain medication, Fentanyl, it's the strongest pain medication available at this time. But even that is only taking the edge off her pain." They looked at each other for a long time before the nurse added, "She is a trooper, though. Even though she can be cranky on her worst days, she still refuses to give up or add more pain meds."

Joe looked over at Betty, then responded to the nurse with a chuckle, "Well, I better grab that checkers set and get back over there before I make her cranky taking too long."

"What took you so long? I don't have a lifetime to wait you know." Betty scolded him as he set up the board and checkers on the little side table that sat between them.

Joe chuckled and answered, "Sorry, madame, but you have as long as I do. But I will do my best not to leave you waiting so long next time."

"Well, that's better." Betty retorted with a gentle smile before making her first move on the checkerboard.

"So, are we playing checkers or Swap Out?" Joe asked. "You never said."

"Swap Out. You need the practice," Betty answered with a laugh. It made Joe feel a warm spot in his heart that he could make her laugh knowing that she felt so miserable.

After losing ten straight games in a row to Betty, Joe could see she was getting very weak and tired. So, he decided to call it a day and let her get some rest. "I give. You are the forever champion of Swap Out. I'm beat. And I must be getting on my way. Plus, I believe it's almost your dinner time."

Betty smiled at him saying, "Okay if you insist. But don't forget I'm here if you need another butt-kicking lesson." Joe collected the game pieces and put them all in their box, then the worn-out game board. He kissed Betty on the cheek, which always made her blush, and said, "I'll see you soon, Champ."

Betty returned the smile and said playfully, "Not if I see you first." And they both laughed.

As he was leaving, one of the charge nurses pulled him aside and told him, "She is always in a much better mood when you have been around to see her. Thank you." Then, she went back to her task. Joe didn't respond, he simply nodded and walked out the front door.

86

#

Joe mulled over in his mind what he had just learned as he walked down Main Street towards the Oakwood Town Library. He knew that the dreaded day of reckoning was getting closer by the minute, so he needed to make up his mind on who would be the sacrificial lamb and how it would take place. After spending time with Betty and learning of her latest prognosis he decided she would be this year's town savior. He wanted to make sure her death was quick and painless. She deserved that. Knowing that her future only contained more pain and misery made Joe feel less like a villain and more like an angel of mercy.

As he climbed the front steps and entered the library through the heavy oak doors, Joe nodded to passers-by who said good afternoon and wished him a good day. He headed straight for the reference section of the library and located a substantially thick book on medication interactions. He wanted to research what over-the-counter medications he could use that would mimic the medication Betty was already taking and put her peacefully to sleep for the last time.

After about an hour of page-turning and in-depth research, Joe found the answer: codeine. It was easily obtained in over-the-counter cough medicine and would intensify the sedative effects of Betty's current pain medications and relax her into the next realm.

His next obstacle was how to unobtrusively introduce the codeine into Betty's system. With her being in a nursing home, the nurses would know that she could not take it without severe drug interactions. This meant that he would need to use a trojan horse of sorts to get her to digest it in something she would eat or drink. That meant he would have to prepare something special for her that he could hide the taste of the codeine in. Joe decided to go visit Betty the next day and discreetly probe her about her favorite foods and beverages. Then, he would bring a special surprise to the residents on the important day with Betty's portion containing one additional ingredient. This would avoid suspicion about the food she ate being a cause of death since everyone else would be having the same thing and no one else would die.

When Joe was satisfied that he had a good plan in place, he put away the book he had spent so much time perusing, left the library, and went home. He spent the rest of his evening trying not to think about what he had to do over the next two days by cleaning the house, working in his garden, and gathering a collection of books and activities that Betty might enjoy doing with him when he went to visit her the next day.

#

The next morning was an unusually overcast and foggy day, which made it easy for Joe to sleep in. The stress over the past few weeks had exhausted him more than he realized. It was after 10 in the morning when the sun began to melt the clouds away and shine through his bedroom window, stirring him from his deep nightmare-filled slumber. When Joe looked at the clock, he couldn't believe he had slept so late. It was something he rarely did. Joe took some extra time this morning to stretch and work out all of the kinks, before climbing out of his soft king-sized bed. He looked out the window and watched as the haze cleared and summer once again made its presence known, thinking to himself that the initial gloomy weather was especially appropriate for this day. He decided to go see Betty after lunch was finished being served at the nursing home.

Joe arrived at the nursing home shortly before one, just as lunch service was being cleared. He brought with him a tote bag filled with books, games, and puzzle books to leave for the residents' enjoyment and placed them on the large card table in the center of the lounge area. This was where the residents congregated and socialized as best, they could since most were in wheelchairs or on walkers of some kind. He often did this to provide stimulation and variety to these interesting individuals who were at the end of their lives. But he somehow felt that today was extra special since it would be Betty's last day of entertainment.

After making the rounds and saying hello to the other residents, Joe found Betty sitting in her regular station watching the children in the schoolyard across the street play. Her love for children made this her favorite place to sit and ponder her life. He brought with him a book of mixed word puzzles, and a couple of large print Harlequin romance novels knowing that these were her favorite. Her eyes had long since given out, which made it difficult for her to do her favorite pastime of reading, but she still enjoyed having a good book of humor and romance read aloud to her. He set them on her lap as he pulled up the chair next to her, startling her out of her private thoughts.

"Good morning, Betty. How are you today?" Joe initiated the conversation.

"Good morning? Don't you mean good afternoon? Or are we back on the west coast?" Betty teased.

"You're right. It is good afternoon. Glad to see you're as sharp as ever today. Now maybe we can finish one of these crosswords together." Joe answered with a flirty smile as he picked up one of the books he had previously placed in her lap.

"Well, if you think you can keep up, then I guess we can try," Betty said.

Joe opened the book in his hands, flipped to a page with a cross-word puzzle that had the title, "Simply Movies," took out a pencil, and read Betty the first clue. "One across, A 1967 crime thriller set in Mississippi, staring Sidney Poitier and Rod Steiger, First letter I, third letter T, 19 letters."

"Oh, I see you have gone for a harder level puzzle today." Betty responded, "Hmm...Let me think." Joe and Betty had done several crosswords over the months in this same manner, he would read her the clues to save her from straining her eyes, and they would put their heads together to figure out the answers. Usually, Betty had the answer before Joe unless they were doing an easier level of difficulty. It wasn't that Joe was not intelligent. He simply wasn't as up to date on trivia as she was. As they started this puzzle, Joe realized he probably should have chosen one that had to do with food. It would have made for a much easier lead-in to finding out her favorites. However, it was too late now.

"How was lunch? Anything especially good today?" Joe interrupted Betty's thought process.

"Are you trying to distract me from coming up with the answer before you?" Betty teased.

"No, of course not," Joe responded in innocent denial. "I was just distracted by a smell coming from the dining room and was trying to figure out what it was."

Betty laughed at Joe's defensiveness and replied, "In the Heat of the Night. Grilled chicken Caesar salad. It wasn't bad." Joe looked at her confused at first, then realized the first half of her statement was the answer to the clue. Betty laughed again when she saw the confusion on Joe's face.

Joe chuckled and said, "You had me there. It took me a minute to figure out what in the heat of the night had to do with grilled chicken Caesar salad. Good job. That fits perfectly."

Betty smiled and asked, "What's the next clue?"

"Ten across, Errol Flynn and Juliette Greco starred in the 1958 adventure movie, 'The *blank* of Heaven'" Then they both looked at each other like two deer in headlights. "That one might take us a bit to figure out." Joe laughed.

"Especially since I have no idea who Juliette Greco is," Betty agreed.

"So, on an easier topic, what kind of foods do you like?" Joe prompted.

"That's an odd question out of nowhere. Are you hungry or something?" Betty said looking at Joe like he had a third eye or something.

Joe chuckled and said, "No, I was thinking about bringing a treat for everyone that they might not get to have here on a normal basis and was curious what you liked."

Betty's expression mellowed as she replied, "The one thing that I never get here and have been craving lately is a really good cherry cheesecake. Not sure how you would be able to get that past the food Nazis, though."

"Well, I have connections," Joe answered with a belly laugh. "So, what's the answer to ten across, madame?"

Betty laughed with Joe and then suddenly said, "Try Roots."

Joe plugged in the word then looked at her saying, "I thought you said you didn't know who Juliette Greco was?"

"I don't, but I know who Errol Flynn is and just had to think of his movies to find a word that fit." She laughed.

The two friends sat and chatted like that for another hour or so working their way through the crossword puzzle before Joe could see Betty was becoming very fatigued. "Well, my dear, you are starting to look as if you need a nap. I say we table this puzzle and I come back tomorrow with your treat, and we finish this then."

Betty appreciated his consideration of her energy levels and said, "If you like. But, if we keep meeting like this someone might think you have a crush on me," then winked with a smile.

Joe looked into Betty's worn-out frosty blue eyes and replied, "What makes you think I don't?" before winking back and walking away.

Joe made a point of stopping by the pharmacy on his way home to pick up a bottle of cherry cough syrup that contained codeine. Then swung by the library to find a cookbook with a cheesecake recipe and to the supermarket to purchase the ingredients for two cherry cheesecakes. Now that he had everything he needed, he headed home to prepare Betty's last dessert.

10

Oakwood 1968, Betty's Last Dessert

Joe had been up late the previous night preparing cheesecakes for the nursing home. Cooking was not something that he was particularly adept at; he ate out a lot since the passing of his wife. His wife had done all the cooking when she was alive, and he just couldn't seem to bring himself to want to spend much time in the kitchen now that she was gone.

This, however, was an important dish for a special lady and he wanted to get it right. After a few tries and a kitchen that looked like a tornado hit it, he managed to end up with two reasonably nice-looking cheesecakes that from the scrapings he tasted, were rather delicious. For the cherry topping, Joe made one batch to put on the cheesecakes that would be served to the other residents and poured some of it into a separate jar that would fit into his pocket where he added the cherry-flavored cough syrup with which to top Betty's portion. He knew he would be serving her, so this was the best way to make sure she would be the only one to get the special topping.

His nerves were beginning to unravel as the time for his visit approached. He had decided the best time for today's visit would be two-ish. That way everyone would have time to enjoy and digest their lunch before indulging in the surprise treat.

In the meantime, he decided he would settle his nerves with a mid-day whiskey. Joe wasn't normally much of a drinker, but today he felt like he could use a little false courage to get him through his day. He poured himself a large drink as he heard the grandfather clock in the other room chime noon. Two more hours until D-day.

At the nursing home, Betty was having a particularly rough day. Her pain levels had skyrocketed, her cancer numbers were off the charts, and her mood was somber. She did her best to stay positive and friendly as her strength waned. Lunch was one of her favorites: chicken pot pie with a wedge salad on the side, but she could only finish half of it before her stomach began doing flip-flops. The staff could see how bad she looked and tried to be as gentle and attentive to her and her needs as they possibly could with fifty other residents to also tend to. She smiled at the orderly halfheartedly when she came over to take her lunch plate and she asked her to help her to her favorite chair by the window. The orderly smiled and said, "Of course, Miss Betty," as she set the dishes back on the table and took her hand assisting her to a standing position and slowly walked her over to the big comfy chair by the window. Betty sat there watching the children at play for what seemed like a long time before nodding off. Even the simple act of eating was exhausting for her and required a nap afterward. The staff and other residents left her alone and let her enjoy her nap as she lightly snored.

Betty was still resting peacefully mumbling when Joe entered the facility at a quarter to two. So, he took the opportunity to check in with her nurse to see how she was doing. The nurse gave Joe a forlorn smile as he approached her. "Good morning Nurse Julie. How are you today?" Joe asked, hoping to lighten the sadness that was apparent on her face.

"I'm well. Busy as usual, but altogether I am good. And you?" Julie was a very kind woman who was in charge of the daily care of twelve of the fifty residents, which kept her continuously busy.

"Other than achy bones from a few decades of working hard and not taking care of myself, I am well also. How's our girl today?" Joe replied.

Julie looked at Joe with a serious look, "She's having a rough day. We had to up her meds again this morning just to make her pain tolerable. Her cancer has now spread throughout her bones and into her liver. I can only imagine how much pain she is constantly in. The doctors don't think she has much longer. Her eldest daughter is supposed to be here tomorrow for an extended visit and her youngest daughter said she would get here when she could, that she's busy with her mother-in-law." The two stood silently watching Betty sleep, respectfully admiring her strength and courage. They couldn't help but feel a sense of awe when they realized how much this woman had accomplished in her short seventy years, and now to be enduring what she was seemed anything but fair.

Joe looked at nurse Julie and asked, "Then I guess it would be alright for her to have an off-menu treat today? I told her I would bring cherry cheesecake today. Maybe it will brighten her day some."

Nurse Julie smiled and nodded, "Yes, I think we can make an exception to the rules for this special treat."

Joe took his time making sure to stop and say hello to the other residents who were seated in the common area as he worked his way over to where Betty sat. He felt his liquid courage wearing off as the dreaded moment came closer and closer. Mustering up the best happy face he could Joe sat down next to Betty saying in a low voice, "Hello, Betty. How are you doing today?"

Betty groggily opened her eyes trying to pretend she hadn't fallen asleep. It took a moment for her to shake off the deep sleep she had been in and then she replied, "Oh...fair to middlin'...can't ask for more than that now, can I? How are you?"

Joe flashed a toothy smile and replied, "Better than some and not as good as others." Betty chuckled knowing that he was quoting one of her standard replies to him when he would ask how she was feeling. "I brought you your cherry cheesecake."

"Well, that was very thoughtful of you. Maybe I'll have some in a little while. I'm still not quite over lunch. How did you get it past the food patrol?"

Joe responded with a small nod as he said, "No problem. I told you I have connections. Are you up for some reading? I'd be glad to read you one of the new Harlequin romance novels that I brought yesterday."

"Sure, if you'd like." Betty weakly replied.

Joe patted her leg before saying, "I'll be right back. Let me put this stuff out for the others and grab a book to read." Betty nodded without responding and Joe walked away. He went to the dining room and placed the cheesecakes on the table with the container of cherry topping he had made for the others, along with a stack of small paper plates, plastic forks, and a knife. He sliced the cakes into small wedges making sure to cut a slightly larger piece for Betty. He slipped the small jar of special topping from his pocket and when he was sure no one was watching poured it on the piece of cheesecake he had cut for Betty, then took the specially made treat, a fork, and napkin, went and picked out a book and rejoined Betty at her perch. "I decided to bring your piece over so that it would still be around when you're ready to eat it."

Betty smiled at his kindness as she watched him set it on the small side table that sat between them. "So, what is the location

22422222222222

for this book?" She knew that most Harlequin romance novels are cookie-cutter storylines set in a variety of locations and settings.

"We have a dude ranch and a New York socialite on vacation. It should be a laugh fest." Joe told her. Then the two chuckled together as he opened the book and began to read it to her. He delighted in watching her demeanor lighten as he read the book's crazy antics and when they both belly laughed after he read the line, "Get on the horse, you silly cow!" It wasn't really his type of book, but he enjoyed reading it to her very much.

Joe had been reading to Betty for a couple of hours when he saw her reach over and pick up her cheesecake. "So...did you make this yourself?" Betty asked.

"Why, actually...yes! Yes, I did. Just for you." Joe answered proudly as Betty took her first bite.

She savored it as if it were a bottle of fine wine before saying, "Not bad. Baked cheesecake can be tricky. Did you make the topping, too?"

"Yes. I made it special just for you." Joe was pleased when he realized she was enjoying it.

"There's a bit of a kick in those cherries," Betty remarked. "It's good, but I can't place it."

Joe grinned and said, "It's a secret ingredient."

Betty retorted, "It's not like I'm going to be around long enough to tell anyone." She saw that the thought of her mortality was something that removed the smile from Joe's face and followed up her previous comment with, "Oh, cheer up. We all must go sometime. And I have had a full life."

This prompted Joe to force a grin for her sake, and he leaned over and whispered in her ear, "Okay. I used cherry brandy in the cherry sauce to intensify the cherry flavor."

Betty raised her eyebrows and responded, "Well, aren't you the culinary expert. It has been a long time since I have had brandy. Thank you for this delicious surprise."

"It's my pleasure, Betty." Joe finally responded with a genuine smile. It made him happy to see that he was able to bring even a small amount of joy into this woman's last hours, even if she had no idea she was being a hero, a sacrifice, and the savior of their small town's citizens. It brought him some peace to know that at least one good thing was coming out of this gruesome task.

Joe could see Betty was getting drowsy as she finished the last of her treat. The nurse came over and let her know it was time for her pain medicine.

"On that, I will take my leave, sweet lady," said Joe. "I bid you a good evening and sweet dreams." He then left, taking the paper plate that contained Betty's serving of cheesecake, and her fork and napkin with him, tucking them along with the jar of leftover sauce, into the grocery sack which he had brought the treat in. He wanted to leave no evidence behind just in case there might be any suspicions about her death.

When Joe reached his house, he headed straight for the whiskey for another shot of courage to take the edge off of what he had just done. He took the bottle and went to the living room where he sat in the corner in a large armchair staring blindly out the window watching the sun go down, awaiting the annual visit of Mr. Blanchard.

No one knew how old Mr. Blanchard was. He looked old enough to have been around for a substantial amount of time, but he never seemed to age. Mr. Blanchard looked the same now as he had that very first meeting between Joe and him.

The phone rang slightly past eight o'clock while Joe was still sitting in the same spot he had settled into when he got home a few hours before. He reached over and picked up the receiver, paused to clear his throat, and said, "Hello."

"Joe? This is Julie over at the Oakwood Nursing Home."

"Hello, Julie. What's up?" He responded feigning curiosity, waiting for the news she was about to give him.

"I'm sorry to have to tell you...Miss Betty passed away about a half-hour ago, peacefully in her sleep. I know the two of you were close friends, so I wanted to let you know."

"Thank you for letting me know. I appreciate your consideration." Joe choked back a tear as he responded before hanging up the phone. His deed was done. The town was safe for one more year. Betty was finally free from her pain and loneliness.

The bottle of whiskey was a little more than half empty as the grandfather clock struck midnight. Joe listened to each ominous bell knowing that a knock on the front door was imminent. And as dependable as ever, when the last bell chimed Joe heard a knock on the front door. "Come in," Joe raised his voice to be heard from where he sat.

A dark ominous figure cloaked in black entered the room. Only his silhouette was visible in the darkness of the room where Joe sat. "I have been informed by my master that you were able to fulfill your end of the agreement again. Although, it looks like you were cutting it close this year."

"Not in the mood for your banter, Blanchard. Let's get this annual nightmare over with."

"Now, now...Joe, is that any way to speak to your guardian angel?"

"I wouldn't call you anyone's angel, you sadistic demon. Are we done here? You have confirmed your information. Now must I suffer through more of your company? I'd rather not be around you any longer than I have to."

"As you wish. Yes. You and your town are safe to live your perfect lives. At least for one more year, that is," Mr. Blanchard waved his hand in a flourish and a stream of transparent smoke began to solidify into a rolled-up piece of leather parchment. He held out the scrolled-up contract extension. "Your annual extension as promised."

Joe reached out and took the document saying, "Don't let the door hit you in the backside on your way out."

At that, Mr. Blanchard turned and left Joe sitting with his sorrows in the dark. For the first time, Joe found himself running his fingers over the texture of the parchment in his hand, wondering what kind of animal it was made from. It like the parchments before it, was unlike any leather he had felt before. His heart almost stopped when the realization hit him that it could be and most likely was made from human skin. Paralyzed by the thought, he let the parchment slip from his fingers, falling to the floor. He couldn't believe he had never thought of this before. Cringing with the image of human leather in his mind, he took another drink and attempted to shift his thoughts.

###

Over the following days while waiting for the next town council meeting, Joe tried his best not to focus on what he had done. Watching the town go about its business as though nothing had happened, children playing in the streets, businessmen tending to their business, shopkeepers selling their wares, and neighbors socializing as normal helped ease his conscience. He knew that his actions kept the town he loved safe for another year.

When the day of the council meeting arrived, Joe arose extra early in order to compile his thoughts before addressing the council members with his update. He dreaded the idea of making plans for future unfortunate souls to be placed upon the list of sacrificial lambs but knew it was required to keep those closest to him and his community forever safe. As these thoughts stiffened his resolve, he placed the signed annual agreement extension into his briefcase and left to meet the other members of the circle of seven.

The usual respectful greetings met Joe as he entered the oak-covered room and took his seat at the round table. He remained quiet and simply answered their welcoming remarks with a nod. The room was especially noisy while waiting for the last of the council to arrive today with chatter about this idea or that idea on how to bring more tourists into the town during the sacred time of year. It was almost as if the men were working for the tourism board to increase business, rather than a plan for committing annual murder. At first, Joe found himself disgusted by the chatter, and then he realized that this was simply the other men's coping measures to deal with the horrible reality of it all.

Mayor Tim Berkshire tapped the gavel on the solid oak table as the last member settled into his seat. The chatter gradually fell to silence as the other six men turned to face Tim.

"Good morning, gentlemen."

A chorus of "good mornings" responded.

Tim began, "Today's agenda is not long, but what is on it is of the most vital importance. So, let's get into it, shall we? I'd like to address the non-recordable agenda first before you start the reading of last week's notes if you please, Mr. Secretary." The rest of the men nodded in agreement. "First things first. Joe, will you please provide us with an update on last week's sacred agreement situation?"

Joe reached for his briefcase and removed a piece of paper before addressing the committee. "As of 7:30 PM last Wednesday the annual contract has been completed." He spoke with a very official and non-emotional tone. "Tom, if you would please pass this to Tim to be placed in the vault of records." Joe handed the gentleman sitting next to him the document and it was passed around the table to the mayor.

Tim reviewed the document and then stood up from the table and went to a large built-in bookshelf that lined the wall behind him.

He firmly pressed on an embedded carving of an eagle which released a shelf exposing a safe behind it. He slowly input the combination and placed the official single sheet of parchment into the vault with a stack of others that lay beside a very old scrolled-up parchment. After closing the safe, Tim returned to the table.

"Thank you, Joe," he said. "Now, I recommend we return to the recorded portion of our meeting. Mr. Secretary."

Tom read the minutes from the previous week and then turned to the current week's agenda. "The first item up for discussion is the topic of August Tourism Ideas. Does anyone have recommendations on how we as a community can improve tourism in the month of August specifically during the week of August 11th thru August 17th?"

Several ideas began to permeate the conversation before landing on the idea of having an annual Oakwood Festival during that time frame and promoting it with an all-expense-paid three-day vacation drawing to attend the festival.

"It's decided then," said Tim, "We will need the support of the local business community to sponsor this idea. Joe, you have the history with our town's business community to convince them to back this plan. Would you be willing to reach out to local shops, restaurants, and inns to solicit donations and involvement?"

Joe looked at Tim with a smile and agreed to reach out to the business community. "Yes, Mr. Mayor. I would be happy to take charge of this wonderful tourism opportunity."

11

Back to 1984, Another Weekend with Mom

The sun was already baking the landscape at 7:00 AM when Jim's blaring alarm clock woke him from a deep sleep filled with unusual dreams of small-town Americana. He yawned and stretched with a grimace as he smacked the alarm to silence its annoyingly loud beeping. Once silence again filled the room, he rolled over and buried his face in the pillow continuing to stretch attempting to wake up. He gradually returned to the world of the living and wandered to his small kitchenette for a cup of coffee. Knowing that he would need a little kickstart before he made the long three-hour drive home to see his mother, he had preemptively set the coffee pot to auto-start at 6:30 AM. The smell of fresh brewing coffee was Jim's favorite way to wake up, and today was no exception.

Jim enjoyed his coffee as he packed at a leisurely pace for his weekend before getting dressed and grabbing his satchel as he headed out the door. He strapped his bags to the rack on the back of his motorbike, then glanced at his watch. 8:45. Fifteen minutes behind schedule. He thought to himself, 'maybe I took things a little too leisurely this morning', but it was a nice day so that should make the drive pleasurable. He decided he would have to wait to call Sharon until he got to his mother's, but should go back inside and make a quick call to his mother to let her know he was leaving a little later than normal so that she wouldn't worry when he wasn't there at his normal time.

"Hello?" His mother answered in her soft, friendly voice.

"Hey, Mom. It's me, Jim."

"Oh, hey, honey. What's up? You're still coming, aren't you?"

Jim chuckled softly before responding, "Yes, Mom. I just woke up a little late and am now getting on the road. So, I wanted to let you know that I would be a little late."

Tess took a deep breath and smiled with relief as she said, "Oh! That's all. No problem. Thank you for letting me know, sweetheart. You know me...a giant worrywart."

"Yes. Yes, I do. That's why I didn't want to leave without letting you know I would be late...even if it made me even later." He loved needling his mom when she was being overprotective. It was their way of showing each other they cared. And, to some extent his way of voicing his frustration at his mother's constant oversight.

"Okay. Well, then I will be looking for you by one instead of noon then," his mother said, looking at the clock seeing it was now ten to nine, and laughing. She always added an hour to the length of the drive to allow for any stops he might need to get gas or stretch his legs, and possible traffic issues. She might be a tad overprotective in her son's eyes, but she wasn't completely unreasonable.

Jim laughed back before saying "I love you" and hanging up the phone and hurrying out the door. He did love his mother very much too. But, after two years of his mother's reminding him to drive safely, reminding him not to speed and to wear his helmet, ever since he bought his motorcycle, Jim just wanted to speed down the road and feel the wind through his hair without worrying about upsetting her, or having an accident. He wanted to be a typical teenager.

Tess kept herself busy puttering around the house waiting for Jim to arrive. She loved her visits with her son. But the idea of him spending hours on the road riding his motorbike made her nervous and overly worried. Jim was her whole life from the time his father had died. She did her best to let him be his own person, explore, and grow up into the strong, competent, caring young man that he had become without passing on to him her own fears and life damage. But she still worried about him, especially now that he was out on his own.

Time seemed to stand still as she vacuumed, dusted, put away laundry, and a list of other household chores. She liked to have the house spic-and-span whenever Jim was home. She managed to complete all of her chores in under two hours. Realizing she still had over two hours to wait, Tess decided to bake some treats and make Tim's favorite dinner. Since he was a little boy, Tim loved his mother's homemade lasagna and handmade rolls. It took her hours to make, but the effort was pure love.

As she gathered the ingredients and placed them on the kitchen island, she found herself thinking about all of the times she and Jim stood in this exact spot mixing batter and rolling out doughs or cutting cookies over the years. Her time spent in the kitchen cooking and baking with her son were some of the fondest memories she had.

Time went much more quickly now that Tess reminisced and was focused on making her son's favorite meal and cookies.

The phone rang again while Tess was putting the last batch of cookies into the oven startling her and causing her to jump, almost dropping the tray. She answered by the third ring, "Hello?"

"Hi Tess. It's Margo from the community garden."

"Oh, hey, Margo. How are you?"

"I'm okay, but I need a favor."

"Sure, if I can help, I'd be glad to."

"I've accidentally double booked myself for my turn to tend to the garden this week, and I was hoping you would be willing to trade days with me. My day is Thursday."

"Let me look at my schedule real quick." Looking at her calendar, Tess saw that she had yoga class on Monday, volunteer duty at the library on Wednesday, and a doctor's appointment on Friday for her annual physical. "Looks like Thursday is free. My normal day at the garden is Tuesday. Will that work for you?"

"Yes! Thank you, Tess. I absentmindedly told my niece that I could drive her to Atlanta that day and I really didn't want to cancel on her. She never asks me for favors."

"Not a problem, Marge. Garden duties moved from Tuesday to Thursday for me this week."

"I owe you one, Tess. Let me know if you ever need anything."

"You're welcome. But I've gotta go. I have cookies in the oven and the timer just went off."

"Okay, bye."

"Bye." Tess hung up the phone and ran over to the oven. She pulled the cookies out just in time to keep them from over browning on the bottom. She enjoyed her shifts at the community garden for two reasons. One, she got to do one of her favorite hobbies, gardening. Two, she was able to get fresh vegetables for free without having a garden in her own yard and had assistance with maintaining the garden.

Additionally, she liked the idea of there being no waste, where if she had her own garden, she would have to do all the work and wouldn't be able to eat or give away all of the harvest. The community garden was a win-win opportunity.

Tess felt badly about cutting her conversation short with Marge. She was one of her best friends and she enjoyed talking to Marge normally, but their talks could go on for hours, and Tess just didn't have the time this morning with Jim coming home for the weekend. She decided she would make it up to her by saving her some cookies and dropping them off after Jim went back to school.

###

The sun sprayed through the trees that lined I-20 as Jim sped along the highway. The shade was genuinely welcome, creating a barrier from the scorching sun. Jim was glad he opted not to wear a jacket. His helmet absorbed enough heat to make him sweat even with the headwind. Although the drive was long, he enjoyed the scenery and the feel of the wind on his face as well as the time to think. His thoughts transitioned from his visit to the campus library to Sharon, who he looked forward to getting to know better. Then back to his article and the topic. He thought it would be a good idea to get a feel for the history of the town by researching the founding fathers, mayors, council members, and the method of local government that maintained the town's almost unfathomable ideal existence.

Jim made a mental note to visit local church archives in addition to his plan of going through library and town hall archives. Then his thoughts again returned to the pretty blonde who always greeted him at the library with a charming smile. It was difficult for him to get those gorgeous blue eyes out of his mind on such a perfect day. He found himself wondering what she would be doing this weekend and vowed to call her when he got settled in at his mother's. That should cause a ruckus. Since his mother and father had been high school sweethearts who married right after graduation then had him the next year, Tess felt like Jim's casual attitude towards dating left something to be desired. His mother tended to try and turn any potential dating relationship Jim had into something serious. He always rolled his eyes and told her, "It will happen when it happens. I have plenty of time for something serious later in life." Jim thought that his father's untimely death at such a young age made his mother's biological grandma clock start ticking faster than most mothers.

The thought of his mother having a biological grandma clock made Jim laugh aloud picturing a grandma clock shaped like a babushka with arms that rotated to phrases like 'you better find a girl, before time runs out', or 'you're not getting any younger and neither am I', instead of numbers surrounding the clock face.

Jim quickly looked down at his watch as he passed an off-ramp sign that he recognized as being thirty minutes from his mother's and was pleased to see that he was ten minutes ahead of when he expected to arrive. He realized he must have picked up speed inadvertently while he was lost in his thoughts and looked at the speedometer. When he saw it read 90 miles per hour, he decided he better ease back on the throttle and stop tempting fate, then slowed to 80; after all, the speed limit was 70, but no one actually drove that.

Jim slowed to an idle as he entered his mother's driveway. He made sure to park his motorbike off to the side near the garage so that his mother had room to pull past if she needed to go out; just as he had done ever since he bought his motorbike shortly after his sixteenth birthday.

His mother, with her hawk-like hearing, heard him pull up and looked out the kitchen window before smiling in relief at seeing her precious boy arrive safely at home. She quickly turned and began arranging their lunch on the table so that it would be ready when he came in.

Jim smiled as he saw his mother busily arranging his plate on the kitchen table just as she had done so many times for him throughout his lifetime. "Hello, Mama,"

"Oh, Jim! I'm glad you're home. How was your drive?"

"It was peaceful and uneventful. I am glad to be home too," Jim answered as he gave his mother a big bear hug and kiss on the cheek before taking his bags to his room.

When Jim reached his bedroom, he threw his bags on the floor beside his bed and dove onto his all too familiar lumpy mattress that had been his loyal servant all through junior high and high school, providing him with many slumber-filled nights. He badly needed to stretch out after that long ride. As much as he loved riding his motorbike, he had to admit that the long road trips played havoc on the body. Jim lay there enjoying the feeling of blood flowing once more to his limbs and fingertips as he stretched in all directions, like a cat in a sunny window after a long nap, until he heard his mother call to him, "Jim, come eat your lunch. The bread on your sandwich is going to dry out."

"Coming, Mom," he responded with a slight chuckle in his tone and roll of his eyes. Stretching one last time then walked to the kitchen. "Looks good, Mom. You didn't have to make me lunch. I'm a big boy now."

Tess smiled back at him and replied, "I know you are, but it's a mom thing. We like to know our kids are eating often and healthy, so we feed them every chance we get. Even when they get old and decrepit like you." She loved to banter with him and couldn't resist the opportunity to play on his words.

Jim laughed along with her. "Well, that is one thing you have always done for this decrepit big boy." He remembered how he and his mother had always played these word games together while he was growing up and cherished the moment to do it again. "Hey, Mom, I need to make a phone call after I finish eating and then we can sit and catch up, okay?"

"No problem. Business or pleasure?" His mom asked with a hint of excitement in her voice. Jim knew she would be probing him for information on his love life and this gave her the perfect opening. He decided to let her keep wondering for a little while longer and took a big bite of his sandwich so that she could not expect an immediate answer without breaking her own rule of no talking with your mouth full.

Savoring the anticipation on his mother's face as she waited for him to answer, Jim intentionally chewed slowly taking some guilty pleasure at his mother's frustration with having to wait for an answer.

After all, it was only fair that he tortured her a little after the many times she tortured him with questions regarding when he would be finding a girlfriend. Just as he thought she could handle it no longer, Jim finally swallowed and replied, "Potentially pleasure, Mother. But don't get all ooey-gooey over this. We have only spoken once or twice and that was in passing."

His mother couldn't hide her excitement but tried her best to contain it. She didn't like to pressure Jim. She simply looked forward to having little ones around again. "Okay...okay...I get it. Cool my jets. But you will invite me to the wedding, won't you?"

Jim rolled his eyes before smiling back at her and taking another bite of his sandwich. "Seriously! You're going to take it there already?" This time ignoring the no talking with your mouth full rule.

Tess could hear the slightly annoyed tone in his voice, "I was just teasing you. Don't be so touchy. And don't talk with your mouth full." That ended their lunch time chit chat and the two ate in silence.

When Jim finished his lunch he took his mother's cordless phone, kissed his mother's cheek as he thanked her, and went outside to make his phone call. "Thanks for another great lunch, Mom. You really are the best," he said with a wink.

He took a seat on the large porch swing, where he had many fond memories of spending evenings chatting alongside his mother, before he called Sharon's number. Butterflies suddenly filled his stomach as he listened to the phone ringing, one...two...he was taken aback by this onset of nerves that he had never had before when calling a girl. Three...four...the phone continued to ring and his mind began to run through scenarios, 'maybe she is working, or on another date, or avoiding my call having only given me her number to be kind, or worse yet maybe she had given me a wrong number.' He shook his head trying to clear his mind of the ridiculous thoughts that were filling his consciousness and get back to feeling like himself again. He was about to hang up after the phone rang for the sixth time, when he heard a soft, out-of-breath voice pick up on the other end, "Hello?"

Jim smiled when he heard the happy tone in her out-of-breath response. "Well, hello there. It's Jim Norton. I was about to hang up thinking you were too busy to take my call," he teased her. He was suddenly feeling like his playful self now.

Sharon chuckled at his response and replied, "I didn't want you to feel too important, so I made a point of letting the phone ring a few times before taking a break just for you." She wasn't typically so quick to banter back, but this guy seemed to bring it out in her. Something that to her surprise she rather liked. "How are you?"

It brought a smile to Jim's face to hear her ask about him. "I'm good, thank you. How is your weekend going?"

"Well let's see...Today I have lunch with the Queen, followed by dinner with the President. But in between, I will be cleaning my apartment, moving out my old roommate's left-behind items, of which there are plenty, and then washing my hair. Does that sound busy enough for you?" she quickly replied with a laugh.

Jim laughed too. "Yes! That sounds quite busy. So, lunch with the Queen and dinner with the President, eh? I had no idea you had such influential friends. How did you manage to mingle in that circle?"

"Well, actually, I was born into that circle since my foster mom thinks she is Queen of all she surveys, and my foster father is Branch President at the local bank." They laughed in unison.

"I thought that you might be working at the library on a Friday. But now that I think of it, I don't recall seeing you there when I have been there on Fridays," Jim said.

"My normal schedule is Monday thru Thursday with Fridays and Saturdays off. When I first started my internship, I had a Friday class, so I was given Friday and Saturday off. And the library is closed on Sunday. When my class was completed, it was just easier for the head librarian not to have to rearrange everyone's schedules. So, I kept the schedule I had."

"That's convenient. How much longer do you have to complete your internship?"

"Another eight months. The short week has extended the number of weeks to complete the internship in order to meet the number of hours required," Sharon answered, sounding a little deflated.

"That works out well, then. I should be finishing my first semester around the same time. I'll get to have your lovely face brighten my long hours of studying and research. Did I just hear you say you were a foster child?"

"Well...of sorts. I was a teenager when I went to live with my godparents. That's a topic for another time though." Sharon didn't want to dump all of her baggage on this guy at once. Better to spread it out over time to keep the interest flowing and not scare him off.

"So, what are you up to Sunday night?"

"Sunday is my one free day this weekend. What did you have in mind?"

"I should be back in town by about three. So, if you would like to have an early dinner about five, and then maybe see a movie or something, I wouldn't complain," Jim said.

Sharon laughed, "Glad to hear you're not a complainer. Where did you go? Sunday, at five sounds good. Shall we meet at the student hall?"

"Sunday at five at the student hall it is. I made the trip back home to see my mom for the weekend. We have a once per month visit agreement. I better go before my mom is out here probing me for details about you; she'll be chiming into our conversation in no time," Jim said with a laugh, "I'll see you then."

Laughing in response, Sharon said, "See you then," before hanging up the phone.

Jim's mother was standing at the kitchen sink smiling at him when he returned. "That sounded as if it went well." She had been standing there listening with great anticipation. "So, is this my chance to probe you for details, since I didn't get my chance to chime in?" She said chiding him as a response to his final comment when speaking to his new young lady.

Jim rolled his eyes at his mother answering, "No, Mom. Let us get to know each other before I have to answer your interrogation."

They smiled at each other affectionately and walked into the family room together to sit down for a long chat and conversation catching up on each other's life events. He talked about his audition article and school events while she updated him on the garden club, book club, and work happening at the library. The library where she volunteered was doing some restorations and redecorating that was causing issues locating books while they were being shifted around in the redesign and construction. The chaos and lack of organization had her flustered saying, "A library of all places should be the picture of organization."

The thought of his mother working in such an environment made Jim shake his head with disbelief, "I can see you going all PTA Mom on the construction guys every time they put something in the wrong place or where you can't find it. They must be running for the hills every time they see you coming." Jim laughed at the image of big burley construction workers running away from his petite mom in fear.

"Haha. Very funny. You try keeping things quiet and organized with men shuffling things all willy-nilly. And, the drilling and hammering is enough to drive anyone to be a...what was it you called me...oh yeah...a PTA mom...whatever that is supposed to mean."

"It means you're a control freak, Mom. Which is fine for a librarian. Just not with construction workers." Jim could see his mother's feelings were getting hurt and decided it was time to do something else. "Should we go to the community garden and pick up some vegetables for tonight's salad?" He knew that would take her mind off of his words that she found offensive. Tess agreed and the two took a leisurely stroll to the garden that was only three blocks away.

Sharon plopped in the oversized chair that sat in front of her balcony window, taking a deep breath after the phone call. She took a moment to catch her breath before putting away the groceries she had been lugging in when the phone rang. It was a pleasant surprise to hear from Jim so soon. She hadn't expected to get a call from him until after the weekend since in her experience, most freshmen liked to play hard to get, make them wait for the call game trying to make themselves seem older. This would be the first freshman she had dated since she was a freshman; and the first younger man ever. This thought brought an unintentional smile to her face as her eyes wandered to the floor by the door where the groceries landed as she leapt for the phone when she came in.

After a brief pause, she hurried to put away the groceries. She searched each bag for the frozen and refrigerated items looking closely for the ice cream. Ice cream was her one special indulgence, a favorite treat of hers since childhood. Being a grad student living on an intern's income had made her a very frugal shopper. Her mother had taught her at an early age how to make a dollar stretch at the grocery store as well as how to make an array of simple dishes to stretch meals and meal plans. She was only fifteen when her mother died of cancer, and she went to live with her godparents. They were very kind people. But they were of meager means as well, even though they kept up appearances. If it hadn't been for Sharon receiving scholarships and grants, she never would have been able to attend college, let alone get her Masters in Library Science.

As she completed her task, she replayed the conversation with Jim in her head, smiling at the flirty banter that the two were able to have with one another. After weeks of watching Jim come and go from the library, rarely even nodding at one another, to finally be receiving a call and going on a date seemed like pretty good forward momentum. She allowed herself a moment or two of indulgent thoughts before looking around her small apartment and taking a deep sigh. Her last roommate had left such a mess everywhere when she moved out the week before and Sharon had not had time until now to clean up.

She set straight to work picking up boxes and scattered newspapers, rearranging personal items and furniture that had been disheveled during Muriel's departure. As roommates go, Muriel hadn't been the best or the worst in Sharon's experience. But she definitely was the messiest she had ever had. The experience had made Sharon decide that she was done with having roommates even if it meant taking on a second job. Now that her Friday night classes were complete, she had a free day or two to find a part-time job to help cover expenses if she had to.

The sun began to set, and Sharon realized that she had been cleaning and shuffling things about for several hours and was ready for a break. She stood and looked around at her handiwork with satisfaction at how much better the place looked, before looking in the mirror that hung in the entryway and seeing her mangled hair and dirty face. 'Time for a shower and then dinner and TV,' she thought slipping out of her T-shirt and heading to the bathroom.

###

When they returned from the community garden, Jim helped his mother in her flower garden and did a few household maintenance projects to help her out as they spoke. It was normal for them to chitchat for hours when he was home catching up on neighborhood gossip, each other's lives, and anything else that happened to cross their paths. This visit was no different.

He enjoyed their talks and helping his mother around the house. He knew she would never ask. "Thank you, Jim, for all your help around here today. It seems to be getting harder and harder to keep up with the everyday things without falling behind on the maintenance projects," his mother said with gratitude.

A smile crossed Jim's face as he watched the woman who raised him pulling weeds from her flower beds before saying, "You know I am always here to help you, Mom. All you need to do is tell me what needs to be done. I'd rather do it than have you hurting yourself trying to do it yourself." His mother had always been very independent and capable, but he worried more and more about her falling and hurting herself trying to do too much. He had always been there to help and having her do it all alone made him feel a slight tinge of self-imposed guilt. His mother would never try to make him feel

116

guilty about having his own life, even if she had dedicated her life to raising him and giving him the best life possible.

The two finished the weeding before Jim helped his mother to her feet and she looked at her watch while brushing dirt from her trousers. "Well, you must be getting hungry. It's about dinner time," she said. "I have some short ribs in the crockpot, and they should be nice and tender by now."

Jim licked his lips. "I hadn't realized I was getting hungry until you said short ribs. I love your short ribs. Is there your famous homemade coleslaw to go with it?"

"Of course, there is. It's been chilling in the fridge since early this morning. Although, I don't know about how famous it is," his mother answered with a chuckle. "And tomorrow night is lasagna. The pasta needed to chill before I could roll out the lasagna noodles, so I ran out of time to make that tonight."

"Well, aren't I a lucky guy? Both your short ribs and lasagna in one weekend. If you're not careful, you will have me thinking you missed me." Jim laughed as he teased his mother.

Side-by-side Jim and his mother dragged the yard bag of weeds to settle beside the trash cans that sat next to the garage. "I'll take this out to the curb for you before I leave on Sunday. I don't want you trying to lift this. Your trash day is still Monday, right?"

"Yes, Monday is trash day, and I would appreciate that a lot. Thank you," replied his mother. The two walked back into the house. "Now, go and wash up. Dinner will be on the table in ten minutes." She washed her hands and face in the kitchen sink before removing the bowl of chilled coleslaw from the refrigerator and placing it on the table. Taking out the large platter from the cupboard above the stove, she placed it next to the crockpot, and gingerly ladled the tender short ribs and baby potatoes from the bottom of the pot onto the platter, before pouring some of the juice the meat and potatoes had been cooking in over the top of the mixture. She placed them on the table calling to Jim, "Dinner is on the table. Come eat."

Jim was at the door as she finished her sentence and grabbed two plates from the cupboard along with two sets of eating utensils from the drawer right below and set them on the table. "What would you like to drink, Mom?"

"I think a cold beer would be acceptable after this hot day of chores. Don't you?" His mother replied.

"Sounds good to me," Jim answered and grabbed a cold beer for her and a root beer for himself out of the fridge before joining her at the table. A cold beer was what he actually wanted, but he knew his mother would not approve. So, he stuck to their tradition of a beer for her and root beer for him whenever they spoke of having a beer together. "Thanks, Mom. This looks delicious. I've missed your cooking." He had barely finished speaking before he was shoving a large bite of short ribs into his mouth, trying not to make too much of a mess. "But where's the salad we went and picked veggies for?"

"I figured since we're having cold slaw tonight, we would have the salad tomorrow with the lasagna. And what did I tell you about talking with your mouth full? It's gross." Tess laughed at his eating habits, shook her head, and began to eat. After dinner, Jim helped his mother with the dishes and the two watched a movie on TV.

The weekend passed in a flash, Jim thought to himself as he awoke to the smell of bacon cooking and fresh coffee brewing on Sunday morning, he took a deep breath in and with his arm blocked the cascading sun from the window that was hitting him in the face as he rolled over. He thought to himself, that he couldn't think of a better way to wake up than his mother's cooking and a hot cup of coffee.

Hurriedly putting on his jeans and a T-shirt he made his way to the kitchen where his mother stood over at the stove pulling the last piece of bacon off the frying pan. There were already eggs and pancakes sitting in the middle of the table, which made Jim's mouth water looking at them as he poured himself and his mother a cup of coffee and set them at their seats at the table. "Smells amazing, Mom. You didn't have to go to all this trouble. But I sure am glad you did."

Laughing his mother said as she picked up the plate of bacon and walked towards the table, "You wouldn't think you were home if you didn't wake up to breakfast and me standing over the stove. But thank you. I enjoy doing it for you and rarely get to anymore." Then she placed a piece of bacon into her mouth as she sat down across from him.

They chatted a little as they ate. When he finished, Jim looked over at the clock and was surprised to see it was 10:00. "Mom, you shouldn't have let me sleep so late. I wanted to help you out around here some more before I leave. I have to leave a little early this weekend. I have plans this evening."

"I know. You have that big date with Sharon tonight. So, I wanted you to be rested. Besides, you helped me enough for one weekend." Jim's mother spoke with a glint in her eye and a sense of hope in her voice.

Jim gave her his usual eye roll knowing exactly what she was alluding to and replied, "It's just a first date, Mom. No pressure. Please?" He had forgotten that he told her the name of the girl he was secretly very much looking forward to seeing.

"No pressure. However, I'd love to hear about how it goes. I haven't seen you dating in a while. So, you can't blame me for being a little excited for you," his mother said with a wink, before clearing the breakfast dishes from the table.

When Jim attempted to help his mother, she said, "No...no...let me take care of this. You go and get ready to go. I don't want you feeling hurried and driving crazy on that darn motorbike of yours." She shook her head with disapproval before adding, "Don't forget to take the garbage cans down before you go, though."

Exasperated by his mother's match-making Jim replied "Yes, Mother," before he left the kitchen and went to his room to pack up his things for the long drive back.

12

The Big First Date...No Pressure

It was about 3:30 when Jim arrived home. His mother wouldn't be too pleased to know that he kept a steady pace of ten to fifteen miles over the speed limit, but he didn't plan on telling her. He took his time stretching, unloading his stuff, and taking it into his apartment before calling his mom. She was a bright woman and could do the math on how far it was from point A to point B to figure out how fast he was driving. So, he wanted to stall a little before calling to let her know he was home safe. He finally picked up the phone and called his mom at about 3:45. "Hey, Mom. I'm home safe and sound."

"You made pretty good time. No traffic?" she asked.

"Nope. Traffic was a breeze. I guess everyone was still in church at that time of the morning," Jim replied. It wasn't exactly a lie, but he had omitted some of the facts. "I can't chat, Mom. I don't have a lot of time to get ready before I meet up with Sharon." He knew this would stir the pot a bit, but would also get his mother off of the phone without too many questions.

With that Jim's mother said, "Okay. Have fun and I want to hear all about it," before hanging up the phone. She knew that her son was taking advantage of her grandmother's bodily clock to get out of a more in-depth conversation about his driving habits. But he was home and safe so she would let it slide this time.

The phone had barely disconnected before, Jim rushed to take a shower and wash off all the bugs and road grime that were inevitable with long rides on a motorcycle. The last thing he wanted was to show up on his first date with Sharon with bugs in his hair and road tar on his arms.

It felt good to be clean, Jim thought as he stepped out of the shower and dried himself. He did a thorough shave, splashed on some aftershave, and then combed his hair before getting dressed and taking a look at the movie section of the paper. "Clue" was playing at the MegaPlex, which made him happy. He had been wanting to see it and it sounded like a good choice for a first date movie from the reviews: suspense, humor, and multiple endings would provide conversation starters for a cup of coffee or drink afterwards if everything went well during dinner and the movie. He looked at his watch and it was a quarter to five, which meant he needed to get out the door if he was going to be on time.

Sharon took her time getting ready for her date. She couldn't decide whether to wear a sundress or jeans and a summer top. Then she remembered that Jim always came into the library carrying a motorcycle helmet and decided jeans would be more prudent. She picked out her favorite pair of Dittos and strappy summer top then paired them with a blue hand-knit sweater in case it cooled off or was cold in the theater.

She combed her hair into a neat, tight ponytail to avoid tangling from riding on the back of Jim's motorbike before applying a natural shade of eyeshadow and lip gloss. She wasn't much for make-up and was lucky enough to have natural looks that didn't need much. After applying a light coat of mascara, which brought out the blue in her eyes, she checked the clock and realized she had ten minutes to dash over to the student hall. She hated being late and would make it just in time if she left now.

#

Jim was just pulling up in front of the student hall and parking his motorbike as Sharon turned the corner coming up to the hall. She took a moment to check her ponytail, fix the edges of her lip gloss, and then proceeded to walk over to Jim.

As Jim removed his helmet and shook his hair out making sure in his side-view mirrors that he didn't have any strange bat wings or helmet hair going, he caught sight of Sharon out of the corner of his eye and quickly stopped primping. He didn't want her to think that he was some kind of pretty boy who played with his hair all the time. He'd rather she thinks of him as a brilliant young journalism student and "James Dean" type. The thought made him roll his eyes at himself before he climbed off his bike and placed his helmet on the seat.

The two met just at the front door of the student hall, "Well look at you...right on time. I didn't know that there were punctual women anymore." Then he winked to let her know he was just teasing her.

"There are still a few of us out there. But be warned we don't like to be kept waiting," Sharon replied feistily and they both chuckled.

"So, do you want to eat here, or do you have someplace else in mind? It is completely up to you," Jim asked.

"I'm good with eating here. I love their pastrami sandwiches and it has been a while since I've had one," Sharon responded.

Jim thought he was imagining things. 'Did she actually just say that?' He may have just found a keeper, he thought to himself, before saying, "A woman after my own heart. Pastrami from the student hall is my favorite. How did you know?"

Sharon took a minute or two to look at him trying to decide if he was teasing her before asking, "Really? I thought I was the only one who preferred this place's pastrami on rye over a steak dinner." Then she laughed and the two entered the hall as Jim held the door open for her.

Realizing that Sharon wasn't sure if he was sincere or not about his love for student hall pastrami he reassured her, "No, really. They are my favorite. I eat them all the time."

The two carried on with some idle chit-chat about how their days went and the weather as they proceeded through the line at the counter. The cafeteria lady made a point of letting Sharon know that Jim was one of her regulars as she made their plates, which made him blush and brought a shy smile to Sharon's face.

"So, you were telling the truth about eating here all the time from what the cafeteria lady had to say, eh?" taking a seat in the corner so that they could talk without interruption as they ate, Sharon teased after they had settled into their seats. She liked that Jim had blushed when the kind cafeteria lady had pointed out how frequently he ate there.

"Would I lie to you? Not that I would lie to anyone. But certainly not you," Jim responded, then backstroked out of a potentially awkward conversation. They each took a bite of their sandwiches before

Jim continued, "So, I thought we could go see the new movie 'Clue' if you're up for it? It's playing at the Megaplex in about an hour."

"I've heard really good things about that movie and been wanting to see it. That sounds great," Sharon responded eagerly before taking another bite of her sandwich. Jim was pleasantly surprised to see a girl who liked to eat as much as he did. Most of the women he took out in the past wanted salads or were timid about eating in front of him. He was rapidly realizing that there were more sides to this beautiful woman that sat before him than he ever expected, and this pleased him greatly.

"So, what made you decide on a degree in library science?" Jim asked with genuine curiosity. The personality that he was gleaning from this woman did not fit the image that he had for most librarians.

"When I went to live with my godparents after my mom died when I was fifteen, I kinda tucked myself away in reading. It was an escape from losing my mom and having to leave everything I knew behind. I spent so much time in the library that I just fell in love with it and decided what better career than to spend every day doing something that I loved in a place that I adored. So, I decided to get my degree in library science," Sharon answered.

The journalist in Jim came to the surface, "Where was your dad while all of this was going on? Were your godparents abusive or something? How did your mom die? Did you have to move far? Sorry, I don't mean to be insensitive. I'm simply curious is all." His sincere interest in this woman's life caused him to pepper her with questions before realizing he wasn't giving her time to answer.

Sharon shook her head as she answered, "No, you're fine. It was all a long time ago. My godparents were great people. I just had a difficult time with the loss of my mom. I never knew my father. He split when my mom told him she was pregnant. So, she and I were all each other had. Then the cancer ordeal followed by losing her...I just didn't know how to cope and found my way through reading anything and everything that I could get my hands on. My godparents lived in Kentucky in a small town, which was a huge difference from living in Denver where I grew up. That only made it more difficult to process everything that was changing in my life in such a short period of time. Although, looking back at it now, leaving the city probably kept me out of a lot of trouble. I think I answered all of your questions. Right?" She smiled and giggled to ease any tension that her story might have caused.

Jim laughed. "Yes, you answered them all like a pro. So how did you end up here from Kentucky? What was it like living in Kentucky? How was it different than Denver? I've never been to either of them."

"Scholarships, grants, and a good library sciences department are the short answer. But I think I also just needed to get out on my own and stretch my wings a bit. Denver is a great place to live. It's where city meets country with lots of things to do from plays and museums to rodeos. That was my favorite part about living there. Where we were in Kentucky was very rural. It was a tiny town of less than five-hundred people, and not much variety on what there was to do there. Lots of horses and farming. What you would think of when you picture Kentucky."

Sharon paused for a brief minute before unintentionally returning the barrage of questions to Jim. "What about you? How did you end up here? What are your parents like? Are you from this area? What made you decide on journalism as a degree? That is your degree subject, right?"

Jim laughed again and said, "Did you ever think about going into journalism? You have the machine-gun questioning technique down cold."

The two laughed at each other and Sharon blushed before saying, "Sorry about that. I didn't mean to throw it back at you like that. I just have a lot of questions, it seems," and blushed again.

"No problem. I'm glad we have that in common," Jim responded making her blush again before he continued, "Let's see...I ended up here because I took too long to decide if I was going to college or not, then discovered it was harder to get into college than I thought. My mom is the best. It's been just her and me since my father died in a car accident when I was five. We're very close and I go home to see her once a month. I grew up about three to four hours northeast of here. Yes, journalism is my major, and why did I decide on journalism? Well, besides the fact that it was the one subject that I could see myself liking, I guess it's because I have always been curious and the idea of digging up the facts and putting them out there for others appeals to me."

He paused and smiled at her as he watched how captivated she was with listening to his answers before catching a glimpse of the clock on the wall in his peripheral vision. "Not to rush you or anything. I am enjoying our talk. But are you almost finished? If we're going to catch that movie we should get going."

Sharon looked over at the clock and replied, "Oh wow, time flew. Yes, I am finished. Let's go. We don't want to miss the previews."

Jim looked at her for a moment in disbelief, that was something else that they had in common. He loved watching the previews. "No, we sure don't." They decided since the theater was close enough to walk and it was such a lovely night that it would be better to walk until Jim could get a second helmet for her to wear while riding the motorcycle. This decision made Sharon happy inside to hear he was already thinking about a second date.

13

Joe's Reflections, 1968

Joe woke up every morning since Betty's death with a sense of dread. He tried hard to shake off the feeling and remind himself that it was for both her good and the greater good of the community. But he just couldn't cope with the fact that he had now taken two people's lives who he knew and liked very much, for the sake of the town. He found that he was drinking more and more and leaving the house less and less. Life began to feel very empty and without meaning.

After all, entering into that horrible contract didn't end up saving his family in the end. His youngest boy had been injured before the signing, which Joe only found out a week later. After his youngest son was sent home in a wheelchair with mental health issues and died of complications a few years later, his wife never recovered and eventually died of grief, while his only daughter moved away to remove herself from all the horrible memories and rarely returned to see him. She and Chris had broken up shortly after her brother returned home and she seemed to separate herself from anything that might connect her to the town of Oakwood; making it easy for her to move on and not look back, leaving Joe to grow old alone and with many regrets.

If only he had known about Eddie's injuries before that fateful day of convincing the council to sign that dreaded evil piece of parchment; would he have still made that decision? Would it have changed the way he thought? Or would he still have done it to save the town? Had he been saying it was to save the town all this time to compensate for his own guilt? These were all thoughts and questions that filled his mind these days from the time he awoke to the time he fell back asleep.

The weight of his decisions and the haunting of his thoughts eventually became too much for Joe to manage. He withdrew from the community and started missing committee meetings regularly; something he had never done in the past. This began to worry the other members of the council and started people talking about his well-being.

Yet another council meeting adjourned without Joe in attendance. The other six council members took turns looking over at Joe's usual seat while they quietly congregated on their way out of the room, conversing about his absence. "It seems strange to have a meeting without Joe in attendance, let alone three in a row," one council member said.

"I know he has been at every meeting since I have been on the town council. He's almost literally a fixture in this place, he's as stoic as the room in which we sit. Something must be wrong," another member replied.

"What are we going to do? Someone should go check on him and make sure he is all right. My wife mentioned he hasn't been going to do his regular volunteer visits at the nursing home lately, either" the first man responded.

Mayor Berkshire was listening carefully to the men's conversation, "I can understand his need for some space from the nursing home for a bit after Betty. But, I agree, it simply isn't normal that he would miss so many meetings; he's never missed a meeting since I have known him. I remember my dad telling me how even after his wife died, he attended every single meeting without fail as if it was his lifeline." The men fell silent for a moment as they stood looking down the corridor before Tim added, "I'll go check on him this evening. As mayor, I can make it seem like we have council business to discuss so that he doesn't find the encounter too intrusive." The men all agreed that would be best and then said their goodbyes.

Tim spent the afternoon dealing with town business, returning phone calls, filling out paperwork, reading and examining accounts and settling claims, etc. As he worked, Joe remained in the back of his mind. Joe had always been a role model of sorts to Tim, and it distressed him to see Joe's reaction to the recent contract fulfillment events. He decided he would leave work early and take Joe some dinner from the diner down the street and bring with him some of the more intricate public request filings to ask for his expertise as an excuse to drop by unannounced. His mother had always said, "Chicken Soup is good for the soul," so maybe chicken pot pie would be equally as beneficial.

He completed the last of the pile on his desk, leaving him at a good stopping point, and called the diner to order a couple of chicken pot pies to go, then he called his wife to let her know that he would be taking dinner over to Joe's so not to hold dinner for him.

He took his time walking to the diner, enjoying the stroll. The sun was sitting low in the sky and the air was cooling from the hot humid day. It was on days like this that he appreciated having a private office where he could work in his shirtsleeves unless he had appointments. He gave a bittersweet smile watching the neighborhood children playing in the park across the street. It brought joy to his heart that he lived where parents could let their children run to the park alone and play without worry. Yet, knowing that their way of life could so easily be upturned by missing one annual contractual sacrifice put a lump in his throat.

Wendy's familiar face met Tim at the front counter as he entered the diner. "Hello, Tim. Nancy not fancying cooking tonight?" She greeted him with a smile.

Tim smiled back and shaking his head said, "No, this is for Joe. I figured I would take him some dinner and see how the old guy is doing. We haven't seen him at the town council meeting in a few weeks and wanted to make sure he's doing alright."

Nancy's face turned somber, "I've been missing seeing his face around here lately too. It's just not normal not to see him in here once or twice a week. I thought he might be out of town visiting his daughter or something."

"So, he's not been in here either, then?"

Tim's concern was obvious, and brought a worried look to Wendy's face. "Here, take him a piece of our cherry pie with his dinner, on the house. It's his favorite and he's one of our favorites. It's the least we can do if it makes him feel better. How about you? Would you like a slice?"

"No, thank you. My belt is already bulging at the last notch." The two chuckled as Tim patted his belly and Wendy walked away for a brief moment returning with two chicken pies, neatly wrapped in aluminum foil, two green salads in takeaway containers, and a piece of homemade cherry pie wrapped in plastic wrap. She grabbed a paper bag from beneath the counter before carefully placing each item into the bag and handing it to Tim.

"Thanks, Wendy. That's kind of you. What do I owe you for the rest?" Tim asked.

"Two chicken pie dinners at $1.70 each plus tax...that comes to...$3.57" Wendy responded.

"Here you go. Keep the change, Wendy," Tim replied, handing her four one-dollar bills.

"Thanks, Tim. Say hello to Joe for me and let him know we are missing him around here," Wendy said, turning to tend to her other customers.

Joe spent the day sitting in his living room with the drapes and windows closed, staring into the abyss, drinking, and pondering his life. The phone rang a few times throughout the day, but Joe simply ignored it, taking another drink and staring into the darkness of the room that had once been filled with children's laughs, love, and joy. The only thing it held now was remorse, sadness, and angst over loved ones lost.

He looked over at the empty bottle that sat in front of him as the clock struck four before standing and walking to the storage closet. As he slowly opened the closet door and reached inside to remove the bundle of extra clothesline rope that lay at the bottom of the closet, he suddenly felt a sense of calm resolve take over. His mind was made up and nothing would change it.

Joe had spent the week trying to remember why he had done all the things he had done over the past twenty-four years, trying to remember what true happiness was, with no success. It was time to end the misery he dwelt in and in the process potentially protect another innocent. After all, what was to say that he wouldn't find another dire instance that required him to end anther friend's life? What had given him the right to make those decisions and perpetuate those acts? His own self-interests? His own selfishness? These were not satisfactory reasons.

Now it was time to do what he should have done weeks ago. It was time to end it all. If he had done it when he should have, Betty would still be living out the remainder of her life, but he had decided to play God and take her life instead of his own. He had decided his life was worth more than hers. And only now did he realize how wrong he was. It was never his decision. It was his arrogance, his self-importance, and his own sins that should have paid the price. Not Betty's, not Chuck's. Chuck had been the one with integrity and yet Joe had seen fit to impose his will upon that virtuous man, in the name of what?

Joe picked up the stepstool from the kitchen and walked back to the living room. He had not been fond of the open beams that lined the vaulted living room ceilings when he and his wife picked out the house. But she loved them, and so he caved in, wanting to please her. Now they turned out to be his favorite part of the house. It was those same beams that would soon usher him out of this complicated world and take him to be with his beloved once more. After all, he had simply been acting as an archangel doing whatever it took to protect the innocent from the evil of this world, so why shouldn't he be forgiven. At least that was the thought that brought solace to Joe's tormented mind, no matter how twisted the logic was.

Yes, it was time, he thought as he wrapped the rope securely around the beam, ensuring it would not slip with the weight. The weight of his body, his sins, his grief, and his regrets. Then he tied a secure loop around his neck wrapping it several times giving it the strength it needed to fulfill its important task; tightening the knot tighter and tighter until he could barely breathe, and the rope strained against his hands. Allowing his arms to fall limp at his sides, he took one last look around the room that had both brought him so much joy and so much angst before stepping from the stool, as you would step from a curb. The beam stood strong, and the rope did its job as his neck cracked under the pressure, leaving only Joe's lifeless body dangling in the center of the room. It was done.

Tim arrived at Joe's house just after five and rang the bell. He stood there for several minutes before knocking and ringing it once more. Knocking, he noticed the door move slightly as if it had not been latched properly. When Joe still did not answer, Tim decided to take it upon himself to go in. Walking into the main living area his concerns were quickly validated. It took only a moment for his eyes to acclimate to the darkness and see Joe's lifeless body hanging in the center of the room.

The shock of what was before him caused Tim to drop the bag containing their diners spilling the contents all over the floor. Mingling colors of cherries and cream from the two pies ran out of the bag resembling coagulated blood. Tim quickly ran to Joe's side and lifted him to try and remove the pressure from his neck. But he was too late. Joe's body was cold and limp. Tim took the pocketknife that he always carried from his pocket and cut the rope that held Joe's lifeless body, then gently placed him on the floor before taking a moment to soak in what had just happened and figuring out what to do next.

His mind raced and his pulse fluctuated between racing and frozen. In a state of shock, he took a couple of deep breaths and bringing himself to his feet went to the phone to call Jerry Jefferies, the chief of police and a fellow council member. "Jerry? It's Tim. We have a situation. I need you to come to Joe's house right away. And come alone," Tim hung up the receiver without waiting for a reply.

It was only about ten minutes before Jerry arrived. The front door was still standing ajar, so he entered cautiously. "Tim, you here?"

"In here, Jerry," Tim's voice was shaking slightly. Jerry stepped in the mixture of cherry pie and creamed chicken as he entered the room, before looking down at the sole of his shoe in disgust.

"What's going on? What's happened here?" asking before seeing Joe's dead body lying at Tim's feet.

"That's the dinner I brought him and dropped when I saw him hanging from the ceiling," Tim explained. "I came in and he was just hanging here cold and lifeless." Tim's face had turned pale, and his mind felt numb. His emotions were scrambled and jumping back and forth faster than he could keep up.

The two men stood staring at the body that lay at their feet before Tim spoke again, "People are going to talk and start asking a lot of questions if it gets out that he killed himself. This is just not something anyone who knew him would have thought he would do. We can't let this get out." Tim's matter of fact tone was a result of his profession. Being mayor, he was often responsible for dealing with emergency matters, which made him respond rather than react.

Jerry agreed, still mildly in shock over the news himself. "How do you want to handle this, Mayor?" Jerry thought it best to revert to official titles rather than friendship at this particular moment. He too was used to handling emergency matters in a businesslike fashion rather than becoming emotional. A skill that was difficult to employ for this situation.

"I've been thinking about it. He's not a young man and everyone has been wondering if he has been feeling well. I think we should remove any signs of the hanging and position him on the bottom of the steps like he fell and broke his neck coming down."

"I agree. That sounds like the best way to deal with this. The less paperwork to document this incident the better. The last thing we need is people starting to ask questions about his state of mind and why he would do such a thing. We don't need someone stumbling upon the real reasons," Sheriff Jefferies responded. With that, the two men set to work cleaning up any evidence that he could have hung himself, before moving his body to look as if he had fallen to his death. When they were done arranging the scene, Sheriff Jefferies called the coroner's office and started the process of filing his report.

The county coroner's office was overworked and understaffed, plus the coroner was a good friend of Sheriff Jefferies. So, when Jerry signed off on the incident report as being an accident, the coroner didn't give it a second thought. He accepted the sheriff's investigation results, signed off on the cause of death and sent Joe's body to cold storage to wait for the crematorium to arrive, without performing an autopsy.

The two men of power watched the coroner's vehicle drive away, then looked at each other, trying to find words to express what they were feeling about what they had just done. They both respected and admired Joe for his strength and dedication to his family and town. Sherriff Jefferies was the first to speak, "I can't believe he's gone, Tim. He's been a fixture in this community my whole life."

Tim blindly nodded, "He was my mentor and helped me settle into my role as mayor after I was elected. I can't imagine not having him around. This is going to hit the community hard."

Jerry agreed, "He was a volunteer coach for my son's basketball team for three years running. On top of that, he headed the food on wheels, and social outreach committees for our church, making sure those who could not get around had food and company. His community involvement was everywhere."

Hearing that snapped Tim to reality for a moment. "He was also the one who notified Blanchard of completion of the annual commitment every year." That sudden recollection made both men freeze in their tracks. "We have to choose another delegate to deal with that demon."

Dealing with Mr. Blanchard was a task that no one wanted to be responsible for. However, Tim felt as mayor it should be his responsibility to be the counsel delegate to deal with this individual. "I'll take over the responsibility. It's something I can do to honor Joe as my mentor. I should have taken that responsibility off his plate a long time ago, but I just couldn't bring myself to do it."

"That's honorable of you Tim. Maybe we as a committee should incorporate it into our guidelines that it's a responsibility of the office of mayor, just like being on the counsel of seven is." The mayoral elections had been rigged to ensure that someone of the secret seven's choosing was always elected to the position ever since the council chose to sign the contract. This was their way of keeping a tight rein on who knew about the contract and secret group.

"That's a good idea. I'll be sure and bring it up at the next committee meeting."

Trying hard to shake the emotional state that they were in, the two men said their good-byes and went their separate ways to deal with their portion of the matters at hand, notifications, temporary replacements for the many positions in town that Joe oversaw, etc.

#

Joe opened his eyes to find himself standing in a long, dark, steam-filled room with the silhouette of a familiar figure standing in the distance. The figure reminded him of someone he had seen in his nightmares, but he couldn't quite place them. Behind the figure was a giant fireplace blazing eerily. "What is this place? Where am I?" Joe asked nervously. This was not the afterlife that he had envisioned.

A familiar voice answered from a corner behind him, "Did you actually think you would be going to be with your wife and boys after what you have done, Joe?" Suddenly Joe recognized the voice. It was Mr. Blanchard.

"What do you mean? I did everything that was asked. Of course, I did," Joe answered in a panic.

The ominous figure that stood before them finally spoke, "You should have read the fine print, Mr. Wilson. There was never anything that indemnified you from your actions, whether it was to fulfill the contract or not. Your actions had consequences and now it is time for you to pay for them. Did you think you wouldn't?"

With hearing this, Joe's shaking stopped. It was true. All actions have consequences and how could he have thought he would have gotten off clean with what he had done? He now understood that he would never be free from his past or see his dearest loved ones again. No matter how wholesome he thought his reasoning for doing these deeds was, he had committed the evilest of all evil and he would have to pay with his immortal soul.

Seeing the realization on Joe's face, the figure looked over at Mr. Blanchard and said, "You have done well, my loyal servant, and shall be rewarded. You can go back to the world of the living now and continue being my eyes and ears. I will take things from here." Then, the figure waved his hand and Mr. Blanchard was gone. With another wave of his hand, the fire in the man-sized fireplace behind him shrank away revealing a long dark hallway behind it. The walls that lined it were made of volcanic rock that was covered in ash and embers. The figure in front of him beckoned Joe to enter. Without a word, Joe slowly obeyed, and the figure followed him in with the fireplace returning to its former self once they were both inside.

Mr. Blanchard found himself standing in front of the mirror above his fireplace after his master had excused him. His eyes glowed with pleasure seeing his grey hair was once again the jet-black color that it had been when he was a child. Something he had always coveted. His master had kept his word and rewarded him with this small gift, making Blake Blanchard secure in his master's satisfaction with a job well done.

###

At the next town council meeting, the members were less chatty and still mourning the loss of their valued member and patriarch. Everyone entered quietly and took a place at the table, then said brief pleasantries to one another without taking the time to stand around catching up on each other's current affairs. They were all waiting for the meeting to start so that they could get the unpleasantness of the day over with and leave.

Tim barely looked up as he entered the meeting room and started taking his papers from his briefcase, which he had set on the table. He passed out the agendas and the minutes from the last meeting, unnecessarily tapped the gavel out of habit, and started the meeting. Looking over at Jerry Jefferies, he began to speak. "I'm sure that everyone here is aware that our friend Joe died last week after falling down the stairs in his home and breaking his neck."

He maintained eye contact with Jerry while saying this as if to confirm they were both still on the same page with their story. The two had decided that only they should be aware of the truth about how Joe died, agreeing that the fewer people who knew the truth about the facts of his death the better. Jerry nodded to both confirm to Tim yes that they were still on the same page, and to the group confirming what Tim had just told them.

"With that news also comes the unhappy business of filling his place on the council," Tim continued.

The men in the room looked from one to the other, not having thought about the fact that there would have to be a new seventh member to the council. This information created a quiet buzz around the table as each man spoke to the man next to him in hushed tones trying to understand how they would accomplish this task and who they could trust to keep such a secret.

Each man found himself internally thinking about when they had been chosen and how they had initially responded to the information contained in the circle of seven's doctrine. The most recent inductee, Norman, remembered only too well how it had been a lot to swallow and he had not been prepared for what was being asked of him. But eventually he was able to justify the Circle of Seven's cause and accepted the information and the position that he now held. The existing members had explained it in such a way that it felt like an honor to protect their community and uphold the pact for the greater good.

It wasn't until after each of their first annual event that they realized how serious their new role was. Now it was up to them to bring someone else into this world of subterfuge and secrecy. As these men sat lost in their thoughts, Tim continued speaking, "I know that everyone at this table understands the importance of choosing the right person before approaching anyone, and in keeping the circle of seven's doctrine secret to anyone who approaches the council, wanting to apply for the position until it can be ascertained that they will accept their role in both positions. I can't be clear enough on the utmost importance of these facts and how we handle filling this new vacancy."

Everyone at the table understood exactly what Tim was explaining. They could not risk letting it get out what the circle of seven was really about. And, with that understanding, how would they fill Joe's position?

"I think it is important that we do not rush into anything, and we spend the next month thinking about who we feel would be a good fit and uphold the trust and secrecy of the circle. So, I recommend that we reconvene in one month's time with our recommendations and spend the time doing thorough research on any potential inaugurals. If anyone asks about why we are taking so long to fill the position, simply tell them it is a respectful grieving period," Tim instructed.

Seeing that the men at the table were all in agreement that this would be the best way to manage the situation, Tim continued speaking, "For now, I think we need to focus our primary energies on establishing the contest and finalizing all of the details to avoid any future situations." The other men at the table nodded in agreement. From there they moved on to the next item on the agenda and finished the meeting business as usual. "And lastly if you agree, I have decided to take on the responsibility of dealing with Mr. Blanchard when it comes to verifying our annual contract. I think it should be incorporated into our guidelines that this role be a part of the position of mayor's role on the Circle of Seven."

The rest of the men at the table looked back and forth at each other, nodding in agreement before putting it to a vote. The suggestion was unanimously accepted passing this burden onto anyone who held the position of mayor going forward.

14

The Heavy Research Begins

Jim called his mother the next day after his date with Sharon. He had contemplated calling her when he got home the night before, thinking she would probably be up waiting for his call, but it had been almost midnight and he didn't want to wake her if he was wrong. "Hey, Mom. Good morning. How are you doing this fine day?"

"Well, someone sounds chipper this morning...I take it the date went well?" Tess answered with a hint of approval in her voice.

"Yes, it went very well indeed. I'm not used to saying this, Mom, but I could see myself dating Sharon." Jim spoke without hesitation.

His mother was shocked and pleased at the same time. "Wow! That's awesome! She must really be something."

"She is, Mom. She really is...I can't believe how much we have in common and how many things we both enjoy. We talked for hours before and after the movie, and she's a movie whisperer too," Jim rambled.

His mother laughed at this, knowing how her son liked to make commentaries under his breath and couldn't wait to ask his questions until after a movie. It annoyed some people, but as his mother, she found it endearing. "That's great! It's important for one movie whisperer to be with another," she responded, remembering how she and Jim's father loved to whisper together during movies.

She had never married after Jim's father died and rarely dated. And even then, only at Jim's insistence. Jim's father had been the love of her life and given her the most important gift anyone ever could before he died, her son. So, she saw no need to continue looking for another man to share her life with. It brought her great joy to hear that Jim could have found his special one so that he could enjoy the happiness that she and his father had shared, no matter how abruptly their life together had ended. "Tell me more about her."

"She's a library science major working in the campus library for her internship. That's how we met. She loves pastrami on rye, she's punctual, loves to banter and tease me, and was orphaned at fifteen, and she loves to eat. No salads and picking at her plate," Jim told his mother in an excited laundry-list fashion. "She's looking forward to taking a ride on my motorcycle with me." Jim immediately regretted his words as they left his mouth, knowing how his mother felt about his motorbike.

"Wow! That's pretty...impressive...sad...and exciting all at the same time," Tess wasn't sure how to respond to that mix of information or how to handle the motorcycle comment, so she chose to ignore it this one time to keep the peace. But it was clear that they had quite a bit in common and that her son was intrigued with this new girl. Jim hated when girls were chronically late. "And imagine that she likes to eat. I would guess that's a good thing if you wanted her to be around long," His mother laughed as she teased her son. "So, she's older than you then?"

"You know what I mean, Mom. Some girls don't want to eat in front of you. They just want to pick at a salad and then be hangry later, and yes, she is a couple of years ahead of me in school," Jim explained, before laughing at how silly he must be sounding. This was not his normal post-date check-in. He couldn't remember ever being so openly twitterpated with anyone and definitely not to his mother, who was crazed with cravings for grandchildren.

Jim decided it was time to rein it in and changed the topic, but not before telling his mother that he had another date with Sharon on Tuesday. "Just so you know, Mom, I am going out of town on Wednesday for the day to do some research for my article. I can't find much information on the town I told you I was writing about, so I have to go there to do my research on-site. It's only two hours away so I'll be home the same day."

Tess loved that her son respected her enough to cater to her over-protectiveness and let her know his comings and goings. Not many nineteen-year-old men away from home for the first time would accommodate their mothers in this manner. "Thank you for letting me know, sweetie. I do appreciate that you keep me in the loop the way you do. You're a good son and a good man. What's the name of the town?"

On the other end of the phone line, Jim blushed and replied, "Thanks, Mom. I just don't like you to worry, and I know you do. Oakdale...Oakland...Something like that. I have it written down in my notebook someplace. I'll be leaving early so I won't be calling before I leave. But I'll be sure to call you when I get home so that you know I made it back safely."

"Thank you. I hate making you feel like you need to check in, but I can't help myself. You are so important to me." Hearing the names that Jim named off gave her a strangely unsettled feeling, like she should know it, but couldn't place why.

"I know, Mom. You're fine. I love you too. I need to get going. So, I'll talk to you later," Jim reassured her that he didn't mind. And he really didn't. He loved that he and his mother were as close as they were and had such a communicative relationship. Plus, she had always made sure to let him know whenever she was going to be going someplace to ensure he would not worry. That made it a mutually respectful relationship, and not simply a grown man having to check in with his mommy all the time. He waited for his mother to hang up before placing the phone receiver back on its cradle.

Jim stashed the new motorcycle helmet that he had picked up for Sharon to use in the compartment under his seat before climbing on and stomping the kick starter. It had only been a little over twenty-four hours since he had seen her, but it felt like a week. Since the only way they could arrange another date before he went to Oakwood was to meet during her lunch hour, he decided to pack a picnic lunch and take her for a short ride on the motorbike. He attached his satchel that contained their lunch to the back of his seat using the strap that was made for such things, put on his helmet, and then made the short drive over to the library.

Sharon could hear Jim's motorbike pull up outside and it gave her a sudden chill of excitement. She quickly smoothed her hair and finished up the work that she was doing so that she would be ready when Jim came in to retrieve her.

The head librarian was standing nearby and saw Jim enter through the front doors, "Good morning. More time at the microfiche machine today?" she asked.

"Not today, thank you. I'm here to pick up Sharon for lunch," he respectfully replied.

About that time Sharon walked over smiling and blushing at the interaction. "I have this, Mrs. Whetherby. Thank you." Mrs. Whetherby smiled with a hint of impishness, recognizing what was happening, nodded, and stepped away.

Jim smiled back at her and asked, "Are you ready to go? I thought we could have a picnic lunch and take a short ride on the motorcycle. Sound good?"

Sharon liked the idea and responded in kind, "That sounds great," telling Mrs. Whetherby that she was leaving for lunch, Mrs. Whetherby told her to take her time and the two walked out the door. The head librarian had been through many interns but had never had one who worked as hard as Sharon, it pleased her to see Sharon have a hint of personal life and she wanted to encourage it.

When they got to Jim's motorbike, he lifted the seat and pulled out the new helmet handing it to Sharon, "Here try this on. I wasn't sure of your size, so I hope it fits."

Sharon was happy to see Jim had taken care to look after her safety. She leaned forward and let Jim place the protective gear upon her head, "Thank you. It fits perfectly," she said as she fastened the buckle.

"Nice!" Jim said double-checking the buckle before they mounted the motorcycle, and he stomped the kickstart pedal.

Sharon wrapped her arms around Jim's waist as he lifted the kickstand, and they took off. Jim had decided to take her to a scenic view that he had recently discovered on one of his rides that sat just outside a nearby national forest for their picnic. Sharon didn't care where they were going, she was simply enjoying the ride and the company. She clung to him even tighter as he wound his way up the curvy mountain roads. He liked the feel of her arms snug around him, which made him accelerate a little bit more.

It only took about fifteen minutes to get to the spot he had in mind, and she couldn't help but mutter, "Wow..." with a sense of awe as she looked at the view. It was indeed a beautiful, wooded location that looked down upon a meadow-filled valley. The view went on for miles and it was the perfect place for a picnic lunch.

Jim parked his motorcycle and the two sat for a minute or two just experiencing the scenery in front of them together. Sliding off the motorbike. Jim had held his hand out to help Sharon get off, but she had already managed to wiggle off the back of the bike on her own. He was impressed by her independent spirit. "If you're up for a tiny downhill hike, there's a great spot over here for picnicking, or we could just have it here?" He asked the beautiful young woman standing beside him still looking out over the valley.

"I'm up for a small hike. So, now is this hike a downhill hike going both ways? I've never seen one of those before," she teased him.

"Yeah...that came out wrong. It's downhill to get there." He blushed as he responded, adding, "But I'm sure that you're more than capable of making the climb back up." His wit was failing him at this moment in order to respond to her banter appropriately. Making him opt for complimenting her abilities instead.

Sharon enjoyed watching him blush before asking, "Where's this spot? I only have an hour for lunch. Although, I'm sure Mrs. Whetherby won't be too upset if I'm a little late."

Jim laughed, "No I'm sure she won't with the wink she gave me on the way out after she told us to take our time."

"She did not! I would have seen it."

"Yes. Yes, she did. It was when I was opening the door for you." He loved that he had seen something that she had missed, "Seemed like she was playing a little matchmaker to me."

Sharon thought about it and realized he was probably right. Mrs. Whetherby had been needling her to have more of a personal life for a month or two, ever since her husband had passed away. They had been married for fifty-three years and he was the only personal life she had outside of the library. But that seemed to be enough for the kind lady.

Sharon remembered Mrs. Whetherby telling her once that she didn't want Sharon to become an old spinster librarian like so many in the field; that marrying her husband was the best decision she ever made, next to becoming a librarian, of course. "Now that I think about it, you're probably right. She has been pushing me to get out more and meet someone." Laughing a nervous, insecure sort of laugh Sharon started to feel embarrassed which indicated to Jim that it was time to start their hike.

It wasn't a long hike, but it was mildly steep. The tiny trail led down the hillside through some trees and shrubbery to a small plateau. There was just enough shade from the trees that overhung the plateau to make it comfortable. Sitting on the small ledge provided the feeling of floating on air as you looked straight down at the valley below.

Jim spread out a small blanket that he had packed in the satchel with their lunches and beckoned her to sit. She had been standing a little too close to the edge for his comfort and wanted to draw her back without insulting her independent nature. Sharon joined him on the blanket as he pulled out the lunch he had prepared and a couple of bottles of Coke. "I thought I remembered you liking Coke. But if not, I have a thermos of water too."

"Coke is perfect. Did you bring a bottle opener?" She teased since that seemed to be what most people forgot when they went to open a bottle of Coca-Cola.

Jim pulled out his key ring saying, "I never leave home without one."

"I love a well-prepared man," Sharon responded. The more time she spent with this interesting young man, the more time she wanted to spend with him. She couldn't remember having felt like this before. It was nice and a little scary at the same time. And so far, it was worth exploring. "So, how did you find this gem of a location?"

"A group of students got together for a motorbike ride a few weeks ago and we stopped for a break on the way back not too far from here. One of the other guys on the ride showed it to us," Jim answered.

"Tell me about your paper. What's the name of this town you are researching? Will you be gone long?" Sharon asked as they enjoyed their lunch.

"I'm writing on a town called Oakwood a couple of hours drive up I-20 that I heard about. I had to recheck the name of it after talking to my mom yesterday, because I just couldn't remember it. Some journalist I am." Jim admonished himself before continuing, "It's supposed to be a 'little slice of heaven' stuck in history like something out of a Norman Rockwell painting. I want to do a comparison on it to modern life and do an in-depth article on how they were able to avoid the pitfalls of modern life, crime, inflation, overpopulation, etc. I'll only be gone for the day. I'm not able to find much about the town here so I want to check out their town records, library, and police reports to get a feel for the types of crime that they do have. I simply can't believe they have no crime. That's absurd."

"Hmmm...That's either going to be a very interesting article or a very boring article. You're going to have to find one heck of an angle to make the editorial panel think it's a newspaper-worthy topic, I've heard they can be a strict bunch when it comes to content for the school paper," Sharon offered her input. "They only take the best of the best. Students who are serious about journalism as a career."

"It's going to be hard work. But for some reason, I feel like there's something here and I just want to flesh it out before I decide to go with another topic," Jim agreed with some hesitance.

"Hey! You're the journalist. You need to go with your gut. Right?!?" Sharon encouraged him. "After all, you have to have good gut instincts to be a good journalist is what I've always heard."

"True. I'm still getting a feel for which of my instincts are newsworthy at this point. So, what kind of cancer did your mom have?" He realized how insensitive his question came out and tried to smooth it over, "Oh crap! I'm sorry. That was completely insensitive of me."

Sharon's face became without expression, "No. You're alright. It's been a long time. She had bone cancer."

"That sounds terrible. I didn't even know that was a type of cancer."

"Yeah, it's normally something that people get from the spread of another type of cancer, but in my mom's case she was one of less than one percent of the population who get bone cancer. It is very rare."

"Wow, that had to suck. Was she sick a long time?"

"Three years, before it spread to her liver and lungs. They think she already had it for a few years before they found it, because of how advanced it was when she was diagnosed."

"How can someone have cancer for years and not know? Did she just never go to the doctor."

This question hit a nerve with Sharon, "She went to the doctor all the time. She was very conscientious about her health and was always in pain. But there's no external signs of bone cancer so you must have special tests that are quite expensive and since the cancer is so rare doctors typically don't run those tests until it's a last resort. Okay!"

"I'm sorry. I didn't mean to imply she was a doctor hater or something." Jim was afraid to talk for the next few minutes and the two sat looking at the view waiting for the mood to shift back to something more pleasant.

Sharon decided since he was being direct, she could too. "How was it growing up without your father? I know what it was like for me as a girl who never knew her father. But, for a boy who did, what was that like?"

"It was rough. My family was always very close, then suddenly it was broken. He was just not there, and mom was a mess trying to deal with her own emotions, my emotions, and figuring out how to be both mom and dad at the same time. It sucked."

"How did you handle it and stay out of trouble? A lot of kids in your shoes end up on drugs, in gangs, or worse."

"I went through a rough patch when I was younger defying my mom at every turn, threatening to drop out of school, because I hated it. When my mom finally hit her wits end, she stuck me in counseling."

"And it helped?"

"Yeah, but don't tell my mom. I put her through hell for doing it for a long time. I'd rather not give her that I-told-you-so moment. She already has enough of those."

The afternoon passed more quickly than they expected. When Sharon looked at her watch, she had already been gone for an hour and a half. With panic in her voice, she looked at Jim and said, "Oh no! I've been gone an hour and a half. We need to get back. Even if she did say 'Take your time' with a wink, I don't want her to think I am taking advantage."

Jim understood her point and hurriedly packed back up the picnic before turning to make the climb back up the hillside. Before he could offer to help Sharon; she was already halfway up the hill in front of him. He chuckled to himself and fell in behind. He managed to get everything packed back onto the bike and their helmets secured on their heads in the blink of an eye, although she needed little help with her helmet. He started the motorbike thinking to himself, 'When she's ready to go, she's ready to go.' And chuckled to himself one more time before taking her back to the library.

Pulling up to the library, Sharon jumped off the back of Jim's motorbike and without thinking, kissed him on the cheek and started trotting off towards the front entrance, before she realized she was still wearing his helmet. She quickly turned around and trotted back, taking off the helmet at the same time, handed it to him before flipping back around and this time jogging towards the entrance, calling out, "Call me! Thank you! Bye!" She was out of breath by the time she got inside and ran into Mrs. Whetherly almost literally. "I'm so sorry ma'am. I completely lost track of time. It won't happen again, I promise," She was stumbling over her words with sincerity.

Mrs. Whetherby simply shook her head and said, "Dear. You're right on time. Stop worrying. And I hope that's one promise that you won't be keeping," before walking away with a grin on her face.

Going back to her work, Sharon relived every moment of her date, wondering if she had messed up by getting too protective of her mom's memory. Even though she was a very attractive young woman and had been all through high school, her dating experiences were few. She had chosen not to interact with her peers and submerse herself into her books, mostly out of fear of being hurt again. This lack of experience gave Sharon an uncharacteristic insecurity when it came to dating, that didn't come through in the rest of her life activities.

A man of his word, Jim was up early and on the road before 7:00. He wanted to have plenty of time to explore the town as well as get the research in that he was going there to do. It was unusually foggy for an August morning, especially for early August, which mandated that he drive slower than normal, turning his two-hour drive into a two-and-a-half-hour drive. As he reached the outskirts of Oakwood, the sun began to break through the overcast. Jim thought to himself, how odd that this mountain valley town would be clear and sunny when everything around it was fog soaked. Normally the fog settled into the valley making them the last to clear.

Pulling into town, Jim noted the old town's essence. From the circle green in the middle of the town square to the historic architecture that every building and storefront that surrounded the green possessed. Everything about the town resembled something that one might picture in the late 1940s and early 1950s.

He decided to start at the library to see what he could find that might spur other research at the church archives and hall of records. Then he decided to make the hall of records his second stop so that he could find out which of the three churches was the oldest because they would have records going back the furthest.

The library itself was only half the size of the university library, yet it was grand in stature. He was greeted by oversized engraved oakwood doors with large wrought iron door latches and knobs. As he entered the library a grand foyer with inlaid marble flooring met him. In the center of the inlay was a large jade green image of a giant oak tree, the town's emblem. The layout of the library was very traditional, with a librarian's station at the front, and rows and rows of bookshelves separated by genre filling the main body of the library. Vaulted ceilings containing prism windows let in natural light for reading without creating glare. Jim stood and admired the grandeur of this place of knowledge before approaching the librarian.

"Hello, Miss. Could you point me to the microfiche machines? I'd like to do some research on this wonderful little town of yours," he asked the woman standing behind the counter. She was older with a silver bun positioned high up on the back of her head. Her clothes were modest and proper. She was exactly what you would have expected to see working in a library in the 1940s and 1950s.

The prim woman looked at Jim for a few seconds before pointing him in the direction of the furthest corner of the library, then said, "The machines are in that corner over there. But you will have to check out any films here at the desk from me. You can only check out one at a time and they must be turned in before you can check out another."

Jim smiled thinking to himself, this could take a while, before responding, "Okay, well then. I need the first roll of film that you have for the history of Oakwood documenting any newspaper clippings, town events, historical documents, etc." He decided in this case it was best to work from a chronological direction rather than backward. Doing so might save him some time with the method of operation that he had to adhere to.

"It will take me a few minutes to locate them. If you would like to get settled at a microfiche station, I will bring them to you. I will need your driver's license since you don't have a library card with us. To hold until you return the films," the librarian responded.

Taking out his wallet, Jim removed his driver's license and handed it to her, then walked back to the corner where a row of microfiche stations sat, while just across from them sat only two computers. Jim looked at the stern difference between this library and the campus library. The campus library had twenty computers always full of students. This library had two with only one being occupied, while three of the six microfiche machines were taken. Jim chose to take the machine in the furthest corner so as to not be disturbed and be able to people-watch as others came and went. He expected to be here for quite a while.

The silver-haired woman appeared a few minutes later carrying a role of microfiche, "This is the oldest one I find with regards to Oakwood. Let me know if you need something else. I should be right up front," she said cordially.

"May I ask your name in case I have any questions?" Jim asked.

"Of course, my name is Nan," she said pointing at a name tag that hung from her cream-colored, lacy, hand-knitted cardigan. He had missed seeing it before. She walked away and Jim unloaded the film from its canister and threaded it into the machine with care. It seemed very old and slightly brittle. The last thing he wanted to do was strip the threads or damage the film in any way.

Some of the images were very faint and faded. Once he saw the dates he understood why. Some of the clippings were from 1894 when the town was first established. They weren't anything of real significance. Mostly they were old advertisement flyers and documents for lumber from the local lumber yard. It was obvious that a good portion of this film was a compilation of historic documents that had been microfilmed much later to protect them from the hands of time. Then Jim came across a posting of public notice for the incorporation of the town by William Oaks. It looked to be a poster that had been hung in a public place. It was still possible to see the nail holes in the corners, even on the microfiche film. He made printouts of these documents thinking they would make for good supporting documentation of his article and went on scrolling for more pertinent information.

As he continued to scroll down, he found a film of the original town plot plan. It was a detailed location for every aspect of the town from the school to the town center, to the first church. This particular find was very interesting to Jim, and he took some time after printing it out to look at where each building was located, planning to compare it to the way the town now sat.

A little farther down, there was the town charter and some more current newspaper clippings from the early 1900s. Most of the first decade of the 1900s was about local events; it wasn't until 1914 that world affairs started to permeate the pages, talking about what was happening in other parts of the world in the great war. Then in 1917, when the U.S. entered World War I, the Great War became the most talked about topic throughout the local papers as with national papers. The four-page paper quickly grew to ten and sometimes twelve pages with listings of families affected by the war, places to go for charitable handouts, updates on enemy advancements, and places to help with the war cause, quickly taking over the happier news of community picnics and local weddings that was once the main portion of local news.

The daily newspaper report was what caught Jim's eye the most; a page or two long section of the paper listing those American soldiers who had died in battle with pictures. If someone didn't know better, it could have easily been mistaken for a high-school yearbook page.

The soldiers were barely out of school and yet their lives were over, due to such hatred and violence. The images portrayed a much different time and way of life than Jim had grown up in, and he owed that to these same people that he now spotted as a simple blip in time while scrolling through antique newspapers on a microfiche machine.

This roll of film seemed to end at the end of 1918 right after the Great War ended. Jim thought that was fitting and decided that he needed a quick break. He had left without eating breakfast and it was after ten. When he took the roll of film to the front desk and returned it to Nan, he asked for someplace to get a quick bite to eat. "Hello, again Nan. Thank you very much for this. May I get the next oldest content roll of film please?" Nan took the film and started to turn to go to the microfiche storage when Jim caught her attention again, "Um! But first, could you point me to where I could get a quick bite to eat and a coffee?"

"The diner is two doors down on the left. You can get either breakfast or lunch there at this time of day, and the coffee is pretty good. It's Folger's," Nan answered, "But don't bring any food or beverages into the library. You may leave your stuff at the microfiche machine if you don't wish to carry it with you. It will be fine there."

Jim nodded, and said, "Thank you. I won't be too long."

He exited the grand building and turned left as instructed. He decided that it would be a good time to compare the town's original plot map to how the town currently looked while he was making his way to the diner. So, he pulled the printout from his pocket where he had put it when he decided to get something to eat and began to line up the buildings with the drawing.

He chose to use Town Hall as the starting point and work clockwise. As Jim looked at the plot plan and matched each building up, he noticed little had changed. The jail was no longer a stand-alone building. It had been incorporated into the Town Hall. Where the jail had sat was now a hardware store. The mercantile was now a department store, and the farmer's market had become a grocery store. The diner simply replaced the original restaurant. He was amazed at how little had changed. Other than some business names and a few more modern stores, it was exactly as it had been planned a hundred years ago.

Jim rolled up the plot map and went into the diner to have his breakfast and coffee. He was delighted to see that it was arranged like a 1950s diner with stools at the counter and mini jukeboxes at the booths, with a few tables in the middle of the room. On each table and along the back edge of the countertop spaced about every other stool sat an upright napkin dispenser, salt, and pepper shakers, a matching creamer dish, and a small bowl containing packets of sugar and sugar substitute. The atmosphere was happy and busy even as late in the morning as it was. He took a seat at the counter where he was promptly approached by a heavyset waitress wearing a pink waitress uniform and apron. "What can I get for you, Hon?"

"I'll have bacon and eggs, over easy, with whole wheat toast. And a cup of coffee please," Jim responded. As quick as she approached, the waitress darted off and swiftly returned. She plopped a white ceramic coffee cup down in front of him and poured some dark black coffee into it as she chatted with the man sitting next to him. "Thank you," Jim said. The waitress simply said, "No problem," in between sentences as she kept speaking with the regular customer next to him.

While Jim sipped his black coffee and people-watched, his breakfast arrived quickly, which made him wish the diner back home was as quick. Everything looked as he ordered. He was pleased to see that they got the eggs perfect. Usually, he had to have a five-minute conversation with the waitress about how he wanted his eggs because it seems that everywhere you go has a different definition of an over-easy egg.

He finished his breakfast and coffee at breakneck speed so that he could get back to the library. He reminded himself to tell Nan that she was right about the coffee: it was pretty good. Once his plate was clean, Jim quickly paid his bill, left a tip for the waitress, and headed back to the library.

It was already a quarter past eleven when Jim returned to the library. He had taken longer to eat and absorb the surroundings than he planned. It was becoming clear that one research trip may not be enough, and he made a mental note to schedule a return visit.

Nan was waiting for Jim at the front desk with his microfiche film and asked, "How was it?" She was proud of her little town and close friends with the people who ran the diner, so she sent visitors there as frequently as she was given the opportunity.

"You were right. It was very good. And I never knew Folger's was such a good coffee. I thought it was simply something old people drank." Almost as soon as the words exited his lips, he regretted saying them. He turned bright red which made Nan chuckle.

"No worries, young man. You're right: old people do drink it. But it doesn't mean it can't also be good." She gave him a wink and went back to her work. Jim was pleasantly surprised at how well she had taken his slip of the tongue. She hadn't shown much in the way of personality since he arrived, so he hadn't been sure what her reaction would be to his unintentionally rude comment.

Jim settled in at the microfiche machine and began his journey through time scrolling through the newspaper films of 1919. This was a year of strife and change around the world that seemed to be thoroughly documented in this smalltown paper. It was apparent to Jim that the War had permanently changed the format of the originally upbeat paper to one of a more serious nature covering world events and local issues at the same time. The paper grew in size to accommodate all of the new topics. This would indeed take longer to go through than the previous roll of film.

He had forgotten about what a tumultuous time 1919 was until now as he read the highlights of each paper. Prohibition started, women's rights to vote were in full swing, the influenza pandemic was still raging on which led to a very long obituary section, racism was running rampant all over the country, and President Woodrow Wilson had his debilitating stroke. The treaty of Versailles was signed, and the League of Nations was established. Even sports were a topic of contention as the Chicago White Socks were caught intentionally throwing a game to the Cincinnati Reds. Disasters contributed to the negative news as fires in New Orleans burnt down the French Opera house, and downtown Chicago caught fire after an aircraft crashed. Hurricanes killed over 600 people in the Gulf Coast areas and volcanic eruptions killed more than 5,000 at Kelud in Java.

Happy to get through the 1919 roll of film and be able to move on to the next; Jim hoped it would be better than what he had just read since it seemed like for every good thing that was happening there were at least three negative occurrences. He found Nan ready with the next roll of film when he reached the front counter. It had taken him just under an hour to get through that roll of film, even skimming through. He made a mental note to stop by 3:00 so that he would at least get to the hall of records this visit. "Thank you, Nan. I appreciate your promptness. I need to be out of here and over to the hall of records at three. So, I'm hoping to get through as many of these as I can in the time I have left." He looked at his watch and it was 12:10, which gave him just under three hours to get in as much research as he could.

Although, 1919 had been filled with strife, Jim found that the year 1920 was the exact opposite. This roll of film was filled with news articles about jazz and other music, along with cultural articles on art and technology, and a fashion section showing women all the new trends in dresses. It was the calm after the storm of war. A time of prosperity and indulgence as people worked around prohibition and made speakeasies and moonshiners rich. The 19th amendment was ratified giving women the right to vote. The 1920s were given the name the "Roaring Twenties" for a reason. People were enjoying the prosperity that comes with post-war peacetimes. Automobiles became commonplace and as such roads needed to be built, which provided more jobs. Times were good, and the obituary section shrank to a small section of the paper. Jim enjoyed reading this roll of film and managed to skim it in a half an hour. He took note of the pictures and printed out the images that were taken in the town of Oakwood to show the way the town had been affected by the world around it. This made Jim wonder at what time it was that the town simply stopped changing.

Sadly, the 1930s were just as hard on Oakwood as the rest of the world, with the Great Depression, after the 1929 stock market crash. Where people were prosperous the year before, they then were barely making a living. Poverty and homelessness became the norm for large portions of the country's citizens while upper, upper-class individuals continued their extravagant acts and places like the Chrysler Building opened. Betty Boop was introduced as entertainment and prohibition was finally seen as a failure and abolished. With this, Jim noticed an influx of advertisements for tonics and cure-all ailments elixirs, that were nothing more than moonshine. These were even sold at the Oakwood pharmacy. And to cap it all off, World War II began in September of 1930 when Nazi Germany invaded Poland.

Jim found that most of the 1940s newspapers were very much like those during the first World War. Except, coming off of the Great Depression straight into another World War made this era much more about saving resources for the war effort and doing your part at home for the boys abroad fighting for the American way of life. Even though the U.S. didn't officially enter the war until the end of 1941, the previous war was still at the forefront of the memory of most people. This made the average American citizen very in tune with what was happening and led them to do everything they could to help bring this terrible time to an end.

THE TOWN THAT TIME FORGOT

He noticed what seemed like an unusually high number of casualties coming from the town of Oakwood until he reached mid-August of 1944. Then suddenly the death toll in Oakwood from the war dissipated to nothing. The obituary section strangely and abruptly transitioned at that time from pages of fallen soldiers back to a normal attrition rate of elderly dying and one maybe two accidents per year.

This piqued Jim's interest, and he began to look more in-depth at the annual deaths that occurred in the obituaries of the following rolls of microfiche, noticing that from August 1944 on to the current year all deaths were listed as natural causes except one per year which happened in August and was caused by a bizarre accident of some kind. All that is except 1968 when the strange accident happened in September instead of August when a man named Joe Wilson fell down his stairs and broke his neck, killing himself. Jim knew that this couldn't be a coincidence, especially spanning over forty years.

The obituary for Joe Wilson stated that he had lost two sons and his wife in previous years, but still had a daughter living somewhere. If she was still around, maybe he could locate her and get some more information on Mr. Wilson's death.

This made him decide to wrap up his research at the library so that he could go straight to the Hall of Records and review public death records. He wanted to know more about this unusual change and the pattern that followed.

Jim gathered his printouts making sure that he had one of each of the obituaries for further research, then he packed everything up and returned the last roll of film to the librarian at the front desk. "Thank you for your help, Nan."

"All done? That last bit seemed to go much more quickly than the first half," Nan inquired as she traded Jim his driver's license for the roll of film.

"Yes, thank you. The last half ended up pointing me in a direction I hadn't planned on, which sped up this portion of my research significantly," Jim replied.

"Well, if you need anything else, you know where we are," Nan said cordially.

Halfway to the door Jim stopped in his tracks and turned to Nan, "You wouldn't happen to know anything about any of the older families that live around here, would you?"

"Well, I've lived here my whole life. So, I might know something if they lived here in my lifetime. Who are you interested in?"

"The Wilson Family. Apparently, Joe Wilson died in 1968 of an accidental fall. I'm curious if his daughter is still around."

"I think you might be looking for Amy Wilson. Her father was mayor before I was born, and I was a small child when he died, but I seem to remember something about him dying in a strange accident. My parents were friends of he and his wife. When he died, his daughter moved back to town and used to babysit me from time to time."

"Is she still around? Can I speak with her?"

"Last I heard she was living in her parents' old house. She would be in her sixties by now I believe."

"Could you give me directions to her house, or her contact information so that I may interview her?"

"Yes. When you come out of the library, you take the first left then follow it until it dead ends and make another left go two blocks and it's the second house from the corner on the right. It's a two-story house."

Scribbling down the directions into his notebook as fast as he could, Jim thanked Nan and left, looking at his watch he saw it was just past two-thirty. He was ahead of his planned schedule for when he wanted to be out of the library, which made him breathe a sigh of relief.

Jim knew that he would only be able to see death records that were twenty-five years old or older because anything more recent wouldn't be considered public record yet. He also knew that accident reports had no restrictions like this. So, he figured he would start with death records from 1944 to 1959, then pull all accident reports between 1944 and current to confirm that there were no incidents that might be missing from the newspaper clippings.

When he reached the service desk at the Hall of Records, he was greeted by a professional-looking, yet stuffy woman in her mid-forties. She wore a pair of horn-rimmed glasses that looked straight out of the 1950s era. "How may I help you?" she asked abruptly.

"I would like to see all of the death records between 1944 and 1959 as well as any incident reports from 1944 to today."

He was told, "You will have to fill out this form and submit it for review. It will take a week to have all the records pulled since they are going back so far into the archives. And there is a twenty-five-dollar fee due when you submit your form to cover the photocopying. But the photocopies will be yours to keep." The woman spoke as if she were reading a script and stood staring at him waiting for his response.

Jim removed his wallet and took out a twenty-dollar bill and five ones. The woman behind the counter handed him the form and explained, "You need to provide all of your contact information in case the archivist has questions, fill in exactly what you want to be pulled and copied, and explain why you want these documents and what they are to be used for." Then she handed him a pen and said, "You can use those desks over there to fill out your form and come back to the window when you're ready."

Jim turned to where she had been pointing and saw a row of tall standing tables like you would see in a bank for filling out deposit slips. He walked over and spent about ten minutes filling out the very inquisitive form, gave it one last look-over, and then returned to the window.

"All done?" The lady took the form from Jim and reviewed it with scrutiny as if he were applying for citizenship or something, then walked over to a copy machine and made a duplicate, stamped it duplicate and paid cash, then took his money and handed him the copy she had just made and stamped. She placed the original in a pile of other forms in a horizontal stacking tray before asking, "Will there be anything else?"

Jim was hoping to have more data on the deaths in this town before he left for this visit. He paused for a moment and then asked, "Where is the oldest church in town?"

The woman pointed back in the direction of the way he had entered the town and said, "Take the main road out of town about two blocks and then turn right. Go about a half a block and you will see the Pentecostal church on the left side of the street."

Jim thanked the woman and then darted back to his motorbike. He was hoping to catch the minister, a groundskeeper, or someone who worked at the church who would be able to let him in to see the church archives. Or at the very least point him in the right direction. He was determined to see more of these death records before he left town. He knew he would be back in a week to pick up the documents from town records but wanted more information to sift through while he waited for the bulk of the information to be ready.

The first thing Jim noticed when he approached the large brick cathedral was that there was a sprawling cemetery that sat to the left of it and continued onto the property across the street. He decided that he would take a short walk through the two cemetery parcels to see how old the dates were on the tombstones. What he found was the plots nearest the church were the oldest with some as old as the 1800s and the newer plots streamed out across the cemetery crossing to the other side of the road. It was obvious that at some point the church had to purchase the extra land to expand the cemetery.

Some movement inside the church caught Jim's eye after he had been wandering through the headstones for about ten or fifteen minutes, so he started toward the church hoping to catch whoever was inside before they left.

When he arrived, he found the front door unlocked and entered silently. Standing near the altar organizing a stack of hymnals was an older gentleman in a dark grey plaid suit. The man looked up at Jim when he began walking towards the Altar. "Hello, young man. May I help you?" His wire-rimmed glasses were dangling halfway down his nose, and his salt and pepper hair was slicked back to one side on top while very short on the sides and back.

"Yes. I'm hoping to be able to review the church archives for any deaths between 1944 and the current day. I'm doing a journalism article for my college paper on the town, and I have come across an intriguing change in the number of deaths starting around August 1944 as well as the causes of death in the obituaries and I want to compare the records," Jim explained, hoping that his explanation would inspire the gentleman to give him full access to the archives.

"Well, I'm not sure what you're expecting to find, young man. The archives are a complete mess. Did you try the town hall?"

This caught Jim off guard. He hadn't expected any pushback from the chapel staff. "I have. There's a waiting period while they pull the records and make the photocopies. I'm on kind of a short deadline and was hoping I could locate some of the information I need here while I wait. Is there a way I could just spend some time with them to see what I can find?" Jim asked then waited for what seemed like an eternity for a reply.

When the man finally spoke, he was quite salty and put off by the idea but agreed to let him have a look, "If you insist. You will need to be extremely careful as some of these documents are very old."

The man took a ring of keys from his pocket and led Jim to the basement. It was musky and covered in dust and cobwebs as if no one had visited this place in centuries. "This is where you will find the oldest documents. You can start here. The newer documents are kept off sight at a storage facility. I'll leave you to it." The man left without waiting for a response, shutting the door behind him.

Jim found himself in the dark as the door closed and began feeling along the wall to find a light switch. When he couldn't locate one, he found the doorknob and opened the door. The light from the hall streamed into the room exposing a string tied to a chain dangling from the ceiling light that hung in the middle of the room. Seeing this Jim left the door open and walked over to the string. The string snapped without triggering the light when Jim pulled it. Jim looked around for something to stand on and found an old orange crate filled with stacks of folders. He slid it over beneath the light and used it as a step ladder which made him the proper height to pull the pull chain and turn on the light. The light was too dim to be of much use, so Jim decided to leave the door open.

To Jim's surprise, the records were in a fairly organized manner making his research easier than he expected upon first sight. Although the boxes weren't all aligned in order, the files within them were very well kept and in both alphabetical and chronological order. This aided in his research tremendously. In just over two hours he had made his way through the 1940s, the 1950s, and was halfway through the 1960s filling an entire notebook with names, dates, and causes of death. Everything before 1940 had been as the obituaries indicated, so he skimmed through those quickly only taking the random note, since he already had most of that information in his printouts from the library. The last box was for 1970, indicating that the rest of the records after that date would be in the storage unit.

He finished reading the last folder and was glad to be done with this portion of his research since the dust was beginning to make his breathing difficult; placing the file back into the box where he found it. Before turning off the light, Jim looked around to make sure he had not missed anything and had placed everything back where he found it; then left the room closing the door behind him.

The man in plaid was waiting for Jim when he returned to the altar room. "Did you find everything you were looking for?" The man gave Jim a chilly greeting.

"Yes, thank you. At least up to 1970. But it's enough to keep me working until I can get the copies from town hall next week. Thank you for your assistance," Jim respectfully replied. He didn't understand this man's change in demeanor after he had asked about the records and didn't want to make matters worse.

At that, the two men nodded at one another and went their separate ways, the plaid-clad man towards the basement door and Jim towards his motorbike. While Jim organized himself and his belongings onto his motorcycle, he noticed that the activity around town had increased. Kids were outside playing, people were working in their yards and returning home from work. It was indeed a small-town suburban haven, he thought to himself. Then he started his bike and headed back to the main square. He had one last stop to make before heading home.

Following the librarian's directions, Jim found the Wilson house and parked his bike on the street out front. Walking to the front door, he noticed a shimmer of light where drapes were parted, and someone was peeking out the front window. It wasn't long after he rang the doorbell before a woman who looked to be in her sixties answered the door. Her hair was silver, and her skin was tanned from working in her garden. "May I help you?"

"Yes. My name is Jim Norton. I'm writing an article on the town of Oakwood for my college paper and was wondering if you could tell me a little about your father and your family? I hear your family goes back quite a way."

Amy opened the screen and stepped out onto the front porch motioning towards the porch swing that sat off to the right of the door. "What would you like to know?"

"How far back does your family's connection to Oakwood go?"

"Well...my parents were both raised here, and as far as I know, I am the only one in my family to have ever moved away from Oakwood. We have relatives in the cemetery that go back to the 1800s."

"So, your family is one of the founding families of the town."

"Yep. That would be us. My father was even mayor of Oakwood for a time while I was growing up."

"That's impressive. What made you move away from here?" Jim was approaching his questions cautiously after the response that he received at the church.

"I needed to get away from here after my brothers and mom died. It was just too many painful memories for me to deal with at that time. So, I moved to New York where no one knew me, and I could get lost in the crowd and live my life without thinking about my past."

"Wow! New York. That's a huge change."

"It was. It was the change that I needed to heal and move on from my grief."

"If it was what you needed what made you come back?"

"I came back after my father died. I felt guilty about not coming home to see him very often while he was alive, and decided I wanted to be close to him and the rest of my family now to help make up for it." Amy's face turned somber, and her eyes glossed over as she thought about how lonely her father must have been here all alone.

"How did your father die? If I may ask?"

"Sherriff Jefferies reported it as an accidental fall down the stairs, but that never really made sense to me."

"Why is that?"

"My father never went upstairs after my mother and brothers died. He couldn't bring himself to walk past their old rooms. So, he moved

169

into the main floor bedroom saying it was easier on his knees. Which makes me wonder why he would have been up there in order to fall?"

"Hmm…That is curious. Maybe he decided to move back upstairs after you moved away. Could that be it?"

"No. His stuff was all still in the downstairs bedroom when I came home, and the rooms upstairs were covered in dust."

"Did you ask Sherriff Jefferies about it?"

"I tried to, but he gave me some story of how he would store stuff up there sometimes, and I wouldn't know that because I never came home and then brushed me off." Amy sat thinking for a minute before adding, "And another thing, why were they so quick to have him cremated?"

"What? I don't understand. Wouldn't you have had to sign off on that as next of kin?"

"Yes! That's what I told them. All they said was it was in his will to be cremated as quickly as possible if I could not be located, and that they could not locate me. I know that was complete bullshit. Daddy always said he wanted to be buried with mama and the boys."

"Did you try and file a complaint or take legal action?"

"I did, but it didn't do any good. The mayor and sheriff at the time closed ranks on me. They had all the proper papers and Dad was already in ashes. The best I could do at that point was place his ashes with Mom and the boys."

"That's incredible! Why do you think they would do that?"

"I've always thought daddy might have discovered that they were doing something underhanded, and they killed him then covered it up. But I could never prove anything. That's another reason I moved back here. To watch them and try and figure it out. Nothing ever surfaced though."

"Do you know if they are still around?"

"The mayor died about eight years ago of a heart attack, and Jefferies was in the Wood Shire long-term medical hospice center with early-onset Alzheimer's."

Jim scribbled down some notes while Amy watched, then she said, "I'm sorry. I seem to have gotten us all off track. What was it you wanted to know about the town?"

Jim realized he better ask her some basic questions about how the town has changed over the years. "Growing up here, you must have a good picture of what changes the town has made over the years. It seems to be very Norman Rockwell-esque. Is that how you remember it being?"

"For the most part, yes. The war affected things for a while with all the boys being sent to fight and so many of them dying over there. But after that, things seemed to get back to what we called normal and have pretty much stayed that way all these years."

"It's unusual for a town not to feel the effects of progress and still be so quaint. How do you think Oakwood accomplished this?"

"I believe it's because the people care about one another and work as a community about all issues. We know our neighbors and speak to one another. Big cities are missing that. It's a big contrast to New York. We've kept our values and morals intact. Plus, our community has been through so much loss, that we support each other when things are tough."

"That's beautifully said, and very insightful. May I quote you on that?"

"Sure, if you think it's print-worthy." Amy chuckled at the thought of being quoted about anything.

"I definitely do. Well, I've taken up enough of your time. Thank you very much for speaking with me." Jim shook Amy's hand and said his goodbyes.

Jim and Amy waved goodbye to each other one last time as he drove back towards town.

He entered the circle to go back to the main highway, noticing that traffic was now reaching its full impact with shoppers going to the grocery store for their evening groceries, townspeople congregating for summer picnics in the center courtyard, and locals socializing at the diner. Jim smiled at the setting on his way out of town.

Jim made sure to call his mom as soon as he was settled in at home, updating her on how quaint and picturesque it was. "Mom, you would love this place. It's like a page out of history. Peaceful, beautiful architecture, and very homespun atmosphere." He told her about the tons of paperwork that he now had to scour through, "There's so much paperwork that I'll be busy going through it for weeks. I've got to go back to collect the rest next week once the photocopies are ready."

"I'm glad you're back and everything went well. Don't forget to call that girl of yours and let her know you are back." Tess replied trying to cover up her unwarranted concern.

Jim laughed and said, "Thanks for the reminder, Mom. I have every plan of calling her when we get off the phone with you. But I appreciate your support in that area."

"Well, you better get to it then, before it gets too late, then, hadn't you?" his mom said eagerly before adding, "I love you. Have a good night and take care of yourself, sweetie."

"I will, Mom. I love you too. I'll call you in a couple of days or so. For sure, before I head back to Oakwood," Jim said before hanging up the receiver. His mother stood silent after she heard his goodbye. The hair was standing up on the back of her neck. 'No, that would be too much of a coincidence,' she thought to herself attempting to calm the alarming feelings that she was having. She went back to what she had been doing when Jim called, wondering if she should tell him what she knew, no longer feeling like her concerns were unwarranted.

###

Ring...Ring...Ring...Ring...The phone rang for the fourth time and Jim looked at his clock on the microwave, noticing that it was almost 7:30. Ring..."Hello. You've reached Sharon. I can't come to the phone right now. But if you leave me a message, I will get back to you as soon as I can."

Jim wasn't prepared for an answering machine and stumbled upon his words, "Um...Hi. It's me, Jim. I just wanted to give you a call and let you know I am back and see how your day went. Give me a call when you get the chance. Have a good night...Bye." He hated talking to those things and hadn't realized that she had one. He hung up the phone wondering where she might be. His ego had expected to find her at home waiting for his call, but his common sense said she had a life and was busy living it. With that, he took a shower to wash off all of the dust, dirt, and road grub, before plopping onto the sofa and vegging out in front of the television.

###

"Sharon! Over here!" One of Sharon's classmates waved her down calling her over to the table where the rest of the party sat. "I can't believe you actually made it."

"Karen wasn't about to let me miss it." Sharon chided while giving Karen a hug and handing her the gift she had made for her a few weeks earlier, "Happy birthday. I hope you like it."

"Did you make it?" Karen asked excitedly. "You always make the coolest gifts."

Blushing Sharon responded, "I don't know about coolest, but yes, I made it."

The rest of the ladies sitting at the table cheered Karen on, "Open it. Let's see what you got. I'm envious. I love Sharon's handmade gifts. She's so talented." Sharon blushed as she took her seat next to Karen. Karen had been saving it for her.

"Oh Sharon! I love it!" Opening the gift bag Karen pulled out a bright blue hand knit cardigan. "It's beautiful and my favorite color. You are the best friend I could ever ask for. Even if I rarely get to see you these days." Karen added the last bit with a wink before giving Sharon a long hug.

"It was nothing. Knitting helps keep my hands busy when I'm sitting watching TV."

"I beg to disagree. That is quality craftmanship. You could sell these for a really good price." The girl who had called Sharon over said while she meticulously looked at the cardigan.

"And she should know. She works for Esprit in their buying office," another girl at the table spoke up.

Sharon did not know this person, and looked at her classmate, "Really? When did this happen?" She was excited for her friend's new adventure.

"Last month. But if you attended girls' night more often you would know this."

"I'm sorry. I've just been very busy lately with homework, my internship, and all."

Karen chimed in, "Yeah...and all...you mean that new hunk of yours."

The rest of the group oohed and awed like a bunch of high school girls. "Tell us more about this guy." They weren't used to Sharon having a man in her life and wanted to hear everything about him.

Being center of attention and having the conversation focused directly on her personal life made Sharon feel very uncomfortable. "It's new, and I'm not ready to talk about it yet. Besides, this is Karen's day. Let's make her the focus tonight." She nodded at Karen hoping she would help bail her out of the mess she threw her into.

"She's right. This is my night. Let's have some fun." Karen waved over the waitress, "We'll have a pitcher of beer and tequila shots all around." Karen leaned over to Sharon and whispered into her ear, "Don't worry about the bill. My dad's paying for tonight. I know you're on a tight budget, but I just couldn't celebrate without my bestie, could I?"

Sharon smiled, and gave Karen a hug of appreciation, "No, I guess not." Sharon didn't like feeling like a charity case, but she knew Karen's father could afford it and that Karen wouldn't take no for an answer, so she just accepted that this was happening.

When the waitress returned with their drinks, Karen raised her shot glass, "To the best group of friends a girl could ever have, and another year of getting into trouble together."

The rest of the group cheered along with her and downed their shots like a group of professional drinkers, Sharon included. It had been a long time since Sharon had been out on the town with the girls and she had forgotten how much fun she and Karen had together when they went out. She had barely completed her thought when Karen ordered another round of shots. "Well, I guess that sets the tone for the night." Sharon laughed as she took a drink of the beer that had just been set in front of her, and she settled in for a long night of drinking and girl shenanigans.

The house smelled like Nan had been cooking all day when Kevin entered. He usually made it home about twenty minutes before Nan these days while she was short-handed at the library. Something that he wasn't too pleased about, but understood that it was only temporary. Nan's assistant was on maternity leave so Nan was having to both open and close the library until she returned. Only three more weeks and things could return to normal. He didn't want to sound too old-fashioned, but he enjoyed coming home to his wife and having dinner ready for the two of them to sit down and spend some quality time together. They hadn't been blessed with children, so the house was quite empty when she wasn't around.

A quiet house was another thing that he wasn't too keen on. He had grown up with six siblings and the house was never quiet, which made coming home to an empty, quiet house particularly uncomfortable. He and Nan had planned to have a whole house of children when they were first married. But God had other plans was how Nan had put it to him the day they found out they couldn't have children.

They discussed adoption a few times; however, it never seemed to be the right time. In the meantime, being home alone all day had become unbearable for Nan which is why she had taken a part-time job at the library, which eventually had become full-time. She needed to keep herself busy to keep from thinking about the one thing that was missing from her perfect life, children. Then, time had passed, and they had settled into the comfort of being alone and discussions of children simply stopped.

Kevin was peeking into the slow cooker when he heard Nan's car pull into the driveway. He knew she would admonish him for sampling the goods as she often put it if she saw him when she came in. So, he quickly replaced the lid and started setting the kitchen table with plates and utensils.

Although he liked coming home to his wife, he also enjoyed helping her when he could, doing little things such as setting the table or switching the laundry from the washer to the dryer, and emptying the dishwasher regularly for her. Even though they lived in a town that resembled the 1950s, he understood that his wife worked just as hard as he did and wanted to make her home life easier wherever he could.

Nan smiled at the sight of Kevin setting the table when she came through the kitchen door from the car park. "Hello, dear. Thank you so much. I should have done that before I left, but I was running late this morning."

Kevin adored how much she liked taking care of the house and him. "It's fine, dear. I like being able to feel useful here at home. How was your day?"

Nan set her purse on the counter and began plating the roast that was in the slow cooker while she told him about her day, "It was the usual for the most part. Seventh-grade school field trips coming in to learn how to use the card files and microfiche machines for researching their next school paper, Mrs. Clayborn coming in to exchange her next set of books for the nursing home, the usual." Mrs. Clayborn was a regular at the library. She was a retired English teacher who volunteered at the retirement home and made a point of bringing a selection of library books each week for the residents who couldn't make it to the library themselves.

"There was one bit of unusual today though. A journalism student from out of town came in and spent the entire morning looking at the Oakwood historical microfiche. He's doing some kind of article on death rates or something in our town. It all sounded a little boring to me, but he seemed to have hit on a turning point for his paper about three-quarters of the way through and finished up in a flash before dashing out to the town hall," She continued while setting the serving dishes in the middle of the table in the cozy breakfast nook. "He seemed extremely interested in Joe Wilson. He even asked for directions to their old place so he could interview Amy."

Kevin's interest was especially peaked over the bit about death rates and Joe Wilson. "What could he possibly want with Oakwood death rate information?" he asked. "Did he say where he was from?"

"I'm not sure. He just said something about them slowing down around 1944 or something like that and wanting to do a comparison for his paper. He didn't say where he was from or why he was doing the article on us. He just scanned the microfiche, made a bunch of printouts, and darted off," Nan replied sitting down to eat.

Kevin didn't want to make Nan feel as though she was being put through an interrogation, so he changed the topic to how happy he was that they invested in the slow cooker. "The house smelled like you had been here cooking all day with the new slow cooker simmering throughout the day," he said. "I'm very glad we decided to get it. Hopefully, it will save you some work on the home front after Leslie returns, too."

Nan loved her husband and appreciated how he always wanted to make her life easier. "As long as the food doesn't suffer for it, I'm all in on that one. Plus, it doesn't heat up the house in the summertime. I just need to finish reading the cookbook that came with it to keep every meal from tasting the same." She laughed.

"Well, you seasoned this roast perfectly. It tastes great and is so tender I don't even need a knife. So far so good when it comes to the food," Kevin reassured her.

The happy couple finished their dinner and spent the rest of their evening, as usual, cleaning up the kitchen, chatting, watching their favorite television shows, and then turning in for the night at about ten o'clock. Even though Kevin was acting like his normal self for Nan's benefit, his mind was swirling with concern over this new turn of events.

###

Bruce approached Christine with the paperwork that he had received earlier that morning, "Hey, Christine. I found this request for archive files in my inbox. Do you know what this guy wants with all these death records? He stated that they are for an article he's doing, but I'm concerned he might be using them for something more unscrupulous like identity fraud or something," he inquired trying not to sound too suspicious. The dates on the request sent up red flags for him from his position on the secret seven council, but he couldn't tell her that.

Christine responded, "He's a college student from out of town doing an article or something and wanted to compare past death rates with current death rates or something like that from what I gathered. I told him he would have to come back to pick them up next week since there were so many of them to compile and copy."

"Thank you. I'll get right on it and give him a call if I have any further questions," Bruce didn't want to give Christine any reason to question why he was asking even though he was more concerned over this young man's interests in their town than before. He walked away to go back to his office and decided he would bring it up at the town council meeting the next day for further guidance from the other six members of the town council.

Bruce worked on gathering the information requested after he returned to his office just in case the council wanted him to move forward with the request, all the while feeling a sense of trepidation that this was something they needed to be worried about.

The feeling nagged at Bruce for the rest of the day and evening and transitioned into a restless night's sleep of tossing and turning mixed with nightmares. He awoke several times in a cold sweat dreaming of their town's secret being discovered, and everyone he knew falling into ruin all because of this college student's school newspaper article. It made him more confident than ever that he needed to speak with the council about this matter.

Bruce awoke groggy and agitated. He got dressed for his meeting and work in a rush, spilling his coffee on his trousers and having to change them before he left. He lived outside of the town square and although it was a short walk, decided to drive into town for the meeting and then walk to work from there. He was a middle-aged man who had never married, making his cars more like his children. As a collector and restorer of antique cars, he loved any chance he had to drive his favorite; a candy apple red '66 Ford Mustang. He had picked it up for a song at the wrecking yard not too far outside of town and refurbished it himself. He thought driving his special baby might take some of the edge off how he was feeling.

As luck would have it, Bruce was able to find a parking space directly in front of the town hall right outside of the council meeting room. This brightened his day, knowing that he would be able to peek out and look at his pride and joy throughout the day, since his office window at the library faced in this direction. He parked, locked up his cherry ride, and went into the town hall.

Most everyone else was already there by the time Bruce entered and was sitting around talking about some out-of-towner who had been researching the history of the town, in particular the deaths that happened in the town. He was surprised to see that the council was already aware of this incident and wondered how they had found out.

He was still wondering when the mayor who was already sitting in his place asked him to go ahead and have a seat so that they could call the meeting to order and get this discussion underway. Bruce nodded and proceeded to take his place at the table as Mayor Winters tapped the gavel on the hardwood table.

"Good morning, gents. I hope you are all doing well this morning," Ed Winters, the new Mayor and head of the town council greeted his fellow councilmen. "This morning we are going to skip reading the minutes and reviewing the agenda to discuss some more pressing matters that have been brought to my attention in the past twenty-four hours, and most of you probably are already aware of." The men around the table other than Bruce glanced at one another, nodding in agreement.

Mayor Winters continued, "Okay, Kevin, go ahead and tell the rest of our circle what you told me last night when you called."

"Thanks, Ed. As you all know, my wife is the town's librarian and last night Nan shared with me that a stranger from out of town had spent the morning going through the microfiche of the town's history researching the death rates in our town. She said he was particularly interested in deaths post-1944." The other men at the table murmured and gasped as Kevin finished informing them about the previous day's events. "As well as with Joe Wilson. He even asked for directions to the Wilson house to see if he could interview Amy Wilson."

Mayor Winters retook the floor, "Thank you, Kevin. Does anyone else have anything to add?"

Bruce spoke up, "I have something to add."

"Go ahead, Bruce. What do you have for us?" Mayor Winters acknowledged him.

"After leaving the library, it seems that this young man visited the town hall of records and requested some copies of archived death records dating from 1944 to 1959. I asked Christine for more information on him after I received the request, and she informed me that he was a university student doing a school newspaper article on our town. The paperwork says his name is Jim Norton, and he's from Milledgeville. He has also requested any accident reports from 1944 to the present day."

The room became so quiet that all that was audible were the soft breaths of seven men sitting around a table staring at one another with looks of despair. Hearing Bruce say the date 1944 was concerning, but to hear that the rest of the request brought fear to their minds. The request for accident reports solidified their fear that this man was a definite threat even if he did not know it.

Mayor Winters again spoke, "Thank you, Bruce, for that alarming information. Gentlemen, it seems we have a dilemma. Do we take this young man at his word? Or do we act as if he is an immediate threat to our society and way of life?" Ed took a breath and let the men who surrounded him take in the information with which they had just been provided. "Does anyone have anything to say before we vote?"

Kevin spoke up, "I don't know that he is currently a threat. But from what Nan said he has got a fire under him to figure out why there was such a sudden and drastic drop in our town's death count in the year 1944 as well as how it has remained so low. This brings me no joy to say, but to me, gentlemen, this makes him a very real threat to our way of life. I say we must deal with it sooner rather than later." Kevin took a brief pause before continuing, "I had many sleepless hours to give this matter some thought last night. I'm not sure if any of the rest of you have noticed the timing of this, but next week is our week of reckoning. I suggest that we entice this young man back to town on contract day and make him this year's annual sacrificial lamb."

"Anyone else have anything to say?" Ed provided the opportunity for everyone to have their say.

"I have something to add," a grey-haired man in a vintage-looking leisure suit spoke up.

"Yes, Owen?" The mayor asked.

Owen cleared his throat before speaking, "I had the opportunity to meet this young man yesterday at the church. He was rather insistent on searching the church archives for any death records he could find. I allowed him to look at the basement files that run through 1970. But he never saw the files that we keep in storage. I checked in a few times while he was there, and he was taking page after page of notes."

"Thank you, Owen, for that very important information. Does anyone else have any additional information that they think would assist with our serious decision?" The mayor waited for a moment to see if there was anything further to discuss. No one else felt the need to speak, so the mayor continued. "Since no one has anything else to add, I put it to a vote. All those in favor of managing this threat now without waiting and having him be this year's annual sacrificial lamb, please raise your hand."

One by one the seven men around the table raised their hands. This was never a pleasant vote. It was a vote to end someone's life. This year would be bittersweet, ending someone so young's life without notice. It was a deed that had to be done, however, to keep their way of life and their families safe. Once the last man's hand was in the air, Mayor Winters tapped his gavel and said, "Motion carried. Jim Norton will be this year's lamb. Bruce, please proceed with the arrangements to have this gentleman in town on the proper date."

After the vote, Kevin shared, "Nan says that the young man was riding a motorbike. So, if you allow me to say, this would be the best unsuspicious accident possible, if you ask me." He hated recommending a method of killing someone, but time was of the essence and a plan needed to be made.

"That's good information and a reasonable solution. Bruce, you notify the gentleman that his records will be ready for pick-up on the day of reckoning and notify me when he arrives. Trevor, I will contact you once I have been notified and we'll need you to use your position as sheriff to monitor this young man's route and when he leaves town so that Denis, Owen, and I can prepare the arrangements for the deed and carry it out. Kevin, you and Steve will hang back here in town at the ready for any unforeseen emergencies that might arise in case things go awry." Mayor Winters then said, "Does everyone know what they are supposed to do?" The rest of the men at the table nodded.

"Okay then, now that we have that sorted out, onto the rest of the business at hand," Ed instructed, "Kevin, please read the minutes from last week's meeting."

For the rest of the meeting the men who had been so conversational when they arrived were quiet and somber. They took care of their day-to-day business that seemed quite menial after dealing with such a serious matter first thing. But they were issues that needed their attention, so they did their best to give them the attention they deserved before adjourning for the week.

# # #

Jim didn't realize how tired he had been until he woke up on the sofa where he fell asleep in front of the TV the night before. He awoke to the news talking about President Regan ordering the U.S. Marines to withdraw from Beirut, followed by a segment about the Olympics being held in Los Angeles. It took him a little while to fully awaken. The day before had been a lot of mental work combined with an abundance of driving. Realizing how zapped his energy levels were, he decided to take a more leisurely approach and ease into the day ahead.

Jim wandered to the kitchen, prepared the coffee pot, and then stood stretching in the doorframe as he watched the invigorating dark brew slowly drip from the filter into the pot below. He found the process somehow rejuvenating and enjoyed letting his senses soak up the sight, aromas, and general experience of brewing a cup of coffee. To him, it was almost as good as drinking a hot cup of joe.

When the last drop of the magnificent brew had hit the darkness beneath, Jim eagerly took hold of the pot's handle and poured himself a large cup. Breathing in the rich aroma, Jim sipped the hot elixir of life and enjoyed the warmth as it ran down his throat and gradually sent energy into his veins. This was the way he liked to have his coffee, immersing himself and allowing himself to fully absorb every aspect of the moment. Unfortunately, most mornings were a mad dash out the door, and he rarely got to allow himself this indulgence.

As his cup got down to about half full, Jim took a box of Frosted Flakes from the cupboard and a carton of milk from the fridge before picking up the cereal bowl and spoon that were in the drying rack on the counter. He returned to the living room with them in one arm and his coffee in the other hand, careful not to spill a drop.

He had been sitting at the coffee table eating his breakfast and watching the news for a while when the phone rang. He looked at the clock on the wall. It was 10:30, and he couldn't think of who would be calling him. Everyone he knew, besides his mother, would be at work or in class. Walking over to answer the phone he pondered who it was, "Hello?"

"Hello, Mr. Norton?" A voice on the other end of the phone responded.

"Yes, this is he. How may I help you?"

"This is Bruce Farnsbee, the archivist for Oakwood. I see you have a request for some copies of some documents here in our archives."

"Yes. I do. Is there a problem?"

"No, sir. I'm calling because I want to confirm all the data that you are looking for so that I can have them complete for pick up next Thursday. Our offices will be closed on Friday for our town's annual festival, and I want to make sure to get these to you before the weekend. I was informed they are of some urgency to you."

"That's very kind of you. Yes, it would help me a lot if I could have them by next weekend." Jim was surprised by the level of service he was receiving, especially from a government worker.

"Good. Then if this is everything you need, you can pick them up any time after eleven on Thursday," Bruce tried to narrow down the time when Jim would be there so that the council would be prepared for his arrival.

"Great! Thank you very much, Mr. Farnsbee. I'll be there," Jim acknowledged before hanging up the phone.

The call shot Jim into motion, making him grab his satchel and pull out the notebooks and copies that he had made. He wanted to go through everything he had to get a clear understanding of what the trend in Oakwood deaths seemed to be. Sliding his breakfast bowl over to the far edge of the table, he spread out the papers and began to go through them.

Flipping through his notebook he fell upon his interview with Amy Wilson and the part about Sherriff Jefferies caught his attention. He set it down beside him and grabbed the phone book to see if there was a listing for Wood Shire Long-term Medical Facility. When none was found he called information and asked them for the number. As he suspected the facility was in Oakwood. That's why the listing wasn't in his phone book. It was too far away to be in there.

He called the number that the information operator had provided and asked the receptionist if it would be possible to speak with Mr. Jefferies, telling her he was his nephew and was calling long distance. "I've only recently found out that he's been in your facility after trying to find him for several months."

"Mr. Jefferies can come to the phone, but he may not know who you are or be able to carry on a coherent conversation. His current state of mind is sporadic."

"That's okay. I just want to hear his voice and let him know I'm thinking about him." Jim carried on his ruse hoping the voice on the other end of the phone would cave and let him speak with him. It would save Jim from having to visit him in person.

"I'll see if I can get him to take your call. Hang on."

Jim sat in anticipation while the receptionist went to do whatever it was, she needed to do to bring Sherriff Jefferies to the phone.

"Hello?" An obviously elderly man's voice answered.

Jim hadn't thought through this part of his phone call. He wasn't sure what to say. So, he said the first thing that came to mind. "Hey Unc! How're you doin'?"

"Fine..." The older man was understandably confused. "How are you?"

His response led Jim to believe that the receptionist had told Sherriff Jefferies that his nephew was on the phone, which was making things go more smoothly. "I'm good. I saw Amy Wilson a few weeks back and she told me you were in Wood Shire."

"Oh, yes...Amy. How is she?"

"She's well. If you didn't know she's living in her old family home. You know Joe Wilson's place." Jim hoped mentioning Joe's name would spark Sherriff Jefferies to talk about him and it worked.

"Oh yes...poor Joe. Amy's living with him now?"

"No Unc. She's living in his house. You know the one he fell down the stairs in?"

"No. You mean hung himself."

"What? I thought he fell and broke his neck? That's what I was always told."

"Oh...yes...yes...you're right. That was the story alright."

"Did I hear it wrong Unc?"

"No...That was the story. I always did feel badly about covering that one up. But it was better for everyone not to know what really happened though. Wait? Who is this again?"

"It's your nephew."

"Oh hello. Do I have a nephew? What were we talking about?"

"We were talking about Joe Wilson."

"Oh, Joe. I knew him. He was a good guy. Where's he living now."

"Unc, he's dead, remember?"

"When did that happen? Poor Hillary must be beside herself."

"Who's Hillary."

"His wife. You know who she is."

At this point Jim could see that Sherriff Jefferies was losing touch with reality and decided to end the call before someone got suspicious. "Okay Unc...I've gotta go. You be good for the nurses." And he hung up before he received a response then picked up his notebook and started jotting down everything that he had just learned from his conversation with the elderly retired Sherriff in one run-on sentence.

'Joe Wilson suicide not accident was a cover up' Next to it he wrote in large letters...WHY?

Sharon awoke late for work and was rushing around trying to get ready. She had been out late the night before with some girlfriends from school and slept through her alarm. It wasn't like her to go out on a school night, let alone stay out late and sleep through the alarm the next day. It was only after much arm-twisting from Karen and her friends that she agreed to go in the first place. They teased her about being too young to be such a hermit and threatened to drag her out by her perfectly coiffed ponytail if she didn't agree to join them on her own. So, she agreed. She had to admit that she did have fun, but now she was paying the price. Her head was heavy and spinning from all the alcohol the night before. She fully believed in the phrase you play you pay, though, and pulled herself together in spite of how terrible she felt.

As she frantically raced around, she noticed the little red indicator light on her message machine blinking. She hadn't noticed it last night when she came in and had gone straight to bed. She quickly pressed the button to hear the message as she gathered her stuff for the day and put on her shoes. She stopped dead in her tracks when she heard Jim's voice. Sharon hadn't expected to hear from him quite so soon but was very glad he had called. She looked at her watch to see if she had time to call him back, and the answer was no. So, she vowed to call him from work on her break and quickly wrote down the number before dashing out the door.

Sharon was five minutes late to work when she arrived and hurriedly put her things away in the staff room before taking her post at the front desk. Mrs. Whetherby was sitting at her desk when Sharon arrived and noticed how rushed she was. "Good morning, Sharon. Have a late-night then, did we?" She teased. "Dinner with that young man of yours I hope." She added with a wink. Mrs. Whetherby thought highly of Sharon and looked at her as an adoptive niece of sorts. Their relationship had grown close over the past few months as the two learned more about each other.

"Yes, ma'am. No, ma'am..." Sharon stammered. "It was a late night. But, not with a boy. It was my friend Karen's birthday dinner and the girls insisted I go, then kept me out later than I intended." Sharon blushed before continuing, "I'm sorry I'm late. I slept through my alarm. It won't happen again."

Mrs. Whetherby shook her head and smiled at Sharon, "It's only five minutes, dear. My clock could be fast for all we know. Stop stressing. You've earned some fun with your friends. I'm just glad to see you getting out." Mrs. Whetherby had been head librarian at the campus library for many years and Sharon was the first intern that she had who took her position so seriously. And, at times it worried her to see this bright, beautiful, interesting, and independent young woman be so withdrawn from her peers. In this way, she reminded her of herself at that age, and had it not been for meeting her would-be husband who drew her out into the world enough to go out with him, she might have ended up a very lonely old spinster. She didn't want to see that happen to Sharon. Sharon had too much to offer someone; too much to offer the world, for that to happen.

Sharon appreciated Mrs. Whetherby's kindness and her always looking out for her. "Thank you, ma'am. I appreciate that. But I'll still do my best to be on time from now on." Then she winked and added, "With your clock." The two shared a chuckle and went back to work.

Sharon had been so engrossed in her work that she worked through her first break and hadn't noticed until Mrs. Whetherby came up to send her on her lunch break. "It's time for your lunch break, dear."

Sharon looked at her watch in disbelief, "Already? Wow, time flew. I brought lunch today and have a phone call to make so if you need me, I'll be in the staff room," she told her. Mrs. Whetherby nodded, and Sharon headed back to the staff room.

Sharon took her lunch sack and sat next to the phone that sat on the folding table next to the wall in the tiny staff room. She opened the sack and removed the piece of scrap paper that she had written Jim's number on, then picked up the receiver and slowly dialed the number. She didn't know if he would be home but figured it was worth a shot. It startled her when she heard him answer the phone since she hadn't expected to reach him.

"Hello?" Jim answered.

"Hello...It's Sharon. Sorry I missed your call last night. I just found the message this morning."

"Oh hey! It's you! I'm glad you called. No worries, I took a shower and fell asleep on the sofa shortly after I called you. It was a long day," Jim naturally reassured her. His nerves disappeared hearing her on the other end of the line; unlike when he was speaking into her machine. "How's your day going?"

"It's going faster than I can keep up with. How is yours? How was your research trip to Oakwood?" Their conversation was fluid as if they had known each other for years, rather than a few weeks, which comforted her.

"My day is slow-moving. I'm sitting here going over my notes and organizing things. Yesterday went well. I stumbled upon a strange cycle of occurrences and sudden change in the number of deaths after 1944 that has me considering a different approach to my paper," Jim shared with her.

"Oh, really? What about them?" Sharon inquired with great interest.

"It seems before 1944 the town of Oakwood was being decimated by an abnormally high death toll from the War that was happening. And then in August of 1944, they just stopped. It was too early for it to have been because of the end of the war. So, what happened to make this happen so abruptly?" Jim asked Sharon simultaneously asking himself the same question.

"That's strange," Sharon agreed.

"That's not all. It seems that from that same timeframe going forward there's a strange pattern of accidental deaths that happen in August. Only one, and on the same date every year, except in 1968 when the single accident happened in the month of September instead," Jim added. "There's something very strange about all of this that falls outside of the realm of coincidence."

"I have to agree with you. This sounds very unusual and unlikely. Do be careful though. If there is something more nefarious going on here, it could be dangerous for you to dig too deeply."

"I know. I'll be careful. I'm sure there's a reasonable explanation. I simply want to know what it is. Plus, danger is all part of the job for a good reporter."

"You're right. I just don't want to see you get hurt is all...You know, if there are some sort of backroom deals that went on back in 1944, and it has been being covered up for the past forty years, there would have to be some higher-ranking officials involved to keep it secret for this long. Do you think that's what the strange line of annual accidents is about? If so, why does it happen in the same month each year? That doesn't track," Sharon speculated.

"Not just the same month, but the same day. I agree with you though. But they have to be connected somehow. I just haven't figured out how yet," Jim answered.

Even though Sharon was enjoying their conversation, her lunch break was almost over, and she still hadn't eaten her lunch. She needed to eat and get back to work. "Hey, my lunch break's half over, and I haven't touched my food. I'm starved, so I'm going to have to go so I can eat, and make a pit stop in the little girl's room before getting back to work. Talk to you later?" she asked, hoping it would be sooner rather than later.

"How about I make you dinner tonight and I can show you what I have gathered so far?" Jim offered.

Sharon's day had just been made. "That sounds great. What's the address?" She asked scrambling for something to write with. She wrote the address that he gave her on the piece of paper that contained his phone number before saying goodbye and hanging up the phone. She had been so focused on their conversation that she had hardly touched her lunch. She quickly scarfed down the remainder of her ham sandwich before putting the rest of her things away and going back to work.

When Jim hung up the phone, he realized he had nothing to make for dinner. With that, he quickly got cleaned up and left for the grocery store. He figured he would make her his spaghetti a la Jim, better known as spaghetti and meatballs with garlic toast. Which was basically spaghetti with a jar of Ragu marinara sauce and frozen meatballs. Cooking was not his forte, but he could do a mean defrost and boil.

#

Jim spent the afternoon jumping between reviewing his notes and cleaning his apartment for Sharon's arrival. He didn't want her to think he was a complete slob nor did he want her to think he was an OCD neatnik. So, he focused most of his cleaning efforts on picking up items that needed to be put away and normal cleaning, dusting, and vacuuming of places like the kitchen, bathroom, and living room areas. Things that he had to admit he hadn't done in a while.

It was nearly 4:30 by the time Jim had completed his cleaning efforts and he decided it would be a good idea to take a shower and clean up himself before Sharon arrived. 'After all, what good is a clean apartment if he was a dirty smelly mess,' he thought to himself before going to take his shower. The hot water from the shower felt magnificent running down his back after spending the afternoon cleaning the apartment. He hadn't realized how dirty he was getting while his apartment was getting clean. Once he was done with his shower and grooming routine, Jim noticed the time and he decided to go ahead and start dinner.

The water was just beginning to boil when Jim heard a soft tap at the front door, followed by the doorbell. He grinned, realizing that she fell victim to the hidden doorbell like most first-time visitors. For some reason that he didn't understand, the doorbell had been positioned to the far right of the door, and a shrub planted in front of it. Once you knew where to look it was easy to find. But, if you didn't know it was there, it was easy to think that there was no bell.

Jim was still grinning as he answered the door, "Eager to see me, are you?" Standing before him was the beautiful blonde that he had been infatuated with for longer than even he realized; only this time she was a crimson shade of red blushing at her mistake.

"I didn't see the doorbell. Why is it hidden like that?"

Jim laughed and said, "So, I can use my cheesy line on everyone who comes to see me." They both chuckled and shook their heads before he added, "I have no idea. Everyone who visits for the first time has the same problem locating that thing. I'd move it if I owned the place. But, since I don't, I get a good giggle when newcomers come over."

"Mmm...Smells good in here. Is that Ragu I smell?"

Jim stopped dead in his tracks. "You have a good nose. How did you know it was Ragu?"

This time it was Sharon's opportunity to giggle at Jim. "Didn't I tell you that I'm a marinara connoisseur?" She chuckled at his blank expression before telling him, "I could see the reflection of the jar on the counter in the refrigerator door."

He laughed. "That's a good one. Most people can't get me that easily. I'm going to have to keep an eye on you." Then he winked at her before ushering her towards the kitchen area.

Sharon took a seat at one of the stools that sat along the kitchen island across from where Jim was chopping vegetables for a salad and placing spaghetti into the boiling water that was bubbling on the gas range. She placed her bag on the counter in front of her before asking, "Is there anything that I can do to help?"

Jim waved her off saying, "No, no. I've got everything under control." Continuing to chop veggies he pointed in the direction of the small coffee table that was located behind Sharon, "My notes are over there on the table. I'd be interested in your take on what you see?" While she turned to look in the direction that he was pointing, he realized he was being slightly rude. "I'm sorry. I should've asked you how your day was and offered you something to drink. How was your day?" It was his turn to blush at his behavior.

"No problem. For the most part, it was a normal day. I just felt like I was running behind the eight ball all day after I slept through my alarm this morning."

"Aren't you the naughty girl sleeping in on a workday?" Jim teased. "Why were you so tired?"

"I had my friend Karen's birthday dinner last night and they insisted on keeping me out later than I'm used to."

This pleased Jim to hear how forthcoming she was being about her previous night's plans as well as that she had been with her girl-friends. "Can I get you something to drink? Soda? Wine? Beer? Water? Anything?"

"White wine if you've got it?" Sharon responded. "Or, red if you don't."

"White it is." He uncorked the bottle and poured Sharon her glass of wine commenting, "It was my perception from meeting Mrs. Whetherby that you are not normally late. She must've been worried about you being late."

"She wasn't nervous as much as inquisitive. I was only five minutes late. So, she was curious who I was out with last night..." Sharon paused before continuing with her sentence, "she thought I might be out with you."

"Oh really?!? Still playing matchmaker, I see." He laughed, "I knew I liked her." He shot her a flirtatious grin before stirring the pasta sauce.

They continued to talk about their days, while he prepared the French baguette into garlic toast and placed it into the oven. "That does it for dinner prep. How about we take a seat in the living room while it finishes cooking and I can show you some of the notes I have?"

"Sounds good to me," Sharon replied and the two wandered into the next room, taking positions next to one another on the sofa. Jim picked up his file full of photocopies and proceeded to show Sharon what he had discovered at her library, and then at the library in Oakwood. Sharon thoroughly reviewed the files he handed her one at a time before speaking, "You're right. There's a strange series of events happening here..." As her voice trailed off, she began sniffing the air. "Do you smell something burning?"

"Oh crap! My garlic bread!" Jim shouted as he dashed to the kitchen. "I forgot about it." He pulled it out of the oven just the burnt side of done, but not too badly burnt to eat. "I hope you like your garlic bread slightly charred," he said as he turned to the pasta, "and your pasta well done." Sharon laughed out loud watching him drain the spaghetti and pour it into a bowl. Jim just shrugged with embarrassment and said, "Help yourself, my dear."

The two made their plates in the kitchen and then returned to the sofa to eat where they could continue reviewing the files. After they had reviewed all the copies that Jim had made, they turned to go through the notebook full of written notes that he had taken down at the church. "The church had some thorough record-keeping, didn't it?" Sharon asked as she flipped through pages of names dates, causes of death, and even transportation records of those deceased people who were shipped to other locations for burial.

Jim replied with exuberance, "Yes, it was like a treasure trove of who's who of the past. I can't imagine that the records I receive from Oakwood Town Records will be half as thorough."

At about that point Sharon stopped flipping pages and asked Jim, "Hey, this is interesting...what town did you say you were from? And what was your dad's name?"

"Mableton. George. Why?"

"Because there was a George Norton who died in a car crash in 1966 and was shipped back to Mableton for burial," Sharon read from the notes that Jim had hurriedly scratched down into his notebook.

"What? That's not possible. There's no way I would have missed that," Jim refuted as he took the notebook back from Sharon. "There's no way this can be a coincidence. I was in a rush. I must have simply been focused on getting all the information I could before I was asked to leave."

"So, you didn't know where your dad died?" Sharon inquired.

"Mom doesn't like to talk about his death. And I don't like to ask her. It makes her cry," Jim answered. "But now I think I'm going to have to talk to her about him."

"What has she told you?" Sharon continued.

"Just that he was a good man, who died in a bad crash while he was out of town for work," Jim answered. "He was an insurance investigator. I know he drove a red mustang from pictures I've seen and when I wanted to get one and Mom had a panic attack about it. She's very superstitious."

"Maybe you should give her a call, and ask her where he was killed and why he was there? The date matches the rest," Sharon said hesitantly, not wanting to upset him or his mother more than she needed to.

Jim sat and thought for a moment, before responding, "This is a conversation I would rather have with her in person. I want to be there for her if she gets upset and starts to cry." Sharon and Jim sat looking at each other for what seemed like an eternity, before Jim spoke again, "I have to go back to Oakwood next Thursday to pick up the records that I requested. I received a call saying that they would be ready by then. That will give me a chance to review them when I get back and I can go see Mom the following weekend to ask her whatever questions I have."

Sharon gave Jim a serious look before leaning forward and kissing him softly on the lips. "I like you a lot, Jim Norton. I know that we haven't known each other very long, but I would be heartbroken if anything happened to you. Please promise me that you'll be extremely careful."

It made Jim's heart skip a beat to hear her words and caught him by surprise to feel her lips against his own. He was unable to hide his pleasure and wrapped his arms tight around her before saying, "I'll be as careful as I possibly can." Then he leaned in for a deep passionate kiss. "I'll give you my mom's number if it makes you feel better. That way you can call her if something happens and you don't hear from me," Jim added softly under his breath going in for another kiss. Sharon nodded and then leaned in to meet him halfway.

Before Sharon left to go home, she offered to help Jim with his research, "There are a lot of notes here to compile. Why don't you let me take the notebook home with me tonight and I can go through compiling what I can find, and you can work on the other batch?"

"That would be great, if you don't mind doing it. A fresh set of eyes on this might notice something else that I'm missing."

"I don't mind at all."

Jim handed the notebook to Sharon, "Are you sure I can't give you a ride home?"

"You're very sweet. But no. You have a lot of work to do, and I like walking. It's how I get most of my exercise."

"Okay, if you're sure. Make sure you call me when you get home, so I know you got home safe."

With one last kiss Sharon left and Jim stood watching her walk away until she was out of sight before closing the door and returning to his work,

#

That night what sleep Jim was able to get was interrupted by one nightmare after another with the main topics being his father's death and Oakwood. In the morning he awoke groggy and irritated, which made him decide not to wait until the following weekend to talk to his mother about his father's death. He remembered how agitated and aloof she had become the other day on their phone call which only deepened his desire to have this discussion with her as soon as possible. His mind was bouncing from one thought to another while he packed up his stuff to make the trip home to see his mother.

It was still early morning when Jim was ready to walk out the door making him decide to wait to call Sharon until he reached his mother's house. Grabbing his backpack, he left making sure he had locked his door, and was surprised to see Sharon walking up the street in front of him. "Sharon!" Jim called out to her as he waved his hand in the air trying to catch her attention.

Sharon looked up and smiled, "I was just coming to see you. I was hoping it wouldn't be too early." Noticing his backpack she asked, "Are you going out of town?"

"I was going to call you when I got to my mom's. I decided not to wait to talk to her. And it's never too early for you to come by. What's up?"

"I stumbled upon something while looking through your notes last night."

"What's that?"

"You know that year when the accidental death was in September? Not August?"

"Yeah...What about it?"

"Well...it wasn't an accidental death. But there was still a death recorded on that suspicious date in August that year."

"Really? Someone else died that year on August 12th? So then, that makes every year that we have records for had a death on August 12th in this small town and only one was not an accident." Jim's face showed deep concentration while he pieced together his thoughts.

"Yep. That's what it looks like to me."

"There's no way this is a coincidence. Something had to have happened that year that disrupted whatever is going on in that town." Suddenly his expression turned to concerned epiphany, "Amy Wilson, might be right about her father's death not being an accident."

Sharon's face became somber, "Jim...if that's the case...wouldn't it mean..."

Hearing Sharon's voice trail off, "Mean what? What are you thinking?"

"Wouldn't it mean...that your dad's death wasn't an accident either? His accident was on August 12th according to the records you found."

This thought hit Jim straight in the heart. He didn't want to believe that it could be possible that his father had been murdered. However, now it was difficult for him to think it was anything else. "I need to go see my mom. I've got to get some answers out of her, whatever it takes. She's going to have to talk to me about Dad's so-called accident now."

"Just remember, she's your mom, Jim. Not some suspect under interrogation. Be gentle on her."

"I'll be as gentle as I can be. But she's not going to get out of talking to me about this, this time." Jim gave Sharon a quick kiss before mounting his motorcycle and speeding off towards Mableton.

15

The Big Confrontation

Jim could see his mother kneeling in the front yard tending to her flower beds when he came around the corner on the way to her house. He knew that once the surprise of seeing him wore off she would be upset at him for not wearing his helmet, and at this moment he didn't care. The ride up to see her hadn't calmed him down like he hoped it would. It had only given him time to think about all the times he asked his mother to tell him about what happened to his father, and she would evade him in one way or another. This time was going to be different.

Tess stood up excitedly with the surprise of seeing Jim approach. He wasn't due home for another couple of weeks and he hadn't called her like he normally would, to let her know he was coming.

She walked over to him as he parked his motorcycle in the driveway. "To what do I owe this pleasant surprise? You didn't call."

"I need to talk to you about Dad's accident, mom, and it couldn't wait."

Tess could hear the urgency in her son's voice, "What's going on? And why aren't you wearing your helmet?"

"Because it's hot, I was in a hurry, and I simply didn't feel like it. OK!"

Tess was taken aback by the rebellious tone targeting her. It was a tone that she rarely heard from her son since sending him to therapy years ago. "Excuse me? Have you forgotten who you are talking to?"

"No, Mom. I haven't."

"Then what's with the disrespectful tone coming out of you?"

"I need to talk to you about Dad's accident. It's important, and I don't want you trying to detour away from the topic like you always do. I need to know what happened and why Dad was in Oakwood."

Hearing Jim say those words made Tess tremble with emotions, prompting Jim to take her by the arm and lead her to the front steps where they could sit down. "I'm not trying to be disrespectful, mom. I just need to know the facts. What happened? Why was Dad there? I know it hurts you to think about it, but I've gotta know."

"Why? Why can't you just remember your father the way you do and forget about this painful memory?"

"Because his death has come up in my research for my article. Please, Mom. Just tell me what you know and remember. It really is important."

"All I know is that he was in Oakwood investigating several accident claims that were filed with his company and he thought looked suspicious. He left that morning going to be home that evening and never made it back."

"What happened? A drunk driver, right?"

"No the police report said that he came around a blind curve going too fast and drove over the edge crashing into a bunch of trees. They suspected that the angle of the sun may have blinded him as he came around the curve and he couldn't tell where the side of the road was." Tess began crying, "Why do you need these details?"

"I just do, Mom. Go on. What happened to his car, and the files I'm assuming he had with him?"

"I don't know. I never saw any files. His car was totaled so they took it to the local junk yard. I didn't want to see it or deal with it. It was simply too painful for me. And I had you to think about."

"And Dad died on August 12, 1966, correct?"

"Yes. It was one of the worst days of my life. So, can we stop talking about it now? Please?" Her plea broke Jim's heart. He knew how difficult this conversation was on his mother and couldn't put her through any more of his interrogation.

"I'm sorry, Mom. I didn't mean to be so abrasive with you. You just won't ever talk to me about it, and I needed to know. Thank you for telling me."

"Why did you need to know so badly?"

"I can't tell you just yet. It's better if I wait until I have all my facts together before I tell you. Plus, you're safer not knowing what I know." His last comment scared Tess. "Come on, Mom. Let's go inside and make some tea and you can catch me up on what's happening with the garden club." Ready to be done with the topic, Tess nodded and went into the house with her son to have a cold glass of sweet tea and chat about something more pleasant.

The rest of the weekend went by peacefully between Jim and his mother, they caught up on neighborhood gossip, watched their favorite TV shows, and played a few games of Scrabble together before Jim needed to leave to head back to his apartment on Sunday. Jim hoped that the pleasantness of the weekend helped wipe out the painful conversation that started their visit. Although, he knew nothing could completely wipe out the pain he had created for his mother.

16

Back to Oakwood

As Jim packed up his blank notebooks and satchel, he thought about the week and how quickly it had passed. He and Sharon had been spending every spare moment together, which made time soar by. He knew how nervous she was about his taking this trip even if it were only for one day and promised he would call her before he left as well as when he returned. The last thing he wanted was to unnecessarily worry her or his mother. Walking over to the phone he thought to himself, now he had two beautiful women in his life, and he wanted to do everything he could to keep them happy.

"Hey, Mom! How are you doing?" Jim said hearing his mother answer the phone.

"I'm good and even better now that I get to hear your handsome voice, little one," his mother replied in her normal way.

"I just wanted to call you and let you know that I am heading to Oakwood to pick up those documents that I requested. I should be back by five or so and I will give you a call as soon as I get back," Jim speed-talked nervously to his mother. He knew that she was not be happy about him returning to Oakwood after their last conversation.

"Did you say Oakwood?"

"Yes, Mom. Oakwood. You knew I would need to go back." Jim answered in a serious tone.

"I really wish you would not go to that place. It scares me to think of you there."

"Mom, I'll be fine. I'll come home this weekend so you can see that I'm okay. We'll talk all about this and I'll tell you what I have found out once I have all the details sorted out. Okay? I'll even bring Sharon with me so you can meet her." Jim knew that the prospect of meeting his new girl would help calm his mother and give her something new to focus on.

"Okay. But you be safe. Just because you know how to play me doesn't mean I won't be worrying. What does your girl like to eat, so I can prepare meals she likes?" If nothing else, his mother was the perfect hostess.

"I don't know, Mom. I'll give you her number and you can call her to find out. Just, first, let me call her and ask her to come with me."

"Okay. Get off the phone and call her," his mother commanded.

Jim gave his mother Sharon's phone number before saying his good-byes and hanging up the phone. He looked at the clock and realized he had only a few minutes to reach Sharon before she darted off to work. This made him grab the phone's receiver and quickly dial her number. "Hello," was the soft lilting voice that Jim had come to adore.

"Hello, sexy," Jim responded. "How did you sleep?"

"I had a restless night thinking about you visiting that place today," Sharon didn't hold back her thoughts and opinions, which was one of the things that attracted Jim so strongly to her.

"I'm sorry. I don't want to be the cause of you having sleepless nights," he responded. "I promise to make it up to you."

"I'm going to make you keep that promise," she replied.

"How about I start now, by asking you to come to my mom's with me this weekend?" he said in a teasing manner.

"Really?!? That would be a start," Sharon answered with a giggle.

"Yes, I have already told her I would bring you and she is all a twitter preparing for your visit. So, don't be surprised if you get a call from her asking what you like to eat," Jim said laughing as the words exited his lips. "Oh, and she is freaking out about my going to Oakwood. So, please don't bring that up with her."

Sharon was still stuck on the first part of what he was saying to her to fully comprehend what else he was saying. "Okay. I'll expect her call..."

And before she could say anything else, Jim said, "Gotta go...Talk to you this evening. I should be back by five." Then hung up.

"Wait! What did you say..." Sharon tried to confirm what he had said about Oakwood, but before she could he had hung up.

Jim knew he would pay later for cutting the call short like that, but he didn't want to worry Sharon any more than she already seemed to be, and he knew she needed to get to work, which both made for good excuses when the time of reckoning arrived.

###

The sun set high in the sky creating gaps of blinding light between the forest shade at each bend in the road as Jim sped down the highway toward Oakwood. Being intermittently blinded by the sun at each bend of the road reminded him of what his mother had said about the police report on his father's death. Seeing how the sun affected visibility in the mid-morning made the findings believable if the same effect happened going the opposite direction in the evening. However, Jim's gut instincts were that this was simply too convenient of a coincidence.

He figured if he arrived by 11:00, he could fit in a visit to the local police station for a copy of his father's death report after going to the hall of records and collecting his documents and still be back on the road no later than 3:00 so that he could keep his promise to his two favorite ladies and be home by five. He knew that as the son of the decedent, he had the right to see the records without a court order and he wanted to have all the information regarding his father's death that he could dig up before he spoke to his mother.

Driving into Oakwood's town square, he couldn't help but notice a bright candy apple red Mustang that sat outside of the public library. It reminded him a lot of his father's car and sitting on his dad's lap as he let him pretend to drive it. Because he was so young when his father died, he didn't have very many firsthand memories, but his dad's car was one that he remembered vividly. He considered it a sign that he was on the right track to finding the details that he was looking for. His mother had taught him from a very young age to believe in signs from the universe because all signs stemmed from a greater power that mankind still struggled to understand. He admired his mother's spiritual guidance and teachings. They had served him well during the most difficult of times in his life so far. Her beliefs bordered on religion and leaned on more natural spiritualism, which made for a very balanced belief system in a highly religious region of the country.

It was 11:00 on the dot when Jim pulled into town. So far, so good. He seemed to be keeping to schedule. Jim parked his motorbike in a spot just outside of the police station and walked to the town hall.

What he didn't notice was the sheriff sitting in his vehicle just across the town square watching his every move.

The professionally stiff woman from his last visit met Jim at the counter as if she had never seen him before, "Hello, how can I help you?" She spoke in a monotone emotionless manner, that reminded Jim of the movie *Stepford Wives*.

"Hello, my name is Jim Norton. I received a call from Bruce Farnsbee that my copies were ready, and I could pick them up any time after 11:00 today," Jim cordially explained to the still stiff woman in front of him.

"Yes. One moment please while I locate them," she replied and walked away.

Jim stood looking around the grey-walled room. Compared to everything else he had seen in this small town the hall of records was a modern government office, with no hardwood of any kind, and with drop tile ceilings and fluorescent lighting. No wonder the woman who ran the front desk seemed so stiff. While he pondered about his surroundings, the woman returned with a stack of files, each labeled with a year, all stacked neatly in a file box. "Here you are, Mr. Norton. Will there be anything else?" The woman said handing him the rather heavy box.

"No, thank you. This is perfect," Jim responded politely and lifted the box from the tall counter in front of him, smiled with a nod, and walked away. He hadn't counted on the files being in a large box that he would have to attach to the back of his bike. So, he walked to the hardware store to purchase some rope or bungee cords so that he could strap the box down on the back of his seat for the drive home before he headed to the police station.

He was still focused on his task at hand and hadn't noticed the man in the sheriff's car now parked around the corner watching his every move. If he had, he might have felt the little hairs on the back of his neck start to prickle.

His impromptu stop at the hardware store didn't take very long, since he was the only customer in the little shop. It was a small mom-and-pop shop that carried small quantities of everything you might need for home repairs. Something that you might see in a late 1940s or early 1950s town square before large box stores started taking over, putting all the small shops out of business.

Jim walked over to his motorbike and tied down the file box, before suddenly feeling as though he was being watched. He gradually scanned his surroundings trying not to be too obvious about what he was looking for and noticed the sheriff's car around the corner. He couldn't see if anyone was in it, but knew he would have to pass it on his way out of town. It seemed odd to see a sheriff's car when the town had a police station just yards away. But Jim knew that the county and city districts often overlapped out here to help cover the large territories with small police forces. He guessed the officer driving the vehicle might simply be in town dealing with business or having lunch at the diner.

Shaking off the strange feeling, Jim walked into the police station and approached the officer at the reception desk. This facility was exactly as he expected it would be, a small- counter at the front to greet people, a corridor on each side leading to offices and holding cells of some sort, and a few chairs in the small waiting area just in front of the reception desk. Instead of the dismal grey walls in the town records office, the walls here were stark white. With placards and informational posters on them.

The officer was busy with paperwork in front of him and paid no attention to Jim as he approached. "Hello, officer," Jim said walking up to the reception desk.

The officer behind the desk looked up and said, "Hello. How can I help you?" in a pleasant, but formal tone.

Jim cleared his throat before answering, "I'm trying to get the police reports for my father's car accident. He was killed in 1966, within the town limits of Oakwood. That's all I know."

"Son, why are you wanting those?" the officer asked.

"I'm researching my father's death for a book I'm writing about his life," Jim replied, thinking quickly on his feet. He hadn't anticipated being asked why he wanted them. Although reflecting back on it, he didn't understand why he wouldn't have since everyone had asked that question for every document he requested in this town. His name was George Norton."

The officer looked at Jim with a look of sincere condolences, just as most people did when they heard about his father's death even after so many years. "I'm sorry son, but those records are in archives, and it will take a while to locate documents that old. You'll have to fill out this paperwork and we'll call you when we have them ready for you to review." The officer handed Jim a three-page form to fill out asking for a lot of information that Jim didn't have.

Jim flipped through the form and told the officer, "I only have minimal information regarding my father's death. I was only five at the time and Mom doesn't talk about it."

"Just fill out what you know, and we'll do the best we can to provide you with the rest," the officer's expression exhibited an apologetic condolence this time. Jim felt like this man genuinely felt for his circumstances and desire to know but couldn't help him. Jim nodded and taking one of the pens from the pencil can, he walked over to the row of chairs, sat down, and began to fill out the form.

His thoughts kept interrupting the process of completing the form, wandering to thinking about how he wouldn't have as much information as he had wanted to have before speaking with his mother again regarding what he thought had really happened to his father. This made the process of completing what he knew take longer than it should have.

###

The sheriff started to become antsy and impatient with how long it was taking this young man to finish his business in the police station. He hadn't anticipated Jim's stop there and it worried Sheriff Manning. After about ten minutes of waiting, he decided to make a stop at the station and nonchalantly see what was happening. He drove over and parked in one of the reserved for official vehicles only spots in front of the station and wandered in.

"Hey, Cameron. How's it going?" the sheriff asked the officer behind the desk as he entered, surveying the office.

"Oh hey, Trevor. It's going well. Just a lot of paperwork to fill out, from the local teens' shenanigans last night at the high school bonfire. What has you coming into town?"

"I was in the area and thought I would swing by and see how everything was going and if you needed me for anything," Sheriff Manning wasn't the ad libber that Jim was. But it seemed to be an acceptable excuse.

"No...Everything here's good. But thanks for checking in with us. Much appreciated," the officer answered cordially.

"Alright. I'll get back out on my route then. You take care and say hello to Claira for me, will ya?" the Sheriff said, as he leaned on the counter and watched Jim filling out forms.

"Will do. Stay safe out there," Cameron replied. Jim had just completed the form as Sheriff Manning exited the building and took them over to the officer behind the desk, who he now knew was named Cameron.

The officer politely took the forms from Jim and stamped them with a time and date before sticking them in a pile of paperwork in a stacking file. "These will be passed on to archives and they will get back to you as soon as they have the information for you. It could take a while, though, we are short-handed at the moment. So, be patient." The officer handed Jim a business card with his name, badge number, and contact information on it, before continuing, "Here's my information if you need anything else, or want to follow up in a week or two."

Jim nodded before saying, "Thank you." He placed the business card in the back pocket of his jeans. When Jim reached the glass door of the station, he noticed the Sheriff's car was gone, but the red Mustang was still sitting across the way and decided to see if he could find out who owned it. This made him spin around and asked the officer, "Sir, do you know who owns that gorgeous Mustang across the way?"

Officer Winslow looked up to see the smiling face of a car enthusiast and replied, "Isn't' that thing cherry? That's Bruce Farnbee's car. He does car restoration as a hobby. That little lady is his pride and joy. You should have seen her when he found her at the local junkyard, having been in a wreck, all rusty, and needing a lot of TLC." Cameron shared, as a fellow car enthusiast.

"Wow, that had to take a lot of work. It looks like the car my father had. Maybe I can convince him to let me take some photos for my book."

"I'm sure that wouldn't be a problem. Bruce is very proud of that car. He even managed to find the same color paint as its original paint job." Officer Winslow replied.

"Well, thank you. Have a good afternoon," Jim said abruptly, exiting the police station. Getting onto his motorcycle Jim couldn't help feeling convinced that the Candy Apple Red Mustang that sat in front of him must have been his father's. There's no way that a town this size would have two identical mustangs in the junk yard from severe car accidents.

His latest revelation prompted Jim to get off his motorbike and stroll over to the nearby car for a closer look. He took his pen and pad with him, then quickly scribbled down the VIN number from the tag on the driver's side dashboard, thinking this would provide him with the information he needed once he received his father's accident report to confirm his suspicions of this being his father's car.

Quickly looking around to verify if he was being watched or not, Jim hurriedly walked back over to where his motorcycle was parked and climbed on. Not seeing the sheriff's patrol car sitting in the town square anywhere, Jim was convinced the sheriff had left town, and that he was simply being overly suspicious. Of course, it was normal for him to be suspicious with all the information that he had recently acquired about this town.

It was nearly three o'clock when Jim finally started for home. He knew he would be pushing it a bit on time but should arrive before Sharon and his mother began to worry too much. He figured he could drive a bit faster than he did on the way to Oakwood so that he would be able to make his calls by five like he had promised. He instinctively took extra care to fasten his helmet tightly, verified his package was stable and secure, then proceeded to leave town. The sun had shifted in the sky to the other side of the road, creating the same conditions for his drive home as he had on the drive there. This made visibility in some places sketchy, confirming his thought that the police report his mother remembered was plausible depending on when his father had left for home.

Sheriff Manning sat tucked behind two oak trees just outside of town in an area shaded by a small grove waiting for Jim to pass. As soon as he knew Jim was safely ahead of him, he switched the channel on his police radio to the rarely used channel that the mayor and he agreed on and radioed Mayor Winters that Jim was on route home. "The chicken has left the roost," Trevor said into the microphone.

"Roger that," Mayor Winters responded. Then, he nodded to Denis and Owen who had been waiting impatiently in the mayor's office under the guise of a planning meeting, and the three left together in Owen's car. It was a non-descript sedan that could easily blend in with other traffic.

The three gentlemen took backroads to the predetermined sight of entanglement to spring the trap that they had planned for the young man who had the potential of destroying their town and its future. The fact that he would also be this year's sacrificial lamb was all that made the current circumstances and events bearable to these otherwise peaceful, law-abiding citizens.

They radioed the sheriff to let him know that they were in place. Since they knew that Jim rode a motorcycle, it was no giant leap to have his death be a motorcycle accident. With nearly four-thousand fatalities due to accidents involving motorcycles so far this year, it wouldn't be difficult to hide this sad occurrence in the statistics.

To avoid any collateral damage to other drivers, the three men took up positions at separate points on the highway and waited for Jim to pass the first checkpoint which was a ten-minute drive from where the collision point was set to happen. The plan was for the circle of seven agent at checkpoint one to close the road and notify the other men after Jim passed to avoid anyone else driving that way. This not only prevented them from being involved in the collision but also minimized the possibility of witnesses. Denis was assigned this task and was dropped off while the other two men drove on to their destination point.

Ed and Owen sat in Owen's car anxiously waiting for Denis's signal. "I hope this goes well," Owen nervously chattered. "I hope it's instant and the boy doesn't suffer too much." Mayor Winters was not receptive to Owen's comments.

"Owen, thinking like that isn't changing or helping the situation. Now be quiet so I can hear the radio," Ed said before clenching his jaw, creating a steely expression. Owen saw the look of annoyance and took the warning as it was intended, becoming quiet and motionless.

Suddenly a voice on the radio said, "The snare is set. It's all up to you two now." It was Denis indicating that Jim had passed the checkpoint and he had put up the blockade. Upon hearing the signal, Ed and Owen quickly exited the car that they had been waiting in and took two large gas cans from the trunk then proceeded to spread the contents across the road in a well-shaded location. The plan was for Jim to skid off the road after hitting a large oil spill in an area with an obstructed view and hazardous roadside. The area they chose was known by locals as a particularly treacherous stretch of road where travelers frequently went off the road or collided with other vehicles.

Once the two assassins were confident that the road would be too hazardous for a motorbike to maintain its course, they got back into their vehicle and drove further down the road to wait for the sacrificial lamb to appear and play his role in their conspiracy.

Sheriff Manning pulled up next to Denis shortly after the signal was sent and waited with him for dispatch to contact him that there had been a motor vehicle accident reported. "Hey, Denis. Everything in place?"

Denis climbed into the passenger side of the patrol car and sat there for a few seconds before responding, "Yeah. I notified the guys a couple of minutes ago, and I didn't see anyone pass before our friend went by. Thankfully it's a slow time of day traffic-wise."

Sheriff Manning looked at Denis with a smirk as he responded, "Yeah, that and the fact that I set up a detour ten miles the other side of Oakwood that bypasses this area."

Denis looked over at Trevor, "When was that part of the plan put in place? I didn't know anything about that." He wasn't too keen on being left out of details, especially for something so serious in nature.

"It was a last-minute decision on my part. Is there a problem?" Sheriff Manning said indignantly. He wasn't used to having his authority as sheriff questioned.

"I just don't like being left out of the loop. That's all," Denis could see the irritation on Trevor's face and wanted to defuse the situation.

"Well, sometimes things happen quickly, and you just have to roll with them," Trevor said cockily.

As the two men flexed their authoritative muscles, the call came in. "Here he comes," the men on the other end of the radio announced from their hidden perch.

Jim's mind wandered as he sped down the highway enjoying the unusual lack of traffic. It was rare that he could drive this highway without dealing with semi-trucks and interstate traffic of all types. Not thinking about why there was no traffic, he naturally took advantage of the open road to drive faster than he normally had the opportunity to.

While his mind drifted between thoughts, his motorcycle abruptly started to skid in all directions, snapping Jim's focus back to the road and the fact that he was about to crash. Instinctively his motorcycle safety classes that his mother had demanded he take when he bought the bike kicked in, and he started steering into the skid to control his impact. He thought to himself, 'this is going to hurt,' as he laid his bike down sideways and continued to slide along the blacktop with his leg pinned beneath the motorcycle heading towards an embankment.

In a last-ditch effort not to go over, Jim grabbed for any nearby low-lying tree branches that he might reach as he got nearer and nearer to the edge of the embankment. He was able to grab ahold of a mass of tangled baby branches just as his bike reached the edge, and using his other foot kicked the motorcycle, freeing himself and avoiding the fall. The speed of the impact when he laid the motorcycle down had caused him to whack the side of his head against the pavement hard enough to leave the helmet with a minor crack. The force of hitting his head made him dizzy and slightly disoriented.

Once he came to a complete stop, he pulled himself away from the edge of the steep embankment cautiously looked down and he struggled with detangling himself from the limbs that had saved him from following his bike over the edge. It was a much farther drop than he anticipated. His prized motorbike lay mangled at the bottom of the gully that at some point had contained a substantial amount of water.

He took his helmet off and was just starting to evaluate his injuries and situation when he heard the voices of two men coming toward him. But before he could call out for help, he was taken aback by what he heard them saying and quickly silenced himself, taking cover.

"Did you see him go over? Hopefully, the crash did the deed for us, and we won't have to finish him off," the mayor was saying to Owen as they came closer.

"That would be the best situation for sure," Owen agreed, still apprehensive about the whole thing and attempting to stay collected.

Jim couldn't believe what he was hearing. He heard a familiar voice come over the radio, "Mayor, is the deed complete? Can we reopen the road?" It surprised him to hear that one of the two men trying to kill him was the mayor of Oakwood.

Ed quickly responded to the inquiries coming over the radio, "The deed's done, but the body's missing. Open the road and come help us look for it. It looks like he went over the edge into the ravine somewhere and we could use some more eyes to locate him." With that, Jim knew he was in deep trouble and had better stay hidden until the coast was clear.

About ten minutes after the exchange on the radio, Jim could hear a car quickly approaching. It parked nearby and two more men started walking toward those who were already looking for him. He was shocked to see that the man on the other end of the radio helping the two men trying to kill him was the sheriff that he had just seen checking in at the Oakwood police station.

His mind swooned partially from his head's contact with the pavement, and with what was happening. He realized that these men were not there to help him, but instead to kill him. This new information caused Jim to quietly slide further back into the undergrowth for additional cover to hide from his four would-be assassins. He lay there for what seemed like hours doing his best to make no noise as his injuries became more and more painful, while these four men searched relentlessly for him.

When another car was heard coming down the highway, Sheriff Manning looked at his fellow assassins and declared, "This is taking too long and now we have traffic approaching. I'm going to have to call this in as a suspicious incident report to explain why I am already here without receiving a dispatch. You three get out of here before someone sees you, and I will handle this." The other three men nodded in agreement and hurriedly got back into Owen's car and drove off in the direction of Oakwood. Jim was relieved that three of the men were gone, but slightly less so when he realized that the man who was still searching for him carried both a badge and a gun.

Several more vehicles passed while Jim lay in the undergrowth bleeding and doing his best to keep from passing out. The last thing he wanted was to pass out and be found by this man. Plus, he had no idea how many others were involved in this conspiracy. He didn't know what exactly he was so close to uncovering, but he was convinced more than ever that there was a cover-up happening in Oakwood and that it had been going on for forty years.

The sun was starting to set when the Oakwood police car arrived on the scene to help process the incident. Jim could feel himself slipping into shock and starting to shiver. "Hey, Sheriff. What do we have here?" It was Cameron, the officer who had been managing the reception desk, arriving to help with the search.

"Hey, Cameron. Sorry to get you out of the office. I came across those skid marks over there on my way out of town that weren't there when I drove in and decided to investigate when I found this," he explained as he pointed to the twisted motorcycle in the gully.

"No problem. I was just getting ready to go out on patrol when the call came in from dispatch saying we had a suspicious incidence within city limits anyway," Cameron replied. "Have you found the driver?"

"Not so far. If he's not down there in the bramble he might have been picked up by a passer-by," the Sheriff said shifting the direction of the search. "I have this here if you want to check the area hospitals for any accident victims recently brought in." Trevor wanted to get Cameron away from the site so he could do a more thorough search for the missing sacrificial lamb. Jim listened intently to attempt to figure out if Cameron was in on the conspiracy or not.

"Since it's within our jurisdiction I better be the one to stay here and continue the search while I wait for our impound tow truck to arrive and get that motorcycle out of there," Cameron disagreed. "You go ahead and see what you can find out with the local hospitals and clinics and radio me if you find out anything, will ya?"

Trevor was not happy with this turn of events. However, he knew if he put up too much of a fight about it, Cameron would become suspicious himself and that was the last thing he needed. "Alright. If you've got this, I'll get going and see what I can find," relenting as he began walking back to his patrol car, before climbing in and driving away.

The sheriff was barely out of sight before the tow truck arrived. Cameron walked over to meet the driver and the two men had a brief conversation that was inaudible to Jim. Jim looked at his watch noticing that it was now dusk. It was six-thirty. He was an hour and a half late calling his mother and Sharon. He knew the two would be worried silly, and for the first time was counting on it to get him out of this sticky situation.

Jim watched as the tow truck driver repelled down the side of the ravine and attached cables to his beloved motorcycle. "Do you see any signs of anyone down there, Gus?" Cameron called down.

"Nothing around here. But it's going to be getting too dark to see much further around here pretty soon with all of this scrub brush around here," Gus continued, "I don't see any tracks or trails where someone might have been dragged down alongside this thing though."

"Alright then. Come on up, and we'll wrap it up for tonight. We can come back in the morning when we can see better and do another search just to be sure," Cameron said.

Once the wreckage had been secured to the flatbed and both the tow truck and the police car drove away, Jim freed himself from the weeds and branches that he had submerged himself into for camouflage. Inching his way towards the road, Jim thought to himself, about how his father had died in a car accident, and now Jim knew firsthand the emotions, pain, and confusion that his father must have felt in those final moments.

His mind had raced through thoughts of how his mother would be destroyed if he were to die, especially in this manner, careening towards the ravine pinned beneath his motorcycle. He realized his father must have thought about him and his mother in those final moments, realizing he would never be able to grow old with the love of his life and their only son. Suddenly the idea of wearing his helmet on a hot summer day didn't seem like such a big deal anymore and he saw what an immature brat he had been with his silently rebelling against his mother's concerns over his safety.

He still wasn't sure what Cameron's role in this whole thing was, but he knew he couldn't stay there much longer without being discovered. It would be vital to his survival that he get help before sunrise when Officer Winslow and possibly the sheriff would be back to search for him.

After dragging himself to the wood's edge, he took up a position close enough to the road to see if someone was coming; yet close enough to cover in case he needed to hide again and leaned himself up against the trunk of an old birch tree. He reached into his pants pocket and pulled out his wallet. Flipping it open, he removed a laminated card and sat looking at it for a long time.

The one thing that he had of his father's that he could always carry with him was his father's old driver's license. Jim had found it in an old box in the garage where his mother had stored his father's belongings after he died. He remembered being about seven or eight and finding it while looking for his football. It was tattered from being put through the washer and dryer so many times over the years, but still comforting to have with him in times of difficulty.

Gazing at the face on the worn-out piece of government parchment, Jim felt a warm presence beside him and looked up to see the face staring down at him. "It's you? But how? You're dead."

"I'm here because you need me, son; that's all I can tell you right now." The translucent face smiled making his aura shine brightly around them.

"Dad? Dad, am I dead?"

"No, son. You're not dead. Yet..." The figure's voice intentionally left his last word hanging on air.

"I'm so tired, Dad...I don't know how much longer I can hold on." Jim's voice was weak as he pleaded to the being that he could only believe was a hallucination.

"You're stronger than you think, Jim. You can do this. The lives of too many depend on you finishing what you started." This time the figure's demeanor became stern and commanding when it spoke.

Feeling a jolt of second wind, Jim's determination began to return, "I don't understand. Whose lives? Help me, Dad."

"You have to do this on your own, son. This is your mission, your destiny. You must be the one who sets the outcome." The image touched Jim's hand that held the driver's license, "I am always with you, Jim. I have faith that you can do this, and then everything will be explained." Then as suddenly as the image appeared it was gone snapping Jim's consciousness to his immediate circumstances.

It was now dark enough that he had the advantage of seeing anyone who approached before they could see him, which allowed him to relax slightly. Before he knew it, he drifted off to sleep waiting for what was going to happen next.

Sharon walked in her front door at five-thirty to find her phone ringing and thirteen messages on her answering machine. Considering she didn't typically receive thirteen messages in a week, this triggered her concern. She just missed getting to the phone on time before the call disconnected, and immediately checked her machine.

Beep... "Sharon, you don't know me. But this is Jim's mom, Tess. He gave me your number so that I could coordinate with you for this weekend's visit. If you would give me a call, we could chat a bit and you can tell me what you like to eat. That way I can do some shopping before you arrive."

The machine cut off right as Tess finished her sentence. Sharon figured the next message would be Tess calling back to complete her previous message. She was half right. *Beep...* "Hi, Sharon, this is Tess again. I don't mean to be a worrywart. But it's five-fifteen and Jim still hasn't called to let me know he's home safe yet. That's just not like him, especially since he knows how worried I was about his going to Oakwood today. If you would call me and let me know if you have heard from him and he's alright, I would be forever grateful." She gave the phone number, then, the message disconnected. The next eleven messages were pretty much the same content, however, with increasing levels of worry and concern.

Sharon was just about to pick up the phone to call Tess back after hearing the last message when the phone began to ring again. "Hello?" Sharon answered, substantially worried herself by now.

"Sharon? This is Tess. I'm so sorry to be such a pain. I'm simply beside myself about not hearing from Jim though. He knew how worried I was when I found out where he was going and would never let me stress this way. He would have stopped to call me from someplace by now if he knew he was going to miss our check-in call," Tess rattled on before Sharon could respond, "Have you heard from him?"

"No, Tess, I haven't heard from him. And I completely understand your concern. I just got your messages and was calling you. I was expecting Jim to call me after he called you, so about now, I guess," Sharon mirrored Tess's worry. "Are you sure he's just not running a little late and unable to get to a phone to call? After all, he's only thirty minutes late calling."

"I don't know if he told you, Sharon. But Oakwood is where his father was killed in a car accident when he was a boy. And the thought of him being in that place completely set me off this morning when he mentioned the name of the town. So, he knows I would be going crazy by now and he would do everything he could to let me know he was running late if he could," Tess explained. Her mother's instincts were in hyperdrive now and she knew her son needed her more than ever. "We've just always had this understanding that we let each other know where we are if we're going out of town, and if we'll be late for any reason. It's a safety precaution thing."

Sharon realized that Tess was seriously worried and with good cause to be. "Okay. How about this, you're closer to Oakwood than I am. If I leave right now, I can head your way and pick you up and we can go to Oakwood together if you haven't heard from Jim by the time I get there? I can check my machine remotely when I get there to confirm he hasn't tried to call me. Will that help?" Sharon was trying to downplay her own concerns while easing Tess's. She knew Jim would want her to do whatever she could to calm his mother from worrying, and that he absolutely would not want Tess driving in the emotional state that she was currently in. She also knew it was better not to tell Tess what she knew about Jim's research and what he had uncovered.

"Yes! That would be great," Tess exclaimed, not meaning to yell.

"Okay then, I am leaving right now and with traffic, I should be there in a couple of hours. Stay calm and stay off the phone so Jim can get through if he tries to reach you. Okay?"

Tess gave Sharon her address and the two hung up.

Sharon only took time enough to change out of her skirt and dress shoes before grabbing her purse and keys and rushing out the door to get to Tess's. If Jim was in trouble, she wanted to be dressed appropriately to be able to help him in whatever way he needed, not be the girl who shows up to help and ends up needing help herself. That wasn't who she was. Sharon's lead foot took over as soon as she was on the highway with her only concern being getting to Tess's as hastily as possible, and ultimately to Jim if he needed her.

17
The Reckoning

Mayor Ed Winters contacted Kevin and Steve as soon as he got back to his office, relaying the same message to each, "We have an issue. The young man's body's missing," Ed said urgently. "The motorcycle went into the ravine, but the body is nowhere to be seen."

Each of the men's responses was the same, "Okay Mayor, what am I to do now?" This prompted the mayor to meet them at the council room to discuss what they should do as soon as they had an update from Sheriff Manning. Owen and Denis were already waiting in the elegant room where government and secret society business regularly took place. But they were not sitting at the table patiently chitchatting this time. Instead, they were taking turns pacing from one end of the room to the other, silently lamenting to themselves about the situation that they had gotten themselves into.

When Steve and Kevin arrived, they could see the strain on the other two men's faces indicating that the situation was indeed dire. "What happened?" Steve asked without pointing the question to anyone in particular.

"Everything went as planned up until we went to check the body to ensure he was dead. Then, when we reached the landing site where the motorcycle was, the young man was nowhere to be seen. The bike was in a ravine where climbing gear was needed to reach it..." Owen's voice trailed off as Denis took over explaining.

"When they couldn't locate him, Ed told Trevor and me to open the road and come help with the search. After about an hour of looking, Trevor took over, telling the rest of us to head back to town, because traffic was coming, and he would handle it..." Denis paused, and Owen jumped back in.

"And now here we sit waiting for an update while the mayor tries to get more information over at his office until the sheriff returns." When Owen finished speaking, the four men simply stood staring at one another lost as to what to do next.

The four men were still standing speechless when the mayor came into the room. "Has anyone heard from Trevor? We need to know what he found so we know how to proceed," Mayor Winters asked.

"Nothing so far..." the men all chimed in at once, before walking over to the table like lemmings and taking their seats, their actions more out of habit than desire.

Ed followed suit before checking his watch for about the tenth time in the past ten minutes. "What could be taking them so long? I expected to hear from Trevor over an hour ago. Has anyone seen Cameron return to town yet?"

They all looked out the window across the room from them, noticing that his patrol car was not in its normal spot. "No. I just thought he was out doing his regular patrol," Owen responded. The rest of the men simply shook their heads.

Bruce couldn't help but notice that the room was about as tense as it could get when he arrived at 8:00. "Sorry I took so long. It was unavoidable." That was all he said, as he guessed that they didn't care about his personal reasons for being delayed, or that his car had had a flat and it took him twenty minutes to remove the lug nuts that were on too tight. He rightly assumed that all this group cared about at this moment was that he was there and that they would hear from Trevor soon with good news. "So, what's going on? Why are we all here? And is there an update?"

Ed took the floor and answered Bruce's questions in order, "What's going on is...the boy's body is missing. We're all here because we need to figure out what to do. And NO! There is no update." Mayor Winters was beginning to lose his cool. It was out of the ordinary for him to raise his voice, especially when acting as mayor. "I'm sorry, Bruce. I didn't mean to raise my voice at you. I'm just..." His voice trailed off at a loss for how to end his sentence.

Bruce nodded in response, "I understand. Is there a contingency plan in case things haven't gone as planned?" Every eye in the room was suddenly staring holes through him as if he had just insulted each of them. "I take it from the looks that I am receiving, that is a no," he replied before shutting up and sitting down.

With every passing moment, the deadline came closer creating a deeper sense of panic in each of these normally controlled men. It was 10:00 when Sheriff Manning finally arrived. You could cut the tension with a knife when he entered the room. Looking around the table he could see the anxious anticipation on each of his fellow council members' faces. Each man was barely breathing and staring intently at him, but he did not speak.

"Well, Trevor, what is the update? What took you so long? Don't keep us waiting. Tell us," Ed was completely out of patience by this time and demanded answers.

229

Sheriff Manning took a glance at his watch seeing that time was passing quickly, then spoke in response, "I don't know," was all that he could muster at that moment.

"You don't know what?" Denis asked.

"I don't know if the young man is dead or alive. I don't have a body to confirm with," he paused then composed himself and gave them his update. "I tried to get Cameron to check the hospitals and leave me at the crash site so I could explore more. But instead, Cameron played the jurisdiction card and took over the crime scene asking me to check the hospitals. I had to agree so as not to send up red flags. Instead of searching local hospitals, since I knew there was no way that he could have left the area, I drove down the road, waited, and watched as he continued searching, had the impound lot retrieve and haul away the motorcycle, and leave. It took hours for them to finish. They did not find a body. So, I went back to the site when I knew the coast was clear and continued searching myself as best as I could with the spotlight and flashlight. There's just too much-overgrown vegetation in that area and the gully is too steep to see into in the dark."

Owen spoke up this time, "Then where does that leave us? Have we fulfilled the contract?" The room was again focused on Mayor Winters.

"I don't know," Ed answered with an almost defeated expression on his face.

Sharon arrived at Tess's exactly an hour and forty-five minutes from when she hung up with her. She saw the light on in the kitchen as she pulled into the driveway. Before she was able to get out of the car completely, Tess was on the front porch with her purse in her hand.

"Sharon?" Tess asked.

"Tess?" Sharon responded, "Yes, I'm glad to meet you. Although, I would hope for different circumstances. I take it that you haven't heard from Jim?"

"Not a word. Should we go?" Tess responded frantically.

"Do you want me to check my machine before we leave?" Sharon asked.

"Only if you think we should. I'm sure he would have called me by now if he could," Tess said anxiously.

"I think we should, in case he left a message that he would be somewhere, where we could locate him." Sharon was still trying to ease his mother's mind.

"Okay. That makes sense," Jim's mother conceded before motioning Sharon into the house and showing her where the phone was. Sharon called her machine and plugged in the code to receive her messages, but the machine was empty.

"No message. Let's go," Sharon said with urgency now in her voice too. The two ladies, now overcome with worry, climbed into Sharon's compact sedan and drove off. Normally Sharon would be more conscious of what Tess thought of her driving and how fast she was going. But this was no time for being self-conscious. They needed to find Jim and make sure he was alright.

Tess was so consumed with concern for her precious boy, that she didn't even notice that Sharon had been driving a minimum of twenty miles per hour over the posted speed limit for most of the drive. This would usually have prompted Tess to ask her to slow down.

Sharon slowed the pace and flipped on her high beams when she saw the signs for Oakwood, and they began to cross into city limits. The two women cautiously scanned each side of the road as they drove past the dense foliage and forests. "Wait! Slow down! What's that?" Tess shouted pointing to something on the other side of the road just ahead.

Sharon slowed to a crawl as she approached the object that was barely visible positioned next to the road against a tree trunk. "Oh my god! It's him! It's Jim!" Sharon echoed Tess's volume and concern.

The car had barely come to a stop before Tess had jumped out and began running across the road towards her son. "Jim! Jim! Are you okay?" She continued to holler, but he was not responding. Tears began to stream down her face as she thought the worst.

Sharon caught up with her and stopped her from getting any closer when she was within a few feet. "Wait, Tess. Let me check him. You don't want to see him like this if you don't have to." Sharon was worried about how seeing Jim's lifeless body would affect Tess and knew that motorcycle accident victims were often very mangled. Tess looked into Sharon's eyes seeing the fear and sincerity that flooded them and nodded in agreement.

Tess stood paralyzed as she waited for Sharon to give her the information that she both wanted and dreaded at the same time. Sharon, rushed to Jim's side once she had his mother at a safe distance to protect her from what might be waiting for them. She slowly checked Jim for a pulse and gasped, calling out, "Tess! He's alive. But he's hurt and unconscious. We need to get him to a hospital. It looks like he has lost a lot of blood," she continued as she looked at his wounds stopping at his leg.

Tess ran to her son's side. Sharon quickly removed her scarf and tied it tightly around Jim's leg above where the gash that was oozing blood was and noticed the bone protruding. "He has a compound fracture on his leg. We need to get him medical attention." Sharon was happy that she had taken a few emergency first aid classes last semester. Tess watched as Sharon kicked into action and then motioned for Tess to elevate Jim's feet while she turned the car around and pulled it closer.

Sharon didn't even look for cross traffic. She just ran to her car and threw it into drive quickly, making a sharp U-turn, before throwing it into park again, getting out and joining Tess on the other side of the car. "Let's get him into the back seat on his back, and you keep his feet elevated. He's in shock and we need to keep his blood from pooling," Sharon instructed as she opened the back passenger side door.

Tess lifted Jim's legs being careful to support his knees and ankles as Sharon lifted him from under his arms and backed into the backseat of her car dragging Jim with her across the seat before she laid his head flat on the seat letting herself out the other side. Tess followed suit, climbing into the back seat and propping his legs up in her lap being careful not to touch or shift the protruding bone that now became her unintentional focal point as Sharon got into the driver's seat and sped off.

Sharon was focused on her own thoughts and glad that Tess was too focused on Jim to want to speak. She knew that if Jim's accident was connected to his research, it would not be safe for him to be in a local area hospital. But she knew he needed help soon. She debated quietly in her mind, before deciding it would be in his best interest to get as far from Oakwood as possible and headed for Milledgeville. It would be an extra thirty minutes to the hospital, but she knew he would be safe there.

She drove as if she had spent years racing in NASCAR, hoping Tess wouldn't notice. The tires screeched as she skidded to a stop directly outside the emergency room entrance, jumped out of the car, and motioned to the staff inside for help. "Help! Please! He's unconscious and bleeding," Sharon screamed through the door.

Several orderlies rushed outside with a stretcher and pulled Jim from his mother's lap asking, "What happened? How long has he been like this? What's his name?"

"He was in a motorcycle accident. We're not sure. We found him like this forty-five minutes ago. Jim. His name is Jim," Sharon answered as Tess climbed out of the back seat and followed them through the sliding doors.

"Ma'am, you can't go in there. You have to stay here," A nurse called from behind the counter.

"I'm his mother!" Tess yelled back.

"I understand. But you need to let the doctors do their work. You two ladies can wait here. We'll need more information from you," the nurse said calmly handing Tess a clipboard with a medical information form attached.

Tess took the pen and clipboard and turned to look at Sharon who was standing behind her staring at the emergency personnel only sign on the doors that had just slammed closed in her face when they rushed Jim into triage. Sharon felt Tess's eyes on her and turned to see the scared mother of the man she had become so close to shaking with tears streaming down both cheeks. Sharon walked over to her, wrapped her arm around her, and led her to one of the waiting area chairs that lined the walls.

Sharon watched as Tess attempted to fill out the important documents in her hand. Her hand that held the pen could barely make contact with the paper, due to the extreme uncontrollable shaking of her hand. "Here...let me take that. How about I do the writing and read you the questions, and you provide the answers?" Sharon offered. Tess nodded, handing Sharon the pen and clipboard.

Sharon read off the questions about Jim's prior medical conditions, medicine allergies, and the tough questions of whether he should be put on life support should it become necessary. 'This is a question no parent should ever have to answer for their child,' Sharon thought as she read the question aloud and felt a tear start to stream down her face.

For the first time, she had been slapped in the face with the reality that Jim could possibly not make it. Sharon and Tess sat looking at one another for a long time not speaking simply commiserating with the other's pain at the thought of losing Jim. Tess finally responded, "We spoke about this a few times, and Jim always said he never wanted to spend his life hooked up to a machine. So, I need honor his wishes and say no."

Now the tears flooded both of their faces while Sharon tried to compose herself. She had to stay strong for Tess's and Jim's sakes. She could break down later when she was alone. "That's the last of the forms. You just need to sign and date it here," Sharon instructed. Tess did as she was asked and Sharon took back the forms, "I'll give them to the nurse. You stay here and I'll be right back."

18

Answers for Jim

Jim awoke to find himself lying in a hospital bed with wires and monitors attached to both arms and his left leg in a full cast. His head was foggy, and he felt as though he was in a daze, which indicated to him that one of the IV drips must contain some kind of strong pain killer. The room was dark, with beeping machines all around him. He had no idea how he had gotten there or what kind of condition or danger he might be in. Then he noticed the Milledgeville logo on one of the curtains that hung in the window separating him from the nurse's station. Relieved, he knew he was safe, and he was able to relax enough to fall back to sleep.

It seemed as though only a minute had passed when Jim opened his eyes to find a strange, ominous-looking man standing over him at his bedside. He was dressed in an undertaker's suit, all black with sleek lines, a black button-up dress shirt, and shiny black shoes. This made the blood-red bowtie that he wore stand out even more. His hair was shoulder length and jet black, which contrasted with his ash-grey skin. The intensity of the man's charcoal eyes peered through Jim and caused him to shiver when he realized there were no whites in the eyes looking so intently at him. He found himself wondering if he had died instead of falling back to sleep and this was hell. "Who are you?" He finally gained the courage to ask.

"My name is Mr. Blanchard, Mr. Norton," the chilly voice spoke. "Do you know how lucky you are?"

Jim thought this was a strange question for this creepy man that he did not know to ask, "I...I...Yes, I know I have been blessed to have my mom, and in so many ways have been luckier than most...I...I guess..." Jim stammered trying to understand the question, not knowing if he was dead or alive.

"Yes, Mr. Norton. You have indeed had a blessed life. However, that is not what I am talking about," Mr. Blanchard responded. "Do you know how lucky you are at this very minute? I don't think you do."

"I don't understand. Who are you? Why are you asking me this? Am I dead?" Jim stammered some more.

Mr. Blanchard let out a deep laugh at the last question, "No, Mr. Norton. You are not dead. You apparently do not understand. So, I will explain, and then you will understand how truly lucky you are and the test that you have passed," he explained.

"Yes, please tell me what is happening," Jim requested.

"You were the chosen one, long before you were the chosen one," the chilly voice said even more chilly than before. Jim's brow narrowed with confusion. His head was still spinning from the concussion and pain meds, and this ominous man seemed to be speaking in riddles. "Long ago, a contract with the one that I serve was signed by seven men who made up the Oakwood City Council to protect their citizens from the evils that plagued the world at that time."

Suddenly, Jim was starting to make sense of what this man was saying, "In 1944, the world war?"

"Yes, that is the world evil that they feared. To remove themselves and protect their descendants from such evils, they agreed to an annual sacrifice to appease my master," Mr. Blanchard continued. "Several years later, your father was honored in such a way as to be the sacrificial lamb. That's what the Sacred Circle of Seven call their victims." Jim's face went pale as he learned that his father's accident was not an accident at all.

"I see that you understand what I am saying, so I will continue. Your father turned out to be a good man and as such, my master was denied his reward, because your father received his."

"Do you mean dad is in heaven?" Jim inquired.

"Yes, that is what I mean. As such, you were at that time marked to be the test between heaven and hell as it be known. When you came of age, you would either take your father's place next to my master or break Oakwood's contract and send him the many souls for which he has been waiting for forty years to collect."

"I don't understand. Who marked me? Why was there a place for my father in your master's domain? I mean, if he was a good man..." Jim probed.

"Ah, I see where I led you astray with my words," Mr. Blanchard acknowledged. "Your father was a good man, and it wasn't his place. It was a place set for that year's sacrifice. Your father was that year's sacrifice, so it should have been his seat to fill if he didn't already have a place in the other domain. Do you see now?"

"I think so. But how does this mark me?" Jim asked.

"Oakwood could not be punished by my master since they had technically fulfilled their contract. They had killed your father. But as a good man he was entitled to his place in heaven, and he was not permitted to join my master. This led to an arrangement between he who I serve and he who your father now sits with, that you shall be the one to prove that there is still good in the world, or that man is evil by nature. You were chosen as the descendant of a pure soul to test the contract of those who do not have a pure soul," Mr. Blanchard explained in his cryptic manner. "Shall I continue?"

"Yes, please..." Jim answered with trepidation.

"Then, continue I shall. You did not simply stumble on the knowledge of the unholy town of Oakwood. You were fed the information that led you to them. You were meant to drive these hypocritical men of honor to make you their lamb," Mr. Blanchard paused to wait for Jim's response to this news. Jim's look of shock confirmed that he understood, so the dark figure continued with his story.

Mr. Blanchard looked at his unusual wristwatch that wrapped his skeleton-thin left wrist to see that it was now one minute past the stroke of midnight. "You have proven to be the stronger of the two foes. You have survived that which the unworthy circle of seven have put you through. You have lived and avoided being captured by these men who wished to impose the role of the sacrificial lamb upon you. You have caused these citizens of death to miss their deadline and now the contract is breached," he completed his tale.

"I have breached the contract, by surviving? What does this mean now...for me and my family?" Jim questioned.

Mr. Blanchard again laughed before speaking, "I do not laugh often, Mr. Norton. But you amuse me. You and your family are now free to go ahead with your lives. Your roles in this arrangement have been fulfilled. I simply could not resist the urge to see with my own eyes the chosen one. So, when I asked, 'Do you know how lucky you are?' I was referring to your being alive. You had a very large target on your back, and, yet you escaped what should have been your fate. For that you are lucky."

Jim closed his eyes for a moment and shook his head slightly to try and clear the fog from his mind and fully comprehend what he was being told. He began to speak as he opened his eyes, only to find he was now alone. Mr. Blanchard had disappeared as mysteriously as he had appeared.

19

Penance

Tick...Tick...Tick...Tock...The room was so silent that the movements on Mayor Winters' watch echoed throughout the room. They waited as the second hand passed the twelve for the last time that day. They waited in anticipation of what might come next. They waited for Mr. Blanchard to arrive. Their apprehension grew as the minutes passed and it was now five after midnight. Mr. Blanchard was never late. He always appeared as if by magic at the stroke of one minute passed the hour. Now, he was late. What could this mean? That was the question that was written on the face of each and every man sitting at the table.

As Kevin opened his mouth to speak, Mr. Blanchard's dark outline approached the room. His silhouette seemed particularly scary this time, with the lights coming through the window at the other end of the hall outlining his form as he walked towards them.

He entered the room this time without the familiar piece of parchment that typically came along with him for this annual meeting. Recognizing this missing document sent a chill throughout the room.

"Well, gentlemen, it would seem that our contract has finally come due. It is my pleasure to notify you that you are in breach of contract." Mr. Blanchard sneered at the men sitting around the solid oak table.

"That can't be!" Ed exclaimed. "We watched him go down. There's no way he could have lived through that crash. We saw the blood trail. It went over the edge." Mayor Winters protested vigorously.

"That may be the case. But your young sacrifice is indeed alive and well and in the arms of his loved ones at Milledgeville Memorial Hospital as we speak. As such your contract is now void and your town is no longer under the protection of my superior. My employer looks forward to seeing all of you very soon, along with your descendants."

"What do you mean see us soon and our descendants? The contract was for protection, not our souls," Trevor argued.

"Your predecessors seem to have missed reading some of the extra-fine print and seem to have left out a vital piece of the balloon payment." Mr. Blanchard sneered as he summoned the contract and pointed at a dark line at the bottom of the document that resembled a boarder. Mr. Blanchard waved his boney fingers, and the line began to expand revealing a hidden paragraph of stipulations.

He paraphrased, "Once the contract is in breach, the souls of those bloodlines who entered into this unholy arrangement and continued to honor the conditions of the contract, become the property of my employer, and although those individuals shall be allowed to live out their lives in their current form, their souls will join my employer in his employ for all eternity." Mr. Blanchard spoke with spite and contempt in his voice. "In other words, your souls and those of your descendants, along with all those descendants of your predecessors who have yet to passed over, now belong to my master." The words trailed off as he turned and stepped back into the darkness from which he originally appeared. "See you soon, gentlemen," was all that was heard as the portal closed.

Dread and horror were now the mood in the room as each man lost in his thoughts quietly rose from his seat at the table and exited the hall and went home to await the uncertainty of tomorrow.

###

Jim was stirred from his slumber by the familiar voices of Sharon and his mother discussing his color, and the length of his hair. At first, he thought it was another dream. Then he realized it was his mother's nervous chatter as she sat waiting to know her boy would be alright. He opened his eyes slowly being blinded by the light streaming through the blinds, then turned to look at the faces of the two women whom he loved more than ever before.

"Jim??" Sharon spoke softly with a smile. Tears of happiness filled her eyes.

"Well, if it isn't my two favorite women together in one room. This isn't exactly how I meant for the two of you to meet. But I'm glad you are here," Jim's throat crackled as he spoke. The combination of the hospital's dry air and the mass amounts of medication surging through his body had given him a dry mouth.

"Oh! My boy! You're awake," his mother exclaimed with joy. "You were sleeping so long. How do you feel?"

"Like I drove a motorcycle off a cliff. Otherwise, I'm good."

Sharon watched, admiring the bond between Jim and his mother. It was something that she had missed having with her own mother for many years now. "Do you think I could get something to drink or some ice chips or something?" Jim couldn't take the tickle in his throat any longer.

"I'll go ask the nurse," Sharon answered.

"Mom, I need to tell you something."

"Just rest, son. You can tell me whatever it is later," Tess insisted.

"No mom. This can't wait. I am so sorry for all the trouble I put you through about school and my motorcycle. I know that you were only looking out for my best interests and didn't mean to come across as overprotective," Jim continued.

Jim and his mother continued to bond and commiserate until Sharon returned with a small can of ginger ale and a cup of ice in her hands. "The nurse said to take it slow and start with a few ice chips. They don't want you to start throwing up from all of the anesthesia and medication in your stomach."

"Thank you, babe," Jim said as Sharon held his head up to assist him with taking a drink. Sharon smiled hearing him call her that, especially in front of his mother. "So, what do you think, Mom? She's pretty awesome, isn't she?" Jim asked his mother as he gazed lovingly into Sharon's eyes.

Sharon blushed as she said, "You're just biased."

Tess agreed with her son, "No, he's right, you are a pretty amazing girl. You saved my son's life with your first aid and incredible driving skills." Then Tess laughed and added, "Just please tell me that you don't normally drive like you're in the Indy500."

"No. I only drive like that when I'm playing ambulance driver and superhero," Sharon quipped back, causing Jim and Tess to laugh out loud.

"Oh crap! That hurts. Please don't make me laugh." Jim cried out in pain unable to keep from laughing.

Sharon and Tess sat on each side of Jim taking turns tending to his needs. Jim decided that he needed to let his mother into the loop about what he had discovered about the town and his father's death.

He told her about the midnight visit from Mr. Blanchard, although she brushed it off as a pharmaceutically induced nightmare. Sharon who had seen his research believed every word that he said and squeezed his hand tight to let him know.

After Jim had told them his story and was ready for sleep again, Sharon turned on the television keeping the volume on low. The news was on. Just as she was about to change the channel, the broadcaster started to read the next local story, which was about the town of Oakwood, so she stopped to listen.

"The town of Oakwood today suffered tragedy after its town center was struck by a freak storm and destroyed by a tornado. Mayor Winters and three of the town council members along with twenty community members were among those lost in the storm. Currently, the town and its residents are without power and clean drinking water, so the local Red Cross is accepting donations to help bring supplies and aid to this small community. Fatality numbers are still coming in, and all injured parties are being medevacked to outlying hospitals," the broadcaster read the story and then moved straight into an update on world affairs.

Sharon and Tess sat looking at one another in complete disbelief while Jim slept and they thanked their lucky stars that Jim was not there when the storm struck, and that they had opted not to take him to one of the local area hospitals.

Acknowledgments

I would like to thank Steve Eisner and his When Words Count Team for reaching out to me and encouraging me to participate in the Meet the Judges competition. The many judges, editors, cover designers, and administrative staff's input have been invaluable to my completion of this book and its sequels. This has been a once in a lifetime experience that I will never forget.

Thank you, to Woodhall Press for choosing to publish my book and especially to Dave LeGere for his genuine interest and desire to make this book happen even as a Silver Place Winner. It has been an honor and pleasure to work with you and I look forward to many more years of collaboration to come.

And, lastly thank you to all of my family and friends who consistently push me to pursue my writing dreams. Without your encouragement and belief in me, I doubt I would ever have been brave enough to venture on this life dream journey.

About the Author

Elizabeth Donley-Leer is a Texas born, California raised grandmother, who spent thirty-years living in Colorado raising her children before moving to the east coast living back and forth between Georgia and Alabama in her RV with her two giant breed puppies. Writing has been a lifelong passion of Elizabeth's. Besides being a former freelance Children's Book Primary Editor her prior writing experiences include online articles for companies such as Go Daddy.com, professional blogging, SEO Ad work, Web-Content, catalog descriptions, and travel destination descriptions for online travel guide sites, and most recently coming in second in the prestigious When Words Count Pitch Week competition with her novel *The Town that Time Forgot*. Elizabeth earned a degree in writing, editing, and publishing for children and young adults from the Institute of Children's Literature. Additionally, she has written and self-published two children's books (*The Fish Who Wanted to Fly*, and *Passing Ships Are Not Always Quiet*), been a reviewer for the 2012 Denver Film Festival, and is a published poet. Retired, she continues to pursue her passion for writing from her cozy country home in Munford, Alabama.